THE STONE OF ESSENCE

THE KINGDOMS OF TALIA

The Stone of Essence

Maya Unadkat

maya Unadkat

Khiona welcomes you!

SilverDust Press

First paperback edition March 2023

ISBN 978-1-7397034-2-4 (Paperback)

First Edition

Written by Maya Unadkat

Published by SilverDust press

ALSO BY
MAYA UNADKAT

The Aura Realm:

Asyra's Call

Drako's Fire

This one is for you. The reader who took a chance on a small indie author.

Contents

Chapter One

It was often said that sirens lived in the lakes and that terrible creatures lurked in their depths. But standing on the bridge, watching the glistening water below twinkle underneath the light of the moon, Chhaya could not fathom such a thing.

The moon was still high in the sky, and the sun had not yet risen, but Chhaya had found herself unable to sleep. Behind her, the soldier that had accompanied her on her walk remained a respectable distance away, his hand placed on the handle of his sword and his feet planted firmly on the ground, ready. Ready for the Blood Magicians that, until recently, had been terrorising the Khiona Kingdom and all of its people.

But Chhaya knew she was perfectly safe. Even before the war, the Blood Magicians would not dare come close to the palace, let alone within the grounds. No, there were far too many soldiers. Soldiers with swords and Magic of their own. It was true, Blood Magic was far more potent than any other form of Magic, but a larger number always had the upper hand.

Underneath her thick woollen cloak and gown, the chill of the icy air bit into her skin, sending a shiver through her. With a sigh, she ran a hand through the curls that had already tangled as she peered over the edge of the bridge.

There was a rustle behind her. Movement. Footsteps crunched through the damp grass.

"Your Highness," a voice greeted. Chhaya turned to face a second guard, whose head was lowered into a bow.

"Good morning," Chhaya said.

The guard raised her head. "Your father requests your presence."

Chhaya frowned, glancing up at the moon, no longer quite so high in the sky but still visible nonetheless. What could her father require so early in the morning?

"Your Highness?" the guard questioned.

Chhaya nodded. "Very well."

Minutes later, Chhaya emerged into the warmer, yet still chilled, hallway, the two soldiers following behind her.

She nodded her good morning to the guards stationed at the entrance and made her way to her father's office.

"His Majesty is awaiting you, Your Highness," the guard outside her father's office, Rodger, announced in a monotone voice.

"Thank you, Rodger," Chhaya replied before knocking on the door and opening it. The soft glow of the rising sun lit up the dark burgundy walls, and the dark cabinets shadowed over her father, who was slumped at his desk, his eyebrows folded in a deep frown, and the bags under his eyes more prominent than usual. For a tall man, he looked small in the early morning light, his deep grey hair casting a shadow over his eyes.

"Chai," he said, brightening at the sight of his only daughter. Chhaya returned his smile. When she was younger, she had detested his nickname for her – 'chai' meant tea, and she hated being called a beverage – but she had grown to love it over the years.

"I hope you have a good reason for requiring me so early in the morning, papa," Chhaya said with raised eyebrows, joking, as her father poured her a cup of chai, adding two glittering cubes of sugar.

He raised a brow in return as he handed over the cup, which she accepted with eager hands. "You wouldn't think I would wake you at this time without having some chai ready for you, surely?" he joked, settling back into his chair with a heavy groan. "*Beta*, there's something I need to discuss with you." His twinkling eyes turned from humorous to something Chhaya couldn't quite identify.

"What is it, papa?" She frowned, not bothering to tell her father she had been awake already.

"Chai, you know, of course, that your twenty-fourth birthday is approaching." Chhaya nodded. "And you know of the war, of course." She nodded again, lifting her cup to her lips and drinking in the rich, spicy, golden liquid. How could she forget the war that had lasted almost an entire decade? The war that began on the night Chhaya would never be able to forget, no matter how much she wished she could. "Well, I believe it is time for you to get married."

Chhaya froze mid-sip. She stared at her father, blinking slowly as he looked back at her, his lips pressed tightly together.

"Are you joking?" she asked, genuinely confused. What did her birthday or the war have to do with her getting married? Surely, he was joking.

"You need to understand, beta. At this age, everybody was expecting you to be married already. You are aware of the ex- pectations — there is great pressure on royalty to marry and have heirs. And with the war, our people need something; they need a distraction of sorts, a way to take their minds away from the horrors many of them suffered. Your wedding will be the perfect opportunity, Chai. It will lift the spirits of everyone in the kingdom. You know they all are so fond of their Princess."

"But papa..." Chhaya couldn't comprehend what he was saying.

"Chai, listen. At some point, you will have to take the throne for yourself. You will," he insisted when Chhaya attempted to interrupt. "I know first-hand how difficult it is to rule alone, beta. Since your mother...." He sighed. "It is not something I would ever wish for you. Having said that, the last thing I want is for you to be unhappy or with someone you did not want to be with. And so, I have a proposal."

Chhaya took a deep breath. This was insanity. Marriage? She wasn't old enough to be married. She didn't want to get married. She hadn't truly lived yet; she hadn't travelled the Kingdoms as she had always dreamed of doing; she hadn't even dated anyone.

Her father continued without waiting for a response, sitting up in his seat. "I propose we invite all the eligible bachelors, and the princes, from the neighbouring kingdoms to stay with us for a month. That way, you will have a chance to meet them all and see who you like."

"But—"

"We will do an extensive background check on each of them, beta. Anybody who doesn't deserve to have the privilege of meeting you or is unfit to help you rule the Kingdom someday will not be invited."

"Papa—"

"Oh, Chai, I am sorry!" her father exclaimed. "I assumed when I should not have. Would you like to invite bachelorettes instead? Or perhaps both? Whatever you would like."

"That's not what I—"

"Unless you already have somebody you wish to marry?" he questioned. "I understand you are good friends with that Lukas boy, are you not? He is no member of royalty, but I have no objection. His father is a baker, is he not? A very respectable family, indeed."

"Papa, I most certainly do *not* wish to marry Lukas."

"Very well, then. Of course, we will only invite the suitors to arrive after your birthday. We will first celebrate properly. And I am aware this idea has an element of risk attached, so I have arranged for a personal bodyguard to be assigned to you for the duration."

"Father!" Chhaya exclaimed. The King stopped in surprise, turning slowly to look at her with furrowed brows. She never called him 'father'. "Listen to me. I do not want to get married. I do not want any princes, princesses, dukes, duchesses, or any men or women *at all* in this castle. Especially not for an entire month. And I certainly do not want a bodyguard."

"Chai—"

"No, father. I don't want to talk about this anymore." Her hands practically vibrated with anger as she stood up and left the room, determined to hear no more of this foolishness.

She was nobody's pawn, nobody's doll to do with what they liked. She was the future ruler of this Kingdom. And she would be treated as such.

Chhaya was sitting at her vanity, staring miserably at her own brown eyes and dark locks in the reflection, when she heard a gentle tapping at her door. Only one person knocked on her door like that, and it was the one person Chhaya wanted to see.

She walked over, opened the door and smiled at the sight of her maid and long-time friend standing in front of her with a sympathetic smile. Her long, dark hair was tied into a low bun, and her cheeks were flush. "Della. I am glad to see you." Chhaya motioned for her to come in before closing the door. "You wouldn't believe what my father wants me to do," Chhaya sighed, slumping into an armchair by the crackling fireplace. Della had been around for as long as Chhaya could remember, and as the daughter of Chhaya's nanny, they had grown up together. When her mother retired, Chhaya's father offered Della the job as Chhaya's maid. She had gratefully accepted.

"I heard what happened, Chhaya," Della spoke, crouching before her.

"Please, Della, sit properly. Would you like some tea?"

"I will pour it, don't worry." Della poured two cups of chai, one for each of them, and sat in the armchair closest to the princess.

"What do I do, Della?" Chhaya asked helplessly, dropping her face into her hands.

"I have known you for many years. You have sought my counsel on numerous occasions. I know this isn't what you want to hear, Chhaya, but I think you should go through with your father's plan."

Chhaya immediately sat up, staring at her friend in shock. "Are you kidding me? Have you gone crazy, too?"

Della exhaled, her shoulders slumping. "Your father is right about the war affecting morale. My family is struggling, and I know others in the village are, too. Everyone is frightened."

"But how could I get married? You know that's not what I want."

"I'm not suggesting you get married. But inviting eligible bachelors, princes, dukes and the like from neighbouring kingdoms to stay will help to lift everyone's spirits. It would be a welcome break from the fear, a distraction. You don't have to marry anyone, simply meet them and enjoy your time with them—allow *your people* to enjoy this event." Chhaya hesitated, but Della spoke again before she could reply. "It will help them to forget. To move on."

"I can meet and host them without promising to marry any of them?"

"Exactly."

Della's words made sense to Chhaya, and although she didn't want to do it, she knew her father wouldn't budge. "Thank goodness for you, Della. I don't know what I would do without you," Chhaya said, relieved to have a plan.

"Her Royal Highness, Princess Chhaya," the guard announced as Chhaya entered her father's study for the second time that day.

"Chhaya," her father said, his voice almost dripping with hope as she walked towards his desk.

"I have made a decision, Papa," she told him in as calm a voice as she could manage. "I will allow the visitors to stay for one month. I will entertain them, consider them seriously as potential marriage candidates, and speak with each of them. However, I have one condition. If I decide I do not want to marry at the end of the month, I should not be forced to do so."

"But—"

"Papa, this is the only way I will agree to it. If you promise not to force me into marriage, I will continue with this plan."

Her father considered her words before replying. "But you will agree to have a bodyguard?"

Chhaya rolled her eyes. "Papa, there are so many soldiers in the castle already. What difference will one more make?"

"That is precisely the point—what harm could it do?"

"I do not like for people to see me so differently, papa. You are aware of that. I do not like to be seen as merely a princess. I work hard to be more than that. I have even been taking lessons on herbology from Gaia so that I may help my people if they require it of me." She exhaled heavily. "Finally, my friends call me by my name and no longer bow to me. It has taken this long for the children at the orphanage not to worry that I will order their heads chopped off if they so much as look at me. Even in the Kingdom now, I am able to walk to see Gaia without people bowing or staring. A bodyguard always following me around will only make other people uncomfortable."

"Chai, I understand you are worried. But people will get used to it. Having him around will be no more intimidating than taking any other soldier with you," he insisted.

"Then what is the point, papa?"

Her father pressed his lips together. "I know this bodyguard personally, beta. He used to be a soldier. His Magic is unlike any other's, and I trust him to protect you."

"I wouldn't need protection if you allowed me to learn how to use magic myself."

"Chai, we have been over this countless times. Magic is dangerous and unpredictable. Not to mention, you would require years of dedicated training to use it effectively in defence."

She sighed. "You truly won't give up this bodyguard idea?" He smiled silently at her and shook his head. "Fine," she gave in. "*If* you agree to host a ball every week and invite the people of the Kingdom. Including the children in the orphanage."

Her father's eyes softened into a fond smile at her commanding tone. "You do so remind me of your mother, you know." He smiled warmly. "It is a deal, daughter."

"Very well. Then I will agree to have a bodyguard, but only for the duration of the month while I consider the suitors. And you must promise not to force me to marry anyone if I do not choose to do so."

"I promise. I want you to be happy, Chhaya. And while I strongly believe a wedding would be a good boost for the Kingdom, if that means you do not want to marry, then so be it."

"Thank you, Father," Chhaya said with a relieved smile. "I promise to give all of the candidates a fair chance and to make a careful decision at the end of the month."

"Now, there's something important I need to discuss with you."

The deep frown etched into his forehead was not a good sign. "Is everything alright, papa?"

"There has been another attack on the Kingdom's northern border."

Chhaya's eyes widened. "That is the third attack this month." Her father nodded.

"I thought the Blood Magicians had all been taken care of," Chhaya said with a frown.

"We believed they had. I even had soldiers search the forests for any remaining camps, but everything seemed clear. It appears we were wrong."

"So, we send more soldiers?" Chhaya suggested. "As many as we can spare. They should go and scout the woods and the borders."

"It's not that simple, Chhaya," her father replied.

"How is it not simple, papa? These are not ordinary people we are dealing with. They are monsters. They must be taken care of." She stood and began pacing the long room.

"A troop of our Kingdom's finest soldiers was sent to the northern border just ten minutes ago," her father explained. "They should arrive there late this evening to scout from the trees. But we cannot merely send every soldier without a second thought. If there *are* many Blood Magicians remaining, we will need our soldiers here. To protect our people." He sighed, rubbing his head with his fingers. "With any luck, it was just one rogue Blood Magician that we missed. The troop should be able to take care of them and return shortly thereafter."

Chhaya nodded, relieved that something was being done. All they could do now was hope that it was just a single Magician left.

A gentle knock echoed through Chhaya's chambers, and she hurried over to the door, swinging it open to be greeted by her father's beaming face.

"Happy birthday, Chai," he said warmly, pulling her lovingly into his arms.

"Thank you, papa." A bright smile lit up her face as she returned his hug.

"These are for you, beta," her father said, presenting her with a bouquet of her favourite blue lilies.

Chhaya took the flowers and carefully arranged them into a vase on her coffee table. "They're beautiful, papa. Thank you."

As she admired the flowers, she noticed a glint in her father's eye that she couldn't quite place. "It's just a little something to start your day," he said.

"I was going to wait until this evening so you could wear them with your ballgown tonight, but I could not help myself." From his pocket, he pulled out a small velvet blue box. "These belonged to your mother." He opened the box to reveal a pair of elegant earrings, each featuring a silver diamond at the centre and delicate pezzottaites along the edges.

Chhaya inhaled in surprise as her father handed her the box. She remembered these earrings. Her mother had worn them almost every day when she was young, and she had admired them for the longest time.

"Your mother always meant for you to have them, Chai. And I can't think of a better time to give them to you. I am so proud of you, beta. You work so hard and bring so much joy to everyone in the Kingdom. You are truly a well-loved, respected, and good person, and if your mother were here today, she would be just as proud of the princess and future queen you have become. I know it in my heart."

"Oh, papa." Chhaya's eyes filled with tears as she hugged her father once again. "Thank you," she whispered, her voice thick with emotion. She cleared her throat and pulled away, gesturing for her father to sit in one of the armchairs. She flicked the box open again and marvelled at the beautiful earrings inside. "And thank you for the extraordinary party that you have planned for tonight. I already know it will be magnificent."

"You are more than welcome, beta. I would also like to remind you that your bodyguard, Favian, will arrive this evening. I will introduce the two of you before the party, and he will escort you throughout the evening. His official duties begin at the ball."

Chhaya let out a frustrated and somewhat childish groan. "Papa, couldn't you give me at least one last night of freedom before Favian arrives?"

Her father chuckled. "You have your freedom as you always have, beta. What is it that you think Favian will do that you are so against?"

Furrowing her eyebrows, Chhaya glared jokingly at him but remained silent.

"Please, Chai. It's only for one month. Will you not humour an old man?"

Chhaya sighed dramatically. "Fine, papa. But only because you are *very* old."

"Wow," Della exclaimed as she shut the door behind herself. "You look gorgeous, Chhaya. As always, of course."

"Thank you, Della," Chhaya replied with a laugh. "It's all thanks to your talented hand with hair. What would I do without you?"

"You would be lost," Della chuckled.

Just then, a knock sounded at the door. Della rushed over to answer it, leaving Chhaya to return to her dark, wooden vanity. She was not in the mood to deal with any further distractions. Chhaya was already feeling anxious about the upcoming week and just wanted to enjoy the evening with her friends.

"Yes, she is in here," Della said at the door. "No, she isn't quite ready yet. No, she needs a few more minutes. I understand, but... no. I don't know..."

"Della, who is it?" Chhaya called out.

"Your Highness... I think you had better come out here," Della said, her forehead wrinkled apologetically.

Chhaya rolled her eyes but put down her lipstick. Who would be disturbing her so soon before the party started? With a sigh, she marched over to the door.

As Chhaya looked at the man standing before her, she couldn't help but feel a sense of unease. He was tall and well-built, his muscles clearly defined through the tight clothes he wore. He stood before her in a rigid, soldier-like stance with his hands clasped in front of him and his back straight, his eyes hidden behind dark lenses.

Chhaya frowned. She was familiar with all of the staff in the castle and was certain she had never seen this man before. She looked around, but the guards that were usually stationed outside her door were nowhere to be seen.

Her heart dropped into her stomach. Could it be possible that this stranger was here to harm her? Had he overpowered the guards and tied them up somewhere? Was he there to abduct her? Did he want to kill her?

Chhaya's thoughts raced, her mind whirring. She took a slow step backwards and reached behind the door, trying to find something she could use as a weapon. Something pointy prodded her finger, and she knew it was the fireplace poker. Grasping it firmly, she held it steady, ready to swing if necessary.

The man continued to study her through his dark lenses as she took a steadying breath.

Why had she not listened to her father and taken those self-defence classes when he had suggested them? They would have come in handy right about now.

"Who are you?" she asked with a slight tremble that she hoped had gone undetected.

He took a step towards her, and Chhaya readied herself.

"Favian, Your Highness," he said in a deep, monotone voice, bowing low to her. Chhaya exhaled in relief, her shoulders relaxing. Favian. That was the bodyguard her father had assigned to her. "Your father has appointed me as your bodyguard for the next month, Your Highness." He stood up straight again, his blank expression unchanged.

Now that Chhaya looked closer, his clothes seemed to be a strange variation of the soldiers' uniform. While they usually wore the royal colour of burgundy, he was dressed entirely in black. His black trousers were almost completely concealed by the long, stiff cloak he wore on top. However, the primary difference between this man and the other soldiers was the lack of a sword. Soldiers were required to carry a sword on their person at all times while on duty. And this man seemed not to have one at all.

"I was unaware you would be here already," she said, putting down the fireplace poker. "My father told me I would be meeting you at the ball."

"Your father instructed me to come and introduce myself to you, Your Highness."

"Okay then. Thank you."

"Of course, Your Highness," Favian replied.

There was an awkward pause during which Favian stared blankly at Chhaya while she shifted between her feet before speaking up again. "Well..." she said uncomfortably.

"Yes, Your Highness?"

"I need to finish getting ready."

"Yes, Your Highness."

"Goodbye then." Chhaya attempted to close the door, but Favian placed a hand on the thick wood before it shut.

"Your Highness?"

Chhaya groaned internally at this infuriating man. "Yes?" she asked through gritted teeth.

"I must come in, Your Highness," he stated.

Chhaya looked at him, squinting in disbelief. "These are my rooms."

"Yes, Your Highness."

"My private rooms," Chhaya emphasised.

"Yes, Your Highness," Favian replied, unaffected.

"Surely you don't expect to be coming into my rooms?"

"I am your bodyguard, Your Highness," Favian reminded her. As if she could have forgotten.

"You can be my bodyguard from outside the door!"

"There are many guests in the castle this evening, Your Highness. Your father wishes for me to take extra precautions."

"This is unnecessarily extreme," Chhaya argued with a huff.

"His Majesty was very clear. I am to stay with you, Your Highness," Favian insisted, unmoved by her protest.

Chhaya couldn't believe what she was hearing. She looked at Della, who looked just as lost as she felt, and glanced back to Favian. "What if I need to change?" she demanded.

"I will not come into the bathing room, Your Highness," Favian stated flatly.

"This is unbelievable," Chhaya muttered, shaking her head in disbelief. But Favian seemed uninterested, his face as blank as ever. "Oh, do what you must." Relenting, she took a step backwards. Almost as soon as he had stepped into the room, the door swung closed behind him. Chhaya flinched, unused to seeing such casual uses of Magic.

She turned back to her vanity without another word to him. Her makeup had already been applied, and Della had already helped her into her dress and styled her hair. She was almost ready to leave.

"Della, what are you wearing tonight?" she asked, turning to her friend and maid.

"Me?"

"Yes, of course. You are coming, aren't you?"

"Oh, I didn't realise I was invited, Chhaya," Della answered, looking down at the floor.

"Of course you are invited! You are one of the most important people in my life. Unless you have other plans, I would very much appreciate your presence tonight. Come, let's see if we can find something for you to wear." She took Della's hand and led her towards the wardrobe. "Baby pink does look spectacular on you, and I think I have just the gown."

"Are you sure?" Della wrinkled her forehead.

"Of course! It would be an honour to have you there as my plus one," Chhaya answered honestly, giving Della a warm smile.

"Well, in that case, it would be an honour to join you."

The orchestra stopped playing the very moment Chhaya stepped onto the grand staircase, and Magicians conjured bursts of silvery light that rained down onto her like delicate snowflakes, vanishing the moment they touched the floor. Colour kissed her cheeks as she stepped through the magnificent archway.

The walls were decorated in striking, yet elegant, white garlands, and a slow stream of the snowy light floated down upon them all, courtesy of the Court Magicians.

Below, the guests watched as she stood in the beautiful silver gown her father had gifted her for the occasion at the railing. Her hair flowed down in soft curls, and her lips curved upwards as she caressed the earrings her father had given her that morning.

She was accompanied by Della, who was dressed in a pale pink gown that perfectly complemented her deep skin tone, with her hair twisted into a thick braid, a change from her usual bun.

"Your Highness," a deep voice from behind her quickly erased the smile from Chhaya's face. "Please wait here, Your Highness. I shall do some reconnaissance before you go downstairs."

Chhaya rolled her eyes as he stepped in front of them. She had been doing that a lot lately. "I thought the point of having a bodyguard was for protection," she whispered to Della. "Not to be annoying."

Della chuckled softly and replied, "He is only doing his job, Chhaya."

They watched him curiously as he stood rigidly, his hands clasped in front of him as he scanned the room through his ridiculous sunglasses. Some of the guests looked up at him in confusion, and Chhaya caught sight of some of her friends, trying not to laugh as they pointed up at him. In contrast to the guests wearing ball gowns and formal tunics and the guards wearing their burgundy uniforms, Favian looked entirely out of place in his long black cloak.

She groaned inwardly. "This is humiliating," she whispered to Della. "He looks like some sort of angel of darkness."

"He is only here to protect you," Della whispered back.

"I know, but does he have to be so very obvious about it? I did not even want a bodyguard in the first place. Goddess knows I don't need one; this castle is already the safest place in the kingdom." Chhaya sighed, her teeth clenched tightly.

"All clear, Your Highness," Favian said, turning swiftly to face them and standing sideways. He held out an arm to gesture for Chhaya to go first.

"Can you at least take those off?" she asked, pointing at the lenses over his eyes. "It is the evening, and we are indoors."

"I am a bodyguard, Your Highness. Bodyguards must conceal their eyes."

Chhaya and Della exchanged a glance before heading down the stairs.

"Ladies and gentlemen, my beautiful daughter, Her Royal Highness, Princess Chhaya," her father announced from the front of the ballroom. All the guests applauded as Chhaya walked down the remaining steps with a red tinge to her cheeks. After twenty-four years of presentations exactly like this one, the attention still flustered her.

Chhaya was painfully aware of Favian's presence only a couple of steps behind her, his mere existence suffocating her like a thick blanket she could not remove.

"Thank you, Papa," she said, embracing her father tightly. "This is all very wonderful."

"Only the best for my favourite daughter," he replied with a smile.

"I'm your only daughter," she pointed out.

"Ah, I see you have met Favian." Her father gestured towards the man, waving him to come closer.

"Your Majesty," Favian said with a bow.

"Favian is the best in all the Kingdoms, Chai," her father continued, patting Favian kindly on the back.

"About that, papa. Is this truly necessary?" she asked again in a hushed tone, knowing full well that her father had made up his mind but unable to resist trying again nonetheless.

Her father chuckled and raised an eyebrow. "You said you would humour an old man, Chai!"

"Fine," Chhaya grumbled. "Come, Della. We had better begin making the rounds." With Favian following behind, the two of them began making their way around the room, greeting every one of the guests.

"Um... you look lovely, Chhaya," said Lukas, leading her around the ballroom with the other dancers in a traditional Khiona Kingdom dance.

"Thank you," Chhaya muttered, her eyes glued to the ground as they moved.

"Listen, Chhaya. We're good friends and all—at least, *I* consider you my good friend. After all, we have known each other since we were young. And it's your birthday, and I'm thrilled to be able to dance with you, but..." He glanced to the side, "does he *have* to do that?"

Chhaya had danced exactly three dances so far this evening, and during every single one, Favian had shadowed their every move. He positioned himself close enough to make Chhaya and her partners feel uncomfortable but far enough away not to get in the way of their dancing. He kept his face turned towards them, his expression unreadable as he followed them around the ballroom. It was all quite unsettling.

Well, Chhaya had *assumed* he was watching, but she couldn't quite tell since he wouldn't take off those silly sunglasses.

She sighed. "I'm sorry. I know it's strange and a little uncomfortable, but he just won't leave me alone."

Lukas chuckled. "That's unfortunate."

"I have no idea what to do. It really is embarrassing," Chhaya grumbled.

"On the bright side, you'll have suitors coming to visit from all over the Three Kingdoms next week," he said with a teasing grin. "If you don't like any of them, your lovely bodyguard here will make them feel so uncomfortable that they'll leave you alone without further effort."

"And what about the ones I do like?" In reality, she had no intention of getting married, so Favian's constant presence did not really affect her apart from how irritating he was.

"Let's hope they like you enough to overlook Favian."

"Favian, this is becoming absurd," Chhaya whispered sharply.

"Your Highness?" Favian asked, looking at her with a blank expression.

"It's my birthday, Favian. I want to dance."

Favian nodded. "Yes, Your Highness," he replied dutifully.

"No, Favian. I do not think you quite understand. I cannot dance with anybody because you are making everybody feel uncomfortable!"

"I am doing my job, Your Highness."

Chhaya groaned and covered her face with her hands. "Can you do your job without following me around the ballroom? You can watch me, but keep some distance, okay? Please?"

Favian was silent for a few moments. Chhaya could almost see him considering her request in his mind.

"I cannot protect you if I am too far away from you, Your Highness."

Chhaya let out an exasperated sigh. "Well, I would still like to dance."

Favian remained silent, staring at her with that same blank expression.

"Fine, then you will have to dance with me," Chhaya said finally, grabbing Favian's hand.

"Wha—Your Highness?!" For the first time since she had met him, Favian showed emotion. His cheeks coloured, and his eyebrows flew up on his forehead. Chhaya tried to ignore the fact that dancing with her caused such a reaction as he attempted to shake her off.

"You won't let me dance with anybody else, so you'll have to dance with me," Chhaya demanded, her voice edged with frustration. Having a bodyguard was not supposed to be so difficult.

"No, Your Highness, I cannot," Favian insisted firmly.

As the orchestra began to play the final dance of the night, Chhaya sighed and shook her head. "Forget it," she said, turning away from Favian. She walked over to her father and hugged him. "Papa, I think it's time for me to retire for the night."

"Already, Chai?" her father asked, surprised. "You're usually the last one standing."

"Yes, Papa, but it's been a long day, and I want to visit Gaia first thing tomorrow morning," Chhaya explained.

Her father smiled at her. "Then sleep well, beta."

Chapter Three

"Good morning!" Della called out cheerfully as she threw open the curtains.

Chhaya groaned loudly, pulling the blanket over her head to block out the light.

"Wake up, Chhaya," Della said, her voice gentle.

"What time is it?" Chhaya asked sleepily, her voice muffled by the thick blanket.

"It's six," Della responded hesitantly.

"In the morning?" Chhaya moaned. "Why does nobody wish for me to sleep anymore?"

"Well..."

"I'm going back to sleep," declared Chhaya.

Just as Chhaya was drifting off into a peaceful slumber, a loud knock at the door jolted her awake. KNOCK, KNOCK, KNOCK. It was loud. KNOCK, KNOCK, KNOCK. And persistent.

Chhaya buried her head under her pillow to drown out the sound, but it wouldn't stop. Finally, she threw the duvet off herself and dragged herself out of bed, storming over to the door. She threw it open, only to reveal Favian stood as rigid as always with his hands behind his back and dark lenses covering his eyes.

This time, however, he was dressed in loose black trousers and a black tunic, the cloak he had been wearing the previous evening missing.

For a moment, Chhaya allowed herself to admire the way Favian looked, dressed in casual clothes rather than his uniform. But the realisation that he was the one who had awoken her from her much-needed sleep hit her, and she narrowed her eyes at him. "What do you want?"

"Good morning, Your Highness. I am glad you are awake," Favian said in his usual monotone voice.

"Of course I am awake—your persistent knocking wouldn't allow me to sleep," Chhaya grumbled, a sound that wasn't very princess-like of her.

"I am just following your father's orders, Your Highness."

"What orders?"

"Your father has requested that I teach you self-defence, Your Highness," he explained.

Chhaya inhaled slowly. "And why does it have to be at six o'clock in the morning?"

"I am merely following your father's orders, Your Highness," Favian repeated.

Chhaya narrowed her eyes before closing the door in his face.

"Can you believe this?" Chhaya asked Della as she crawled back into bed. She snuggled under the warm blankets, feeling the tension drain away as she basked in the cosy warmth.

It didn't last long.

KNOCK, KNOCK, KNOCK.

"I think I'm going to kill him," Chhaya muttered as she made her way over to the door for the second time.

She pulled the door open and folded her arms over her chest. "What?"

"I just wanted to ensure you were getting ready, Your Highness."

"Getting ready for what?"

"For your self-defence lesson, Your Highness."

Chhaya sighed. "Are you truly serious about this?"

"Yes, Your Highness. Your father's orders, Your Highness," Favian said, his expression unchanging.

"Fine," Chhaya replied through gritted teeth. "Give me ten minutes." She closed the door with a loud slam and headed to the bathing room, where Della was already preparing some loose cotton clothes for her.

Chaya's dislike for Favian only grew stronger after their training session. The warm-up he had forced her to do consisted of running, something Chhaya had never even attempted before. He had then forced her into several rounds of fencing and watched as she chopped several logs of wood—which she expected would later be used for her own fireplace—before showing her to lift and throw heavy stones. It had been an unbearable two hours.

"I don't see why we cannot do exercises I actually enjoy," Chhaya spoke between desperate gasps for breath as she lay on the grass, red-faced and sweaty.

"What do you enjoy, Your Highness?" asked Favian, not even slightly out of breath.

"Yoga."

"Yes, Your Highness. We can incorporate that into your routine."

"Horse riding."

"Horse riding is a spectacular training exercise, Your Highness."

"Swimming?"

"Again, Your Highness, a very efficient exercise."

"So, are we to stop running and chopping wood? Because I'm unsure I will even be able to move for the rest of the day."

Favian thought about it before announcing, "Perhaps we could decrease your run, replace the wood chopping and stone-throwing with horse riding and finish each morning with a swim in the lake. But the fencing must remain."

Relief coursed through Chhaya so intensely that she would have hugged him if she had even a droplet of control over her sore and aching body.

"And when were you intending to begin the self-defence portion of this training?" she asked, forcing herself to sit up and prop herself against a tree. "After all, I believe you mentioned that was the primary purpose for all of this."

"You cannot defend yourself if you have no strength," he responded. "Your Highness."

Chhaya could have sworn she saw his unmoving lips twitch ever so slightly, and her eyes narrowed into a dangerous glare. "Are you implying your princess is weak?"

Favian stayed silent but looked down at her, still bright red and breathing heavily on the ground and raised an eyebrow.

He had a point.

"The first matter of discussion," Chhaya began as Favian entered the room. Fortunately for her, he had returned to his own room to bathe, so when he returned to hers, he smelled fresh again. But *unfortunately* for her, he was dressed in his black uniform once again, cloak and all. She felt like pounding her head into the wall. He would scare everybody away if he went into the kingdom wearing that. "You need to get rid of the cloak," she stated firmly, crossing her arms.

"It's my uniform, Your Highness," Favian responded, his face remaining impassive and his voice emotionless as usual.

"I have no thoughts for your so-called uniform, Favian. I want the cloak gone," she insisted. "You look terribly frightening, and it's far too dramatic."

"I am a bodyguard, Your Highness. Bodyguards wear uniforms."

Chhaya breathed in heavily, clenching her jaw. "You also need to remove the lenses," she told him, her patience wearing thin.

"It's part of my uniform, Your Highness. Bodyguards cover—"

"Yes, yes, I see where you are leading. Bodyguards cover their eyes," she interrupted, her fists clenched as she paced the room, wondering where in the Kingdoms her father had found this man. A thought occurred to her. "I am your employer, am I not? Do you not have to follow my instructions?" She turned to face him, her eyes blazing with determination.

"Your father is my employer, Your Highness," he replied, his tone unchanged.

Chhaya sighed, closing her eyes and pinching the bridge of her nose. "Fine." He could wear the dreadful article of clothing and those lenses for the moment, but she would eventually find a way to get rid of them.

She opened the door and felt Favian follow closely behind her. "As you know, guests will arrive from across the Three Kingdoms next week."

Favian nodded and followed behind her with a straight back and stiff shoulders.

"Right. Until then, I will be going about with my usual routine."

"Yes, Your Highness."

"After breakfast, we will leave immediately to visit Gaia, the Kingdom's most-skilled herbologist. She is not far; her apothecary is in Courtfell, the town just outside the castle grounds. Okay?" In actual fact, he didn't have a choice. He had been instructed to accompany her wherever she decided to go.

"Yes, Your Highness."

"Good." A small smile graced her lips in relief that at least one thing was going according to plan. She stopped in front of the doors to the breakfast room and turned towards Favian, her nerves suddenly taking over. "Please, just... act normal," she pleaded, hoping he would at least try to blend in and not draw too much attention to himself.

He nodded once in response, leaving Chhaya feeling anything but reassured. She sighed and opened the doors, seeing Della already in the room, filling a mug with coffee. Chhaya insisted that Della join her for breakfast, and the two of them walked over to Chhaya's usual table with her friends, which was surprisingly full for such an early time in the morning.

"Good morning," they all chorused, greeting Chhaya and Della with warm smiles.

Chhaya smiled back at them, but she couldn't help feeling nervous as she looked over her right shoulder to see what Favian would do. She felt a brief moment of relief when she couldn't see him and hoped he had decided to eat breakfast elsewhere. "Thank goodness," she breathed. "I thought he would never—" she stopped talking as she noticed all her friends were looking above her head rather than at her. She turned slowly, already knowing what she would see, but still felt herself deflate when she saw Favian standing behind her left shoulder. He had moved so silently.

"Will you not have breakfast?" she asked, trying her best to maintain a polite tone.

"I had breakfast after the training session, Your Highness."

The title made Lukas widen his eyes, and she decided she had had it. Chhaya leapt to her feet and grabbed Favian's arm, pulling him to the side of the large room. "No more 'Your Highness'."

"But Your Highness—"

"No. I understand that the cloak, the lenses, and the stance are all a part of your role. But please, do not call me 'Highness' in front of anyone. *Please.*"

Favian hesitated momentarily but bowed nonetheless. "Yes, Your High— uh—"

"Chhaya," Chhaya said with softened eyes. She couldn't help but smile at his discomfort.

Favian cleared his throat. "Yes. Chhaya." He held out his arm for her, again gesturing for her to go first. Chhaya cleared her throat and walked back to the table. That was one thing she wouldn't have to worry about, at least.

"Is everything okay?" Della asked in a hushed voice as Chhaya took her seat.

"Never been better."

"Good morning, Gaia!" Chhaya called out in a bubbly voice as she walked into the herbologist's apothecary and smiled at the familiar sound of the bell jingling above the door. She inhaled deeply, breathing in the smells of fresh herbs and plants and spices. There was an especially minty scent in the air today.

"Good morning Princess!" Gaia called back in a trembling voice, her words muffled and distant.

Chhaya made sure the door was firmly closed behind them, shutting out the icy winter air, and led the way through the shop and around the shelves, chuckling at Favian, who was forced to duck his head under the herbs that were drying on the metal railings on the ceiling. The dark wooden floorboards creaked loudly under Favian's feet as he manoeuvred around the large wooden workbench near the back. The two walked through the stone archway at the back of the shop and emerged in Gaia's lab.

"I smell mint," Chhaya commented, offering the older lady a warm hug. "Are you making an elixir for a stomach ailment?"

"Ah, you are learning quickly," Gaia exclaimed proudly, returning the hug with one arm while continuing to stir the contents of the large metal cauldron over the fire in front of her with the other. Chhaya didn't know anybody else who, at Gaia's age, would be able to continue with such heavy work; it was admirable. "But no. That is the smell of the fresh mint tea I put on." She indicated to a pot of tea sitting on the table nearby.

Chhaya grinned at the herbologist and approached the table, lifting the top and deeply inhaling its potent scent. "It smells perfect," she said appreciatively, pouring three cups of the tea.

"Now tell me, who is this you have brought along with you today?" Gaia asked before removing the cauldron from the fire and bringing it over to the worktop, where she decanted it into four different vials.

Chhaya turned to look at Favian, who was standing a few feet away, his arms crossed over his chest and a blank expression on his face.

"Favian," she replied, simultaneously answering Gaia's question and handing him his cup of tea. At first, he simply stared at the tea, not taking it, but Chhaya raised her brows and kept it held out towards him.

"Hello," he said, finally accepting the drink from her.

"Hello, Favian. Are you Chhaya's... *significant other*?" Gaia asked, glancing at Chhaya with eyes filled with hope, causing Chhaya's cheeks to pink as her face filled with horror.

"No, no," Favian quickly responded, flustered, at the same time that Chhaya protested.

"Favian is my bodyguard," Chhaya answered.

"I see you haven't changed your mind then," Gaia chuckled but looked away, her shoulders drooping. "Bodyguard?"

"Papa insisted," Chhaya grumbled, rolling her eyes.

"Well now, Favian, how are you enjoying the Khiona Kingdom?" Gaia asked, taking her cup of tea from Chhaya.

"Very well, thank you. I grew up here," Favian responded, his voice less rigid.

"You did?" Chhaya asked, turning to him. She was unsure why it was so surprising to her. He just hadn't seemed comfortable since he had arrived, and Chhaya had assumed he simply felt out of sorts in a new place.

"Well, it must be nice to be back home, in that case," Gaia said with a kind smile.

Favian awkwardly nodded once before sipping his tea. Chhaya watched him for a moment, trying to gauge his mood. He seemed more at ease now, less like a stiff and emotionless bodyguard who cared only about his job, and she couldn't help but feel a twinge of guilt. She had been anything but kind to him since his arrival, and it was clear she had only made things worse, both for him *and* herself.

"What is it that you have made?" Chhaya questioned, nodding at the vials Gaia had filled.

"A blood replenishment tincture," Gaia replied. She looked up at Chhaya, then glanced at Favian before looking back at Chhaya with sad eyes. "In this age, you never know when you will need it. This particular tincture takes only 24 hours to brew, but I have another that has been brewing for two weeks already. It will require a further two weeks before it is ready."

"It takes four weeks to make?" asked Chhaya.

"Yes, because it is very potent. One drop of the Moon Orchard Potion will be enough to replenish an entire body with blood for a week."

"I hope you won't have to use it," Favian said suddenly, his voice thick and his comment surprising Chhaya. Since he had arrived, he had only spoken if he felt it necessary.

Gaia raised her eyebrows at him. "As do I, Favian. But one never really knows. Better to have it on hand." Her lips thinned. "So, are you ready for today's lesson?"

"Gaia seems nice," Favian commented, breaking the silence between them as they walked.

"She is," Chhaya agreed, somewhat surprised that Favian had initiated a conversation. "And she has been kind enough to teach me over the past months."

"Princess!" a voice called, and a little boy suddenly came running up to her, throwing himself into her legs and burying his face into the cotton dress that was concealing warm trousers.

"Sebastian!" Chhaya laughed, caught off guard by the enthusiastic greeting. "You've been getting very strong lately. Any day now, we will go flying if you barrel into me like that." Favian immediately tensed beside her, but Chhaya rolled her eyes at him. Surely he wasn't considering this child a threat? "This is Sebastian," she said calmly. "He gets excited but means no harm."

"Are you coming to visit us?" Sebastian asked excitedly, grabbing Chhaya's hand and pulling her along the cobblestone roads with him.

"Of course! Where else would I be going?" Chhaya replied with a smile.

Sebastian, as if for the first time noticing Favian, stopped and examined him through narrowed eyes. He tugged on Chhaya's hand and pulled her down into a crouch. "Who is that?" he whispered into her ear.

"That's Favian," responded Chhaya, whispering back to him. She looked over her shoulder at Favian, who stared uncomfortably at the ground, and back to Sebastian. "He's my bodyguard."

Sebastian's eyes widened in surprise, and he looked back at Favian with newfound curiosity. "He's your bodyguard? What does he do?"

"He protects me," Chhaya explained, ruffling Sebastian's hair affectionately.

"Oh," Sebastian said, his eyes lighting up with understanding. "Like a hero!"

Chhaya chuckled and stood up, still holding onto Sebastian's hand as she adjusted the thick velvet cloak on her shoulders. "Yes, like a hero."

Sebastian narrowed his eyes at him, analysing his dark, collared cloak and lenses before turning back to Chhaya. "He looks mean," he grumbled.

"He isn't," Chhaya reassured.

"Why are you here?" Sebastian asked, addressing Favian this time.

"To protect the Princess," Favian responded simply.

"From what?" he asked, his eyes wide with curiosity.

"Assassins, murderers, Blood Magicians—" Favian began.

"He's just joking!" Chhaya interrupted, shooting daggers at Favian. The last thing the children needed to worry about was Blood Magicians. It seemed the damage was already done, however, as Sebastian watched Favian in horror. "Sebastian, I was thinking perhaps we could show Favian your brand-new toy?"

"That's a great idea!" exclaimed Sebastian, jumping eagerly and pulling Chhaya along once again. "Kat said she thinks it's the best kite she's ever seen! She wanted one too, but I let her share mine."

"That's very kind of you, Sebastian. Isn't it, Favian?" Chhaya raised her eyebrows challengingly at him.

He looked at her silently for a few moments before nodding once. "Yes."

Chhaya fought the urge to roll her eyes. It seemed that was the only response she would be getting from him.

Chapter Four

"From today, eligible suitors from all over the Three Kingdoms will be coming to the castle," Chhaya told Favian after their training session, her arms folded firmly across her chest. "They will all be here to meet me, and one of them may even become my husband. The future King." She already knew they wouldn't, but at the risk of Favian reporting back to her father, she had to at least act as though she was considering it. "Please," she said earnestly, walking over to him and placing one hand on his shoulder. "Please, don't embarrass me."

Favian turned his head ever so slightly to look at her hand, which was still resting on his shoulder. She quickly removed it.

"Yes, Chhaya."

"There'll be a few different events and activities," she said as they began to walk to the breakfast room. "Today, I will meet everyone, and tomorrow we will have an informal tea. In the coming weeks, there will be picnics, afternoon teas, dinners, balls, and breakfasts. It is going to be busy." She looked back at Favian, but he had no reaction. Of course, she didn't expect one.

"And I thought I told you to get rid of the cloak and the lenses," she hissed at him as they walked into the breakfast room.

"Uniform, Your Highness."

"Seriously, Chhaya, you have got to do something about that cloak," Mia laughed. The two of them and Della were in the restroom, the only place they could speak freely without Favian overhearing. "I don't believe I have ever seen the children look so scared as when the two of you came to the orphanage last week."

"Tell me about it," Chhaya sighed. The moment they had entered the orphanage, all the children had stopped to stare at him. If the darkness of the offending item of clothing hadn't been enough, the collar certainly had. He had looked rather frightening, standing tall in the doorway and staring at everybody. Some of the children had even hidden behind her and Mia. "No matter how much I try, he will not take it off."

"Have you tried... simply... disposing of the cloak?" Mia asked.

Chhaya widened her eyes. "You absolute genius."

"Tell me something I don't know; I can't believe you didn't think of it before."

"Neither can I. Now I just need some way to rid myself of him altogether," she joked.

"Oh, come on, Chhaya. He's not so bad," laughed Della. "The poor man has done nothing but follow instructions since he got here."

"A little too well, I believe," Chhaya said. "At this rate, all the men who arrive tomorrow will merely turn around and leave."

"I was under the impression you didn't want to get married anyway," Mia interjected, wagging her eyebrows. "Has someone changed her mind?"

"Of course I do not want to get married," Chhaya responded with a scoff. "After everything... well, I have never wanted to marry, you both know that. But in order for this to work—in order for the people to have the distraction they need—this event must last the month. Besides, the fact that I do not want to marry does not mean I cannot have a nice time over the next few weeks. Picnics and lunches and balls and afternoon teas. And hopefully, new friends. How could anyone complain?"

"You never know, Chhaya, you might just meet your future husband tomorrow," teased Della.

"And on the bright side, Favian can be seen from a mile away in that ghastly cloak. He's the perfect way to frighten away any of the suitors you don't want here," Mia joked.

"Are you sure this is a good idea?" Della whispered as she and Chhaya hurried through the castle corridors.

"Come on!" Chhaya whispered back. "This is our only opportunity. My father has called him into a meeting before the bachelors arrive, so this is our only chance to get into his room."

They hurried along the corridor and, sure nobody was watching them, Chhaya opened the door to her bodyguard's room.

Della wrinkled her forehead. "This is—"

"Empty?" Chhaya finished. She closed the door behind them to analyse the bare walls, the plain, pristinely made bed and the clear tables. "I suppose he doesn't have many personal items?"

"It's a little sad, though," Della commented as Chhaya hurried to the dark, wooden wardrobe.

From inside, she removed two cloaks, both exactly the same, and placed them on the bed. Other than the cloaks, the only other items the wardrobe contained were the loose black tunics and black trousers he wore to their training sessions, the tight black trousers he wore under the collared cloak, two pairs of black leather boots, and the thick tunics he wore under his cloak.

"It's probably best not to dwell. At least, not right now. We must leave before he returns."

"Are you taking the other garments?" Della questioned, gesturing to the wardrobe.

Chhaya tilted her head. "If I take everything, he will be left with nothing." She closed the wardrobe again and took the cloaks in her arms.

"What are you going to do with those?" asked Della as they ran back through the corridors.

"Good question," replied Chhaya. They arrived back at her room, and Chhaya dumped the suits onto her bed. "What to do with them?"

Just then, there was a knock at the door. Chhaya looked at Della, whose lips twisted in alarm. Nonetheless, Della headed over to the door and opened it. "Favian!" she cried, looking back at Chhaya with wide eyes.

"Favian!" Chhaya called, too, hurrying out the door to avoid him coming inside and seeing the pile of black fabric on her bed. She locked eyes with Della, who nodded and dashed back inside to hide the cloaks.

"Hello, Your... I mean, hello, Chhaya. I just came to your room to inform you that my meeting with your father is over. You will be needed shortly to greet the first potential suitors. But first, I must go to my room. A waiter spilt tea on my clothes, and I must change."

"You're going to change now?" Chhaya asked, her eyes wide. She couldn't believe her luck; he would be out of that ridiculous cloak by the time she met the first group of bachelors.

"Yes. Please wait here for me, and I will accompany you downstairs."

"Of course, Favian."

Favian furrowed his eyebrows at her, and Chhaya was sure he could sense that something was different, but he bowed and marched away.

Chhaya closed the door behind him and burst into laughter. Neither she nor Della could help it.

"Maybe you should wait for him, Chhaya," Della said as she fastened Chhaya's dress. Her hair and makeup had already been done simply to compliment her natural features and loose curls. The dress she chose to wear was certainly casual—a walking dress rather than a gown—but paired with a formal coat, she looked effortlessly put together.

"He has been gone for far too long, Della. I would have had time for you to style my hair three times already. I don't know why I'm so nervous; I don't plan to marry any of them. But I may as well enjoy myself while they are here, mightn't I?"

"I suppose so, Chhaya, but—"

"Well, how do I look?" she asked, twirling around when Della finished the fastenings.

Della smiled. "You look as though you merely threw on those clothes without thinking twice about it because you are so carefree and uninterested. But you still happened to look flawless. Accidentally."

"Precisely what I was hoping for." Chhaya grinned. "I suppose I shall see you later then."

"You're really not going to wait for him?" asked Della.

Chhaya shrugged. "There's no need, really, is there? When he arrives, please do tell him I have already gone down."

"Okay," Della called when Chhaya was already halfway out the door. "Good luck!"

A cool chill travelled down the corridor, and Chhaya buttoned up her jacket as she walked. The final button was stubborn, and she couldn't quite get it through the buttonhole. All of a sudden, she hit something large and hard and felt herself falling backwards before two strong hands grabbed her, one on her waist and one on her back, and lifted her back onto her feet, steadying her easily.

"Chhaya? Are you okay?" Favian questioned, still holding her upright.

Chhaya looked up at him with wide eyes. "Sorry," she whispered. "I was not looking where I was going."

"It was my fault, Chhaya. Are you hurt?"

Chhaya cleared her throat, looking at where Favian's hands were now resting on her shoulders to keep her steady, suddenly extremely aware of them and how close to him she was standing. He quickly dropped his hands and took a step back.

"I'm fine, Favian. Thank you, but—" she stopped when she looked at him properly. "What are you wearing?"

Favian cleared his throat. "I'm sorry, Chhaya. It has not been pressed, but my other cloaks have all been taken. I do not know where they have gone. This was laundered but not pressed. I hope I will not embarrass you by being dressed like this."

Chhaya couldn't believe it. After so much trouble, he had still turned up wearing the cloak. She huffed and turned away from him, marching down the stairs. She did feel a sense of comfort, however, at feeling him walking behind her. His once irritating and unrelenting presence now... somewhat less irritating and unrelenting to her.

She hadn't wanted him around, but she felt more at ease having someone she was familiar with coming with her to meet the suitors.

Chapter Five

"It is lovely to meet you, Damon," Chhaya said as the blonde-haired man stood up from his bow.

"The pleasure is all mine, Your Highness," he said in a deep, smooth voice that Chhaya knew she would never tire of listening to as he flashed her a handsome smile. She couldn't help the blush that warmed her face and gave him another smile before greeting the next person.

As expected, she felt Favian's presence as he moved with her, standing, as usual, two steps behind her. She saw the next guest, a shorter boy with dark hair who looked as though he might have only just turned sixteen years of age, barely old enough to be invited as a suitor. He stared wide-eyed, his gaze fixed behind her as he chewed on the inside of his cheek. She couldn't blame him; Favian hardly looked like the most friendly person in the Kingdoms.

"Hello," she said in a gentle voice that she referred to as her 'princess voice'. It was the soft-spoken tone she used to greet people or speak to the villagers who were not familiar with her.

The small boy in front of her jumped as if she'd come up behind him to scare him. He swallowed. "Your... Your Highness," he stammered out, sinking into a deep bow. She waited for him to stand again, but he stayed in that position.

Chhaya bit her cheek to hide her laughter and turned around so the poor boy wouldn't see her or feel embarrassed. She caught—at least she *thought* she caught since she couldn't really tell through the dark lenses—Favian's eyes and his lips twitched into an amused curve. It was all Chhaya could do not to burst out laughing.

She turned around again and cleared her throat. "Please do stand," she told him in a surprisingly steady voice. "I'm Chhaya. It's a pleasure to meet you."

"Princess Chhaya!" The boy said, straightening up again. "Yes, I am Viraj." His face was so pale Chhaya was worried he wasn't breathing. She decided to nod politely before moving on to the next person before the poor child passed out.

To her relief, the next guest was a fully grown man, a duke, and he didn't look as though he were about to explode in fear. She offered him her practised smile, which was wide enough that it looked genuine but wasn't too wide that it would hurt her mouth after an hour.

"Your Highness, it's a pleasure to meet—" he stuck out his hand and, before Chhaya could even think twice, was on the floor with a loud thud and restrained by none other than Favian.

"Favian!" Chhaya hissed, covering her hand over her mouth as she stared at the display in front of her. Favian stood as if he had been called to attention, bringing the man with him and clasping his wrists in a tight hold. "Favian, I think he only intended to shake my hand," she whispered, partly shocked, partly mortified and partly trying her hardest not to laugh at the looks on their faces.

The duke tried to stand and shake Favian off, but it was useless. In a split second, Favian twisted his wrist and sent him to the ground, dropping after him to check his pockets and hands.

It was not long before Favian jumped back up to his feet, moving to stand behind Chhaya once again and leaving the duke on the floor. "He is clear," he said as if he had not just tackled a person to the floor and left him there.

Was Chhaya to help him up? Should she apologise? It wasn't her fault, after all.

But the Duke on the floor cleared his throat and leapt easily to his feet, swiftly brushing off his clothes and running a quick hand through his waves, somehow managing to look like he hadn't just been tackled to the ground. "It's no matter," he said, smiling at Chhaya. Amusement flickered in his eyes, and Chhaya exhaled, pleased to find he had a sense of humour. "I understand. These days, one must take precautions." He looked at Favian, this time with a raised brow, before holding his hand out to Chhaya. "I am Aamir. It's an honour, Your Highness."

With shining eyes, she accepted his handshake.

"Well, that was eventful," Chhaya chuckled, walking back into her room, where Della had already lit the fire and prepared a warm bath.

"Eventful how?" Della asked.

"Where do I begin?"

Della removed her coat and began to work on the fastenings of her dress. "One of the guests left immediately after meeting me and did not even bother to wait until the end of the engagement.

Another only cared about when dinner would be served because, according to his neighbour, the feasts served in the palace were greater than any other. Another wanted to clarify I was certain I was next in line to the throne and that he would definitely become the King," she told Della, amused, before getting into the bathtub. "He left when I told him my husband would only become the King after my father abdicated and I was crowned the Queen. One boy, who, by the way, was far too young to be here, nearly fainted at the sight of Favian and then again at the sight of me! Oh, and speaking of Favian, he tackled someone to the ground for attempting to shake my hand."

"He did what?" exclaimed Della.

"Can you believe it?" Chhaya called as she sunk into the water, closing her eyes and sighing as the warmth caressed every inch of her aching muscles. "He later informed me that papa had instructed him to be particularly vigilant in case of any Blood Magicians. He thought the poor man might have had a knife." While she had been embarrassed at first, Chhaya could now see why Favian had been concerned; if a Blood Magician had been to get inside and slice through the palm of their hand, producing their own blood, they would have been able to use their Blood Magic. It was not an outcome any of them were willing to allow.

"Where is he now?"

"He is expected to report to my father each time we meet visitors, so he's with him now. I warned him to stay outside the bedroom when he was done so I could bathe and change again."

"At least he's listening to you now."

"Somewhat. He still refuses to relinquish the cloak. Or the lenses."

"I feel for him, Chhaya. His room was so bare. It's like his life is empty. Not even a picture or a glass or a mug or a note. Nothing."

"Perhaps that's exactly what he needs, Della," Chhaya responded as she began to lather her arms with soap. "Something to make him happy."

"Perhaps it is not a some*thing*, but a some*one* that will make him happy."

Chhaya scoffed. "I think love is the last thing that man wants." She closed her eyes once again, leaning her head back against the edge of the tub and making the most of the warmth; it was freezing outside, worse than any previous winter in the Khiona Kingdom, and she would take every last drop of heat she could get. Besides, she was still stiff from her daily training, and the hot water worked to soothe her muscles.

"You have a point. I don't think I have ever seen him smile," Della said consideringly.

"Precisely," Chhaya responded. "It's a little sad, truly. If only there were something we could do."

"Maybe you could offer him some time off?" suggested Della.

"I'm not so sure... You remember what he was like the day we met him; he refused to leave, and we were forced to allow him into the room to wait while I finished getting ready. He takes his job far too seriously."

"He certainly needs some sort of distraction."

"A distraction," muttered Chhaya, biting her bottom lip in thought. "He may not know it yet, but he could undoubtedly use a distraction."

"Even if it's a hobby. You never know; he may like watercolour painting."

Chhaya couldn't help but laugh at that. The thought of Favian, the huge and emotionless Favian, painting cherry blossoms while wearing his long cloak and tinted lenses with a delicate little brush was too much. He would likely break the paintbrush in half.

"Okay, maybe not watercolours," laughed Della.

"But perhaps you're right, Della. Maybe Favian merely needs somebody's attention." For a few minutes, she imagined what Favian would be like if someone *did* have a crush on him. Would he enjoy the attention? Or would he feel uncomfortable? Her eyes opened, and she smiled, sitting up in the bathtub. "I've got the perfect idea."

Since not all the guests had arrived yet, the King had allowed Chhaya to have lunch with her friends and then dinner with them later that evening, her last night of comfort before things truly began in the castle.

From tomorrow, there were to be events in the day, such as horse rides and picnics, as well as nightly dinners, dancing and entertainment. Chhaya couldn't quite claim she was dreading the days to come, but at the same time, she wasn't entirely excited either.

"Favian, please do sit down and eat lunch with us," Chhaya pleaded, gesturing to the chair by her side. Favian hesitated, scanning the room through his lenses. "You'll be right next to me! You can't get any closer than that."

Favian's eyebrows rose an almost imperceptible amount, and Chhaya heard muffled chuckles from her friends around the table. Rather than feel embarrassed, she smiled at the twinge of Favian's lips.

"If you insist, Chhaya," he said, bowing before sitting beside her. Chhaya felt relief course through her body. If she could get him to sit next to her during all of their meals, maybe this whole thing wouldn't be so bad. At least then, he wouldn't look like an ominous statue staring at everybody while they ate and conversed.

While he was in the mood to listen to her, she decided to try her luck. "Do you not think the cloak is a little too bold?" she leaned over and asked him in a hushed voice.

"Bold?" he repeated.

"Well, if somebody were here to abduct me or assassinate me or whatever it is that you are here to protect me from, they'll see your dramatic cloak immediately, know who you are and therefore know my exact location."

Chhaya observed as Favian considered what she had said. Whether or not he agreed with her now, he would certainly share her point of view from tomorrow.

"They'll also know to target you before me," she continued when he stayed silent. "To eliminate you as my bodyguard first."

"I do not believe anyone would be looking for my cloak."

"Perhaps not on purpose, but that's not to say they wouldn't notice you more easily."

"Many people wear cloaks."

Chhaya purposefully made a show of looking around the room and raised her eyebrows, shrugging dramatically. "Not like yours." Even Lukas was wearing a cloak today, but his smooth purple fabric differed vastly from Favian's menacing collar and stiff fabric, enveloping the bodyguard as if it were a frightening extension of himself. He truly did look like the epitome of death. "I merely thought I would bring it to your attention." She looked away, casually biting into a warm bread roll slathered with a generous layer of butter.

"Chhaya, are you listening?" Lukas asked from across the table. She looked up in time to see him throw a bread roll towards her. Immediately, a breeze flew across her face as she felt herself being moved backwards. Only no hands moved her. It was as though a gust of wind had arrived from nowhere to move her out of the way, as a hand shot out in front of her and caught the roll just millimetres away from her face. Favian closed his hand around the bread roll and dropped it onto the table in front of her in silence.

Chhaya watched him, slack-jawed, as he picked up his own bread roll as if nothing had happened and bit into it. He seemed so calm, so collected, and yet he had acted at an unimaginable speed. And had he used Magic to move her? Her father had been right; his Magic was at a level she had never before witnessed.

She glanced at Lukas, who was watching Favian with wide eyes and a panicked frown, and bit the inside of her cheek.

"A reflex," Favian said eventually, breaking the silence with his deep yet somehow soft voice.

Chhaya picked up the discarded roll from the table in front of her and examined it. Before long, she couldn't keep it back any longer and started laughing, throwing her head back in utter delight.

"That's what you get," she said between laughs, throwing the roll back at Lukas, who yelped and clutched his eye.

"Chhaya!" he exclaimed with a chuckle. "I'm going to need some ice. Who knew you and bread could be such a deadly combination."

Chhaya chuckled. "You certainly do not want to know what I can do with a full loaf."

"Goddess, don't let your band of fawning fans hear you discuss such matters!" Mia interjected, feigning shock.

Chhaya immediately made a face, scrunching her nose. "Could you call them anything else?"

"That poor boy you mentioned would faint if he caught you throwing a roll across the table," laughed Della.

Even Favian's lips twitched at that comment.

Chhaya grinned at her; it wasn't often that Della felt comfortable enough around her friends to join in the conversation. She was glad she was beginning to feel relaxed enough to consider them her peers rather than merely Chhaya's.

"While on the topic of your potential husbands," began Lukas, placing his head on his hand and causing Chhaya to sour her face, "are you truly serious about all of this?"

"We all know you never intended on marrying. What inspired this change?" Mia asked.

Chhaya glanced at Favian, who was quietly drinking his water and eating his bread, keeping his head down. Was he listening to the conversation? Was he also curious about her motivations? Would he report back to her father? Did he even care if she married or not?

She shrugged her shoulders ever so slightly, pressing her lips into a tight smile as she looked back at the others. "I told my father I would seriously consider it, and I will."

"What a revelation. Chhaya is considering marriage." Mia waggled her eyebrows, and Chhaya couldn't resist the smile that spread to her eyes.

"Please." Chhaya rolled her eyes. "This is not so big of a revelation. In truth, nobody knows what life has in store for them, so we must simply wait and see what happens."

Lukas scoffed. "For as long as I have known you, you have had no interest in marrying. In fact, it's even more than that; you've been actively *against* the prospect of marriage. For yourself, at least."

From the corner of her eye, Chhaya noticed that while he appeared to be eating indifferently and paying no attention whatsoever, Favian's back had straightened. Perhaps he *was* intending to report back to her father.

She cleared her throat and took a sip of water, casting her eyes away from the bodyguard. "My previous thoughts no longer matter. I have told my father I will consider all of my guests, and that is what I will do." She finally turned back to Favian. "We had better hurry. The rest of the suitors will be arriving soon, and we are to meet them after lunch."

Chapter Six

Everything had gone exactly how Chhaya had intended. She had planted the seed of doubt in Favian's mind during lunch earlier, and while he had disagreed with her, the thought had at least stayed with him. Of that, she was sure.

All that was left to do was reinforce the idea, make him certain that she had been right after all. And what better way to do so than in a way that would make Favian feel most uncomfortable?

Dressed in her silk night robe, thick gown and warm slippers, Chhaya sat at the large, wooden writing desk pressed against the wall in her room. The fire flickered gently behind her, and the moon shone brightly through the window—the perfect ambience.

All that was left to do now was to write.

Favian

No, that was much too informal. She flipped the sheet and started again.

Dear Favian

No. She scrunched up the parchment. That didn't feel right, either. She needed something that sounded as though she was indeed in love with him.

Dearest Bodyguard.

That was it.

I hope you will forgive me for reaching out in such a way. I couldn't help myself any longer. I simply had to write to you.

She tapped the quill on her cheek as she stared at the inked letters in front of her.

From the moment you arrived in this castle, I have been drawn to you. Those mysterious eyes you hide behind those dark lenses of yours, the way your lips twitch when you are trying not to laugh, the way your fists clench when you are concerned, the way you tense your jaw when you're stressed. I cannot help but notice.

She chewed on her bottom lip. Was that too much detail? But she dipped her quill in the deep black ink once again and continued to pen the letter.

Just the sight of your dark suit in the room makes my heart flutter. You look ever so handsome in that uniform of yours, that majestic cloak you wear, and I feel as though I could spot you a mile away. It is so freeing, so reassuring to be able to identify you so easily, knowing you are there.

You may not know me very well, Favian, but I know you. I see you even if you do not see me. I can only hope that one day, you will see me too.

I must go, Favian, but I will see you later. You will see me too, of course, only you will not know it.

Until then.

"Good evening Chhaya," Della said, entering the room with a slice of cake on a plate. It was Chhaya's favourite, but she had been too tired after dinner to stay for dessert.

Chhaya startled, leaping up and splattering ink on the parchment in the process.

"Della," she sighed, one hand on her racing heart in an attempt to calm it and the other blotting up the excess ink from the letter with a tissue. "I did not hear you come in. Thank you." Chhaya accepted the cake with a grateful grin. It was covered in a rich, warm custard and truly was the perfect thing on such an icy night.

"How was it meeting the rest of the guests this afternoon?"

"Not quite as eventful as this morning," Chhaya told her with an amused grin. "But, of course, everyone was still terrified of Favian."

Della chuckled. "He doesn't have to try, does he?"

"I don't think he means to be frightening," Chhaya agreed.

"And how are you feeling about the first official event tomorrow? It's afternoon tea, isn't it?"

Chhaya slumped sideways on the sofa and leaned her head against the back. "I'm not sure how I feel about tomorrow, Della. Actually, I don't feel any kind of emotion towards it. It merely feels like any other day. I have no reason to be nervous because I don't particularly want to marry, and there is no need to be excited because... well... for the same reason, I suppose."

Della sat on the opposite end of the sofa with a warm smile. "On the bright side, you will have the chance to spend the afternoon in the garden, which you love."

Chhaya smiled in return. "That's true. And there's always Favian to keep me company if the others become too boring," she joked but wrinkled her forehead. Why was Favian on her mind at all? Perhaps because of the letter. She glanced over at where it lay to dry.

"What would you like to wear tomorrow? I'll make sure it's pressed and ready for you."

"I believe I am expected to wear a dress, so I shall wear my riding trousers."

Della raised her eyebrows. "Your riding trousers with what?"

"Perhaps a short tunic and a thick cloak of some sort. It'll keep me warm, and then I can go for a ride."

"If you insist." Della nodded. "Well, if there is nothing else you need, I'll leave you to enjoy your evening. Relax and make the most of it while you can, will you?"

"Actually, Della, there is one more thing," Chhaya said, a small and cheeky smile spreading across her face as she stood up and walked over to her writing desk. She folded the now-dry letter and held it out to her maid. "Before you return to your room tonight, could you perhaps slip this under Favian's door?"

Della narrowed her eyes but took the folded sheet nonetheless. "What is this?" she asked, unfolding it.

"Just a short letter I wrote to my bodyguard." Chhaya blinked innocently.

"And you are not delivering it because?"

"I do not want to be caught and would have less of a reason to be out of my quarters than you would."

"So you won't mind if I read it then?"

"Of course not. As long as you do not tell him it's from me." She watched in anticipation as Della read the letter.

Finally, Della put the letter down and sighed. "I don't think this is a good idea, Chhaya."

Chhaya frowned. "Why not?"

"It's just... it's not nice of you to do this to him."

Chhaya scoffed. "Oh, come on, Della. It is perfectly innocent. He won't even know who wrote it and will never discover the truth. All I want is for him to remove the cloak. It makes everyone uncomfortable. He looks terrifying wearing that ghastly thing."

"First of all, the man would look terrifying even if he wore bright blue night clothes. And secondly, surely there is a better way to deal with this?"

"Such as?"

"Such as speaking with your father, maybe?"

Chhaya rolled her eyes. "My father does not care about what Favian wears. And if he cared enough about the people being frightened of him to enforce any changes, he would not have assigned Favian to me in the first place."

Della sighed and folded her arms, looking at the piece of parchment once again. "Are you sure about this?"

There was a twinge in Chhaya's stomach. Was this the right decision? But she folded her arms over. "I'm sure, Della. It was your idea in the first place, besides."

"My idea?" exclaimed Della, her eyes bugging.

"You were the one to suggest he could do with some attention!"

Della exhaled. "I did say that, didn't I?"

"Come on. It won't harm anyone."

"If you would like me to deliver this for you, I will. But please note I'm still very much against it."

"You'll see, Della. It'll work. And who's to say, perhaps we'll even see the mighty Favian smile. Please just trust me. Tomorrow, he will be out of the suit, I won't write any more letters, and he will forget about it. If nothing else, he'll at least feel good about himself."

"Okay, Chhaya. I'll deliver this on my way down."

"Chhaya, it's time to get up," a muffled voice told her through her thick blanket.

"Why?" Chhaya complained with a groan, pulling the blanket even tighter around her.

"It's time for your training with Favian." It was Della. She eased the duvet off Chhaya's face and opened the curtains.

"But I still ache from yesterday. My muscles feel as though they are on fire."

"It could be worse; he could be forcing you up at five in the morning for this rather than six."

"But he still forces me to run," she whined. "That shouldn't be allowed at any time of the day."

"I have a feeling he'll make you run double the length if you're late."

"Fine," Chhaya grumbled, the threat of additional running enough to wake her. "But if these early starts and training sessions don't kill me first, I will be forced to kill him."

"You may try, Your Highness," said a voice from the doorway.

"Favian, what are you doing here?!" Chhaya exclaimed, pulling the blanket back up around her.

"I only came to see if you were ready to go. The door was already open," he replied, his tone as monotone as usual, but a hint of a smile graced his lips.

"Well, I am *not* ready, Favian. Get out!" She threw a pillow in his direction, but he managed to close the door just in time for it to hit the back of the wood with a pathetic thud. She turned slowly and looked helplessly at Della. "I *am* going to kill him."

She emerged from her room minutes later wearing a loose tunic with her riding boots and glared at him as if her eyes could burn a hole through him if she tried hard enough. He stared back at her in silence, his hands clasped behind his back once again, although he didn't look as ridiculous when he wasn't wearing the cloak. In fact, he looked rather good in his training clothes, even if they were still black. The sleeves were tight against his arms, and the tunic fitted him perfectly around the torso.

He cleared his throat, breaking her reverie, and Chhaya fought the urge to hit her head against the wall in embarrassment when she saw his raised eyebrow. He had caught her ogling him. She really could be rather idiotic this early in the morning.

"What are you smirking about?" she snapped, turning to walk down the corridor.

"Nothing, Your Highness," he replied in an amused tone, following behind her. "Are you ready to run?"

She sighed. She was definitely going to kill him.

"Did he mention it?" Della asked the moment Chhaya returned.

"Mention what?" Chhaya slipped off her leather boots and entered the bathing room, overjoyed to see a steaming bath already prepared for her. Favian had been determined to make every muscle burn.

"You know. The thing," Della whispered.

"The letter?" Chhaya slipped into her steamy bath with an appreciative sigh. "Of course not." She lay back, allowing herself to completely submerge in the hot water, keeping just her face above it.

"So he is not aware it was me?" Della called from the other room.

"I don't think so."

"You're sure?"

"Did he see you leaving the note?" asked Chhaya after a beat, closing her eyes as she allowed the heat to soothe her aches.

"I don't believe so."

"Then I am sure he does not know. Besides, I am sure he would have mentioned it if he had seen you."

"And do you think it worked?"

Chhaya took a breath and sank into the water, fully submerging herself and exhaling, allowing the bubbles to float up to the surface before emerging again. "He seemed normal this morning. Apart from the fact that he forced me to work twice as hard as usual, nothing seems to have changed. It is possible he has not even had the chance to read the letter yet."

"I suppose you'll find out when it's time for breakfast," Della declared, poking her head into the bathing room and gathering the clothes Chhaya had left on the floor. "Shall I get some tea?"

"I could use a coffee this morning. I'm still not used to waking this early."

Della nodded. "I won't be long."

Moments later, Chhaya heard the door to her quarters open and close as Della left, leaving her in blissful quiet. She could hear the faint crackling of the fire, which was always lit this time of year, and the bird chirping happily outside.

When the water cooled, Chhaya emerged, somewhat reluctantly, from the bath and dressed in the clothes Della had left for her, not waiting for Della to return to dress her; the last thing she wanted today was to be late for breakfast, or her father would never let her forget it. She had promised him that she would give everyone a fair chance and was determined to do so.

When Della returned, she twisted Chhaya's hair into a braid and pulled a few strands out to frame her face, keeping the freshly-washed hair out of her face while still looking elegant. She admired herself in her vanity, the deep green tunic perfectly complimenting her skin tone and matching the riding trousers, emerald green cloak, and brown riding boots. She was giving them a chance, but she was not going to dress up in a ballgown every time she met any of them.

There was a knock at the door, and Chhaya allowed Della to open it, although she quickly realised that had been a mistake as Della began stuttering and panicking the moment she saw Favian on the other side of the door.

"Favian. Hello. What— I mean— how— will you— Chhaya is—"

"Come in, Favian," Chhaya called, inviting him in before Della could say much more. When she got nervous, she did have a tendency to speak too much, and this wasn't quite the ideal moment to reveal to Favian that she had written the letter. "I won't need much longer, so you can—"

This time it was she who was unable to produce a complete sentence. When she turned, she found him standing mere steps away but wearing only his black trousers and tight black tunic rather than his usual attire.

Somehow, the lack of the cloak made him seem even taller as he towered over Chhaya. She swallowed. It appeared Della had not been stammering because of the letter.

"There is no rush, Your Highness," he said with a nod.

Chhaya cleared her throat. She had seen him out of that suit during their early-morning training sessions, yes, but she certainly had not been prepared for this.

"Is everything okay, Your Highness?" he asked, looking around as if expecting someone to see an intruder.

"Yes," she mumbled, turning back to her dressing table. "Everything is fine."

"Chhaya, do you need any help?" asked Della, who was still staring at Favian, her eyes slightly wide.

"No, thank you," Chhaya responded in a tone she hoped was calm. "I'm ready. Favian, shall we go to breakfast?" She chose not to invite Della this time, telling herself it was to prevent her from accidentally revealing the author of the letter to Favian and not because of the way she was still staring after him.

"Your Highness," he said with a slight bow as he opened the door for her.

"I believe we already spoke about that, Favian."

"Your Highness?"

"I recall asking you not to call me by my title."

"You asked me not to call you by your title in front of your friends. You did not mention what to call you when we are alone."

"Chhaya is still fine, Favian."

Guards were stationed around the castle, and even more were patrolling. She still felt that Favian's presence was unnecessary.

"I notice you have finally decided to remove the cloak?" she asked in a nonchalant tone, keeping her eyes fixed on the grey stone walls and marble flooring, determined to look anywhere but at him. Della really was terrible at keeping secrets, but Chhaya wasn't much better herself.

"You were right," he responded after a moment of thought. "The cloak was too easily visible, and I could have been identified quickly."

In that moment, Chhaya could only thank the Goddess that he could not see her face—she couldn't keep the smile off her lips. It wasn't that he had quite lied to her, but she still found it amusing that he had chosen to keep his admirer a secret.

"Well." Feeling bold, she turned back to him when they reached the door to the breakfast room. "I must say, you look rather good without it, Favian."

A touch of pink kissed his cheeks, but Chhaya didn't give him a chance to respond, instead turning again and entering the room for breakfast.

"Good morning!" Mia greeted her brightly, barely glancing at Favian before looking at Chhaya. Slowly, her eyes widened in realisation as she turned back to Favian, her jaw slack. "Good morning Favian," she said in a low voice. Her eyebrows wrinkled, and her cheeks coloured.

Favian nodded stiffly but stayed silent. Mia continued to stare, glancing between Favian and Chhaya with her confused eyes. Favian refused to remove his gaze from Mia.

Chhaya wrinkled her brows at him. Why was he staring at Mia like that? As if he was studying her, analysing—suddenly, it struck her. She had to stifle a laugh behind her hand when she realised what Favian was doing. He was trying to figure out if Mia could be the one who had written the letter.

"Shall we sit?" Chhaya asked her friend, biting her cheek to stop the chuckle from escaping her lips. Some of the suitors stood as she walked past, and most of them smiled or said good morning, all hoping she would sit with them. But Chhaya continued walking to her usual table. It wasn't quite the same, as the breakfast room was filled with even more tables than usual and was, as expected, much louder. Even so, this small glimmer of familiarity provided her with a level of peace.

"That's quite a difference," Mia whispered as they approached their table, Favian following behind and vigilantly looking around as usual. He had finally stopped staring, apparently having decided Mia was not the author of the letter.

"Oh, trust me, I am aware," Chhaya replied.

"You don't exactly look as though you're complaining," Mia teased.

Chhaya immediately felt heat rise in her cheeks. "Of course not. I have been trying to convince him to remove that horrid cloak since the day he arrived." She sat down and buttered a slice of toast, hoping the makeup Della had put on her this morning was enough to hide the redness in her face.

"Mmhmm," Mia hummed knowingly, taking her toast and slathering it with orange marmalade.

Chhaya asked a waiter for a cup of chai for herself and an orange juice for Mia. "Favian, what will you have?" she asked.

"Chai, please," he said to the waiter. "Thank you."

Mia leaned in close enough so nobody else would hear her. "That blush on your face tells me you're not as calm as you're pretending to be."

So it had not gone unnoticed.

Chapter Seven

"Thank the Goddess that is over," Chhaya muttered. The entire afternoon had been filled with awkward, strange and unpleasant conversation and Chhaya, for one, was not looking forward to doing it again.

When she had first agreed to this idea, she had not known more than a hundred bachelors would arrive. She sighed, closing her eyes. All she could think about now was getting away from the castle—and all of the people in it—and taking Shadow for a ride.

Favian remained silent next to her, staring out at the group behind her, watching as they all walked back into the castle. "When I agreed to do this, I was under the impression I would enjoy myself a little bit at least. But I only feel exhausted." She started walking towards the stables, the opposite direction from the castle, feeling more than hearing Favian's presence as he walked beside her. "Instead, it seems I have agreed to surround myself with arrogant people who either want my title, my wealth, or my castle."

Of the fifteen suitors she had had the privilege of speaking with this afternoon, only two had actually taken an interest in her as a person and asked her something about herself that was unrelated to riches or royalty. She sighed. One month to go.

"Your Highness!" a voice called from behind. Chhaya glanced at Favian, who had immediately turned, before turning herself to see Damon, one of the suitors she had met the day before, jogging across the grass towards her, his blond hair looking even brighter in the sunlight.

Chhaya smiled at him as he stopped before her and sank into a bow before straightening up and smiling brightly. Chhaya was sure the afternoon would have been much easier had she had the chance to spend time with him.

His eyes flicked to a spot behind her left shoulder, where Favian stood behind her, alert as usual, before looking back at her, seemingly unbothered by his presence. Relief coursed through her. "It's lovely to see you again, Your Highness."

"Likewise," she replied. "Was there anything I could do for you?"

"I was wondering if perhaps you were free for a stroll?"

She hesitated. After spending so much of her afternoon feeling crowded and overwhelmed, Chhaya had been looking forward to spending some time alone. However, she had promised her father that she would try, and it did seem as though Damon was not like the others. She turned to look at Favian, but as usual, he had no reaction, simply staring ahead at Damon, his arms clasped in front of him.

She turned back with a smile. "That would be lovely."

Damon walked over to stand beside her and held out his arm.

"Where would you like to go?" she asked, placing her hand lightly on his elbow and leading him forward.

"Actually, I haven't had the chance to explore much since I arrived here. I was hoping you could lead the way and show me your favourite places. You are, after all, familiar with the grounds."

Chhaya beamed. "In that case, I think we'll go over to the stables." She would get to see Shadow, after all.

"I love horses," replied Damon, "although I don't get the opportunity to ride as often as I would like."

"That's a shame. I'm not sure what I would do without Shadow; I tend to see him at least once a day."

"Shadow? What a brilliant name for a horse!"

Chhaya chuckled. "He's surprisingly quiet. That's where his name came from—he moves like a shadow."

"I look forward to meeting him."

"I'm glad, because Shadow is the best judge of character I know. Only if he approves of you will I consider approving of you," she teased.

"*Consider*? You wound me, princess," Damon laughed.

The familiar smell of freshly-cut hay wafted into her nose, and Chhaya inhaled deeply. She let go of his arm, turning to him with a bright smile. "Are you ready to meet Shadow?"

The door to the stable swung open, and a brown-haired man emerged. "Princess, we didn't expect to see you here today," he said, his long black boots caked in mud and his covered hands carrying a large rake.

"Daniel, this is Damon. Damon, Daniel," Chhaya introduced. "Daniel is in charge of the stables and takes wonderful care of all of the horses here, especially Shadow."

"Our princess is being modest," Daniel chuckled. "She spends so much time with Shadow that I barely need to see to him at all."

Chhaya shrugged. "I brush him and feed him when I can, but you know very well that he loves you."

"Hey, Favian," Daniel greeted, only just having spotted the man hovering behind them. Favian nodded, wordless as usual. It was odd, having Favian with her but not truly *with* her; she was used to conversing with him, even if the conversation was largely one-sided.

Without the cloak today, Favian had blended easily into the crowd, and Chhaya had noticed he had been staying back as much as possible. Whether it was because he was distracted or had been instructed to do so by her father, Chhaya was unsure. But neither was she complaining.

"I already brushed Shadow today; I didn't think you would have the time, so I went ahead," Daniel said apologetically.

"Thank you for brushing him, Daniel. I was hoping to take him for a ride."

Damon raised his eyebrows. "Right now?" he asked.

"You did say you enjoy riding but don't often have the chance."

"Yes, but—"

"We have plenty of horses for you to choose from," Daniel added helpfully, directly addressing Damon.

Damon looked hesitantly at Chhaya before his frown eased into a smile. "Thank you."

"Daniel, I can prepare Shadow, but it would be helpful if you would help Damon get situated?"

"Of course, Chhaya," Daniel replied with a small bow before leading Damon to the far side of the stable, while Chhaya and Favian headed to the front. "You do know how to ride, don't you?" she asked Favian. He never joined her for her morning rides, but Chhaya stayed close, so there was never any need to.

"Yes," he replied.

"You can ride Sanya then." She gestured towards the horse opposite Shadow, which was bigger than Shadow, the perfect size for Favian. "The saddle should be hanging inside."

Favian emerged with the saddle and held it up in front of his face, peering through the stirrup with a frown.

Chhaya bit her lip and resisted the urge to laugh, putting down Shadow's saddle and turning to face Favian, her arms crossed. "You are sure you know how to ride?" She raised an eyebrow.

He cleared his throat, his lips pinched and his neck pink. "I have not had much practice."

Chhaya sighed with a smile as she walked over to him and took the saddle from his hands, making quick work of preparing Sanya. "It really is simple," she said, moving onto Shadow's harness. "I will get on Shadow first, and you can see how I have done it before you try." She smoothly lifted herself onto Shadow in one swift movement.

Favian nodded and placed a foot in the stirrup. But somehow, when he pulled himself up, he managed to get himself tangled in the reins and landed with a loud thud on the ground.

Chhaya's eyes softened as she watched Favian attempt to disentangle himself before she leapt off Shadow.

"Here," she said when Favian stood up, finally free from the reins. "Put this hand here." She guided his hands gently with her own. "And put your foot in the stirrup. Now pull yourself up. Gently so as not to hurt the horse."

Favian exhaled in relief when he was finally sitting in the correct position. Chhaya, once again, jumped elegantly onto Shadow and guided him towards Sanya.

"Riding is much easier than getting on," she lied, much to Favian's obvious relief. Although it was obvious to her, she wasn't sure it would be obvious to anybody else. Would others notice the way he unclenched his jaw and dropped his tense shoulders?

Without thinking, she leaned over to pick a stray piece of straw from Favian's tunic and froze awkwardly, her hand still on his shoulder and her face far too close to his. Straightening up, she cleared her throat. "Let's get out there before Damon does, and I will show you the basics."

She showed him how to hold the reins—and the saddle, should he need to—where to keep his feet and how to tell Sanya to move forward.

"Why don't we try it," she said, leading Shadow forward. Favian followed on Sanya, slowly but steadily. At least she knew he wouldn't fall. "See? I told you it was easier." She rolled her eyes when he remained silent, although she couldn't have claimed to expect any different.

"Come," she told Favian, leading Shadow forward and waiting for him and Sanya to follow. He was still unconfident but certainly becoming used to the movements. "We'll continue to take it easy; hold onto the reins." Within minutes, they were out into the field. "To turn left, gently tug on the left rein."

Favian tugged a little too hard, almost falling off Sanya, but managed to centre himself just in time. Chhaya quickly cantered over. "Are you okay?"

Favian nodded once and pulled on the right rein, much more gently this time, and turned smoothly towards her. "Fine," he replied.

Chhaya nodded. "We'll go slowly anyway, so you don't need to worry. Besides, Sanya likes to follow Shadow, so you shouldn't have to do very much steering." He nodded at her again, and Chhaya bit her lip to stop herself from laughing; he didn't look so intimidating without the cloak and while trying his best to stay balanced on top of Sanya, even with the dark lenses still covering his eyes.

"Here you are!" called Damon, emerging from the stables on top of a beautiful chestnut mare. Daniel led them out through the gate before heading back inside. "Well, what are we waiting for?" He lightly flicked the reins and manoeuvred himself around Favian to be beside Chhaya.

"Let's stop here," said Chhaya, shaking her hair, now wild from the wind, from her face and pressing her warm hands onto her iced cheeks. She slowed Shadow and looked back at Favian, making sure he was alright and that Sanya was following Shadow's lead and also coming to a stop. Swinging herself down from Shadow, she held onto Sanya so that Favian could do the same, albeit slightly less gracefully, as he almost fell flat on his face.

"There's a stream here that I like to bring Shadow for a fresh drink. He loves it." She led both Shadow and Sanya through a clearing in the trees. Damon followed with his horse, and Favian came through to the stream last. She let go of Shadow and Sanya, allowing them free reign to drink and rest while she sat down at the base of a thick tree and leaned back.

"This place is beautiful," said Damon, taking a seat next to her. "How did you find it?"

"It is, isn't it?" Chhaya looked around her, feeling a sense of peace in this secret little area. It was as if this place was infused with its own magic; the trees were greener, the water was clearer, and the flowers sparkled brightly in the glowing rays of the sun. "Shadow showed me one day. It was after an attack in the town during the war. I had spent all day in the infirmary and needed a break, so I decided to go for a ride. Only I had no idea where I was going. But Shadow knew what I needed, I suppose, and brought me here."

Damon smiled. "It's very peaceful."

"It's wonderful," replied Chhaya.

Chhaya inhaled deeply, breathing in the fresh air. Being as far away from the castle and its temporary inhabitants as they were, it was as though a heavy weight had been lifted from her shoulders.

"So, why is it that you like horses so much?" Damon asked, gently breaking her from her reverie.

"The freedom, I think," replied Chhaya without a second thought. "There is something about being able to gallop freely through the fields, just me and Shadow, that clears my mind."

"I can imagine that; I imagine you don't have very much freedom otherwise as the Princess of Khiona."

"But I wouldn't trade it for the world," she answered quickly. "I love what I do, and I love my people. And I still have the chance to go out and be around others. It's just... it's *different* with Shadow."

Damon smiled gently. "I understand. I am only a Lord, not a Prince, but there always have been things I have not been allowed to do because of my title.

Chhaya pressed her lips together. "Thank you for understanding."

Damon nodded. "It's sort of strange, all of this. Don't you think?" he asked with a nervous laugh.

"All of what?"

"This." He waved his arms. "The entire... *competition,* I suppose one would call it, to become the King."

Chhaya's smile faded. "I do not believe I would refer to it as a competition. And even if it were, the result is certainly not to become the King."

"Sorry, that's not what I meant!" Damon exclaimed.

"Well, what did you mean?"

He ran his hand through his hair. "What I mean is that I realise we are all here for you and not to become the King."

Chhaya raised an eyebrow, but before she could speak, Favian cleared his throat behind her, startling her. "Chhaya. The sun is beginning to set. It will be dark soon; perhaps we had better be going."

Chhaya stood. "I think you're right, Favian." She walked over to the stream and took Shadow's reins first, then Sanya's, before leaving the clearing, not waiting to see whether or not Damon was following.

She held onto Sanya's reins and waited for Favian to climb on. He didn't need her to help him; he had done it before without her after all, but she stayed there just in case he needed her.

"I don't know much about horses, but Shadow is beautiful," said Damon, emerging with his mare. He walked over to Shadow and placed a hand between his ears.

All of a sudden, Shadow squealed loudly and reared back. "Shadow!" Chhaya called, running over to him. But it was too late. Before she could do anything, Shadow kicked his feet at Damon, who had moved out of the way, and missed, hitting Sanya instead.

Sanya reared, violently throwing Favian off her back, and ran in the opposite direction to the castle.

"Shh, shh," Chhaya whispered, calming Shadow and rubbing his head until he was settled before running over to Favian, who was lying unconscious on the grass.

She knelt next to him; there was a large bump on his forehead, and his ankle was twisted awkwardly, but he was breathing.

"Favian?" she said his name gently, placing her cold hand on his forehead. "Favian?" She moved her hand to his cheek, rubbing her thumb gently over a small scratch.

His eyes flickered open, and she exhaled in relief. "Are you okay?"

He winced but pulled himself into a sitting position. "I'll be fine. The horse?"

"Don't worry about Sanya; she'll come back. The horses are all trained to return to the castle stables if they get too far."

Favian nodded and, with difficulty, got to his feet, refusing Chhaya's help. She saw him wince with every movement but said nothing.

"Come on," she said when he was steady. "You can ride back with me and Shadow."

"I cannot ride with you," he said, shaking his head and wincing once again. He also seemed to be holding his arm tenderly. At this rate, merely getting him onto the horse would be a challenge.

"And just why not?" she challenged.

"You are the princess. I am your bodyguard."

"So?"

"It is not proper."

Chhaya sighed and pinched the bridge of her nose between her finger and thumb, resisting the urge to slap some sense into him. He was already injured, after all. "Well, Favian, in case you have not noticed, you have just been thrown from a horse. You need to be checked by a medic. So you may ride with me or on Shadow while I walk. Although that will be significantly slower."

"I cannot allow you to walk."

"Then climb on." She gestured towards Shadow and waited patiently as Favian limped over, although he tried to hide it, and hoisted himself onto Shadow. She stayed prepared, just in case he needed help. While his legs seemed to be stable for the most part, she noticed his hands were cut up and slightly bruised as he struggled to hold onto the saddle while waiting for her to join him.

"I'm so sorry about what happened," Damon trotted over, already having mounted his horse. "Is Favian alright?"

"It's fine, Damon," Chhaya replied before lifting herself onto Shadow and sitting in front of Favian. "I don't know what got into Shadow; sometimes he gets spooked around strangers," she lied. It was extremely rare that Shadow acted like that, and it was almost always when he was around a person he did not trust. She patted Shadow's head, stroking his head calmingly just in case he reacted to Damon's presence again. "You aren't hurt, are you?"

Damon furrowed his eyebrows at them, looking strangely at Favian sitting behind Chhaya on the saddle, but said nothing. "I'm fine. Favian, I hope you're okay?"

Favian nodded but stayed silent.

"I am taking him to see the medic," Chhaya replied as if Favian had given no response at all. "You may go ahead to the stable. We will come slowly to ensure neither Favian nor Shadow are injured any further."

"I can stay behind and come with you. So you don't have to come alone."

"Thank you, Damon, but that is unnecessary. I am not alone; I have Favian with me." She offered a tight-lipped smile. "It would, however, be helpful if you could go ahead and let Daniel know what happened so he can have the medic ready for Favian and anything he needs ready for Shadow."

"Oh, right. Of course," Damon agreed with a nod before galloping forward.

"Are you alright?" she asked Favian when Damon was out of earshot. With nothing to hold onto, Favian slipped from the saddle with every step.

"Yes," he replied.

Chhaya rolled her eyes. "You are allowed to put your arms around me, Favian."

Favian inhaled sharply. "No, Chhaya."

"You will fall off," she warned.

"That's okay, Chhaya."

"Falling off and injuring yourself further is a more desirable circumstance than putting even one arm around me to maintain your balance?"

He stayed silent.

With a sigh, she reached behind her, took hold of the hand that wasn't covered in cuts and pulled it forward, not around her but far enough to hold onto one of the reins.

"Chhaya—"

"Favian, please do not give me a speech about this being improper. You are not even touching me. But if you fall again, I do not know how I will be able to get you back to the castle. Please."

He didn't reply but reached around with his other hand, so he was holding onto the reins with both hands. Chhaya exhaled involuntarily at the warmth radiating from him, shielding her from the harsh wind.

"What's wrong?" he asked, his lips almost touching her ear because of how far forward he was leaning.

"Nothing," she replied, her voice barely audible.

"I thought you made a noise."

She swallowed. "No."

Chhaya was reading when the knock came at the door. She was already dressed for dinner, having opted for a fitted white kurti top with lace trimming and gold detailing. Now she was waiting for Favian to arrive so they could go to dinner.

She had stayed with him at first to make sure he was not too severely harmed when the medic did his first check. It was only when she knew he was safe that she left him, giving him privacy while the medic began to heal any cuts, bruises or breaks. Fortunately, Gaia had provided the castle with a fresh crate of tinctures that very morning. Combined with the medic's Magic, it should have been a relatively simple and painless process for Favian.

"I have a message for Her Highness," said a female voice on the other side of the door to Della, who had answered.

"What is the problem?" asked Chhaya, putting down her book.

"Your Highness, there is no problem per se. It's just that the bodyguard has broken his fingers." It was a footwoman.

Chhaya's mouth dropped open. She had seen him wince earlier, but she thought that had been because of the scrapes and his ankle. The fact that he had broken his fingers and held onto the reins so tightly without a single complaint surprised her. "Is he okay?" Usually, the medic was able to heal broken bones fairly easily unless there were any complications.

"He will be fine, Your Highness. The medic has already healed him." Chhaya exhaled in relief. "However, he has instructed Favian to keep his hands bandaged for the evening and to avoid using magic of any sort." It made sense. As Favian's Magic was more potent than any others, the risk of his Magic causing harm to his fingers in this state was too great. "The swelling and pain are expected to decrease by the morning, but the medic believes he should not be on duty tonight."

"Of course he should not! He should take some time to rest. Besides, if anything were to happen, he would be rather useless without his hands anyway."

"Exactly, Your Highness. But the King has decided that due to this situation, you should remain here, where it is safe. He does not want you alone with all the guests without Favian."

Chhaya thought about arguing, but was feeling tired herself, particularly after the events of the day. She would benefit from having time away from the suitors and away from the tension. She looked at Della, who shrugged, before nodding to the servant who had come to deliver the news.

"Della, you please go to dinner. I will have a quiet evening and will have my food brought here."

"But Chhaya, I can bring it for you. And I can stay so you are not alone."

"Really, Della, there's no need. Please, go and enjoy your evening. Papa has planned some exciting entertainment, and I would like to hear about it."

Della bit her lip with a frown but nodded. "Thank you," she said before she left.

Chhaya looked back at the footwoman. "Would you take me to his rooms?" she asked.

She looked bewildered but nodded readily. "Of course, Your Highness. This way."

Chhaya already knew where Favian's rooms were—she had snuck into them to steal his clothes—but she didn't need anybody else to know that.

The footwoman knocked on the door and waited to hear a confirmation before opening the door for Chhaya and closing it after her again.

Favian was sitting at the table with his back to the door. He had a bowl of warm pumpkin soup in front of him and slices of bread and butter, chicken, salad and a glass of wine. "Thank you for the food. I—" He turned around and did a double take at the sight of Chhaya. He immediately jumped up from his chair. "Chhaya!" As usual, he stood with his hands in front of him, and Chhaya cocked her head, one eyebrow high on her forehead. Even with his hands bandaged up as they were, he had managed to clasp them together.

"Please sit down, Favian."

"I—"

"Please?" she asked softly, raising her eyebrows as she sat in the chair next to his.

Favian looked behind him at the door before finally nodding and taking his seat. He was no longer on official royal duty and therefore had removed his tinted lenses. His eyes were bright and swirled like grey storms, and Chhaya could only wonder why he kept them covered; they were lovely.

"I heard you were not feeling very well?"

"I'm fine," he said, sitting still and not even attempting to eat the food before him. "The medic is overreacting; the pain is almost nonexistent."

"I am glad to hear it, but I would prefer you listened to the expert and took the evening off."

"Of course, Chhaya. I am sorry that you are unable to attend dinner tonight."

Chhaya waved her hand and picked up the spoon in the bowl in front of him. "I was tired, anyway." She scooped up some of the soup with the spoon and held it out to him.

Favian looked at her blankly for a moment before speaking. "You don't—"

"Favian, for the Goddess's sake, please eat. You certainly will not be able to eat with your hands in bandages like this." She gestured to his wrapped-up arms with one hand while keeping her other hand, holding the spoon extended towards him, waiting.

Finally, he leaned forward and drank the soup. She offered him another spoonful before buttering a slice of bread and holding it out for him. Still, he looked hesitant. "I washed my hands. I promise," she joked.

He took a bite of the bread but kept his eyes on her as he did so, as if afraid she was going to hit him with it or something. "Why have you come?" he asked suspiciously.

"I cannot be downstairs."

"You could have remained in your room."

"I was bored."

"You could have requested that Della stay with you."

Chhaya sighed. "Yes, I could have. But I did not want to. I *wanted* to come and see how you were doing, and when I saw that you were sitting here so helplessly, unable to eat your own food because of me, I decided to stay. Is that quite alright?" she asked. "Is there a reason why you do not want me in here?"

He looked surprised then, lifting one eyebrow. "No." He turned then and looked towards the door before taking the next bite from her.

Chhaya glanced at the door, too, creasing her eyebrows. "Are you waiting for somebody?"

"No," he responded quickly.

"Why do you keep looking at the door?" she asked.

"In case anybody arrives."

And then it dawned on her. He was waiting for his secret admirer to leave another letter. And he wanted to catch them. She bit her lip to stop the smile from spreading. "I see. Well, if you do not have any plans for this evening, perhaps you wouldn't be opposed to my company for some dessert?"

"I don't eat dessert," he responded expressionlessly.

Chhaya stared at him with an open mouth. "You don't eat dessert?"

She chuckled when Favian's only reaction was to flex a muscle in his arm and shrug. It was true he was very physically fit and had to be for his job, but no dessert seemed extreme for Chhaya.

"But never?" she asked.

"Never," he confirmed.

"This simply will not do," Chhaya sighed as he finished the soup, and she gave him a bite of the salad. "Wait here," she said, giving him another bite and putting the fork down. She got up and opened the door, asking the footwoman that was still waiting there to bring them a portion of the evening's desert. In the castle, they were able to have cheeses, fresh fruits and nuts regularly, but this evening the head chef had made a particular delicacy Chhaya refused to miss.

By the time the chocolate cake arrived, covered in a thick layer of the rich custard Chhaya could never resist, Favian had finished his salad. She thanked the footman, who bowed and left the room.

"You will have to try this," she said insistently to Favian.

"I have tried cake before," he replied as she held out a spoonful for him.

"Not like this," she responded, eagerly awaiting his reaction. But when he simply looked at her blankly, she sighed. "Just one bite?"

He looked at her curiously but took the bite in his mouth. First, his eyes closed, then opened wide. "This is delicious."

"I told you," Chhaya replied in a sing-song voice.

"I cannot believe I have been missing this."

"Neither can I. A castle delicacy, you see."

Favian looked between Chhaya and the slice of cake patiently, but she refused to give in so easily. She broke off another piece of the soft, gooey cake with the spoon, but just as Favian leaned in to take the bite, she popped it into her mouth. "I am certainly fortunate you only wanted one bite," she said, pretending not to have noticed. She looked up at him and feigned innocence. "Whatever is the matter?"

He shook his head and stretched one arm out towards the door. Chhaya immediately put one hand on his wrist and lowered it. "What are you doing?"

"Summoning the footman. To request another slice of cake," he replied sheepishly.

"No magic," she told him, letting go of his arm. "Remember? Just until tomorrow morning."

Favian frowned. "Thank you for reminding me."

"I will request more cake." She laughed.

When the footman returned with more dessert for the two of them, Chhaya helped Favian to eat half of it since they had also shared the first slice.

"I wish I could use magic," she said offhandedly. She had always dreamed of learning, but her father didn't want her occupied with such things as a princess. Magic could be draining and dangerous.

"Why can't you?" Favian asked. It must have been so strange to him that people lived without magic at all. As a soldier, he would have been taught to master and manipulate Magic from a young age. Chhaya had previously overheard other soldiers discuss Magic as if it were another limb for them.

"I have not been taught."

"I can teach you," Favian responded, and Chhaya's eyes lit up. "You would truly do that?"

"I cannot see a reason against the idea," he responded, taking another bite of the cake Chhaya held out to him. "Your father asked me to train you in self-defence, and Magic is one of the most useful and efficient ways to defend oneself."

Chhaya could not believe it. For so long, she had tried to convince her father to let her learn magic, and now, finally, she was being given a chance. "Where do we start?" she asked eagerly.

"You wish to begin now?"

"Why not? We both have the evening free from any engagements, and you do not have to *use* any magic in order to teach me. You merely need to explain it to me."

"Very well. Begin by closing your eyes." She did as instructed. "Inside each and every one of us, there is a single strand of magic woven into our souls. Look for your strand. Search inside you for the strand of gold."

"I cannot find anything." She felt ridiculous.

"Try to feel it. It will feel like warmth, similar to a welcoming presence, something that has always been there, that has always been a part of you. It will feel familiar and yet so strange. Focus on your breathing, not on finding it. Let the Magic find you."

Favian's deep baritone voice helped Chhaya to sink further and further into herself, focusing on her breath. As if something clicked all of a sudden, she felt it. A warmth that enveloped her like an embrace.

"I feel it," she whispered.

"Good. Hold onto it and open your eyes."

She opened her eyes and instantly gasped. Everything around her was more vivid. The melted chocolate remaining on the plate was a beautiful molten brown, and the moon shone through the window like she had never seen it shine before. But even more spectacular were his eyes. The stormy grey irises were like pale clouds in the sky, shining in the rays of the moonlight.

"Your eyes are gold," he said softly.

"They are? Why?"

"Your magic. It's flowing through you."

"What do I do now?"

"Lift the glass," he said, nodding his head towards it. Chhaya moved to pick up the glass, but he put his bandaged hands on hers. "With your magic."

"How can I do that?"

"Have you tried?"

He had a point. She looked at the glass and focused, allowing that warmth to envelop her even further. Finally, *finally*, it budged. She couldn't lift it all the way or even move it very far, but the glass moved ever so slightly, and to Chhaya, it felt like a victory.

She smiled brightly at Favian, and he smiled a small smile in return. "Congratulations, Chhaya." The feeling from the magic was gone, but she still felt something warm in her stomach and smiled even brighter.

Chapter Eight

I f Chhaya had thought that she would have had a lie-in due to Favian's injury, she was wrong.

At precisely six o'clock, a steady knocking came from her door. She struggled to open her eyes, feeling a deep and constant pounding in her head, starting at the base of her skull. Every muscle in her body ached like they had never ached before, and she could feel her limbs tremble from the effort as she attempted to lift herself up into a sitting position.

The pounding continued, and Chhaya winced, unable to block out the sound from her heavy mind.

This was her own fault. Even after growing up with the constant warning that Magic was draining and dangerous and could absorb your energy if you weren't properly trained, she had spent the duration of the previous night practising and trying to hone it.

As soon as she had left Favian to rest for the remainder of the evening, she hurried back to her room, far too excited and wired with her successful movement of the glass to go to sleep. Della had returned from dinner and left again, leaving the fire lit and the room warmed for her, but otherwise, she had been alone.

The perfect opportunity to practise.

Eventually, she had succeeded in moving a glass from one side of the table to the other, but it had taken hours, and Chhaya had all but collapsed into her bed immediately after.

But this morning, as awful as she was feeling, she couldn't bring herself to regret it. However, there was no way in the Kingdoms that she would be able to handle a training session now, especially not followed by a day of socialising.

Slowly, she dragged herself from the bed, leaning against the wall for support, as her legs were unable to bear her weight, and stumbled her way over to the door. Her arms and shoulders burned like they never had before with the effort of opening the heavy door in front of her. Why had Della not arrived yet? It was usually her opening the door to Favian and waking her.

"Good morning," said Favian in his training clothes.

"Favian," Chhaya said breathlessly, clinging to the door and forcing herself to remain upright. "I need this morning off."

Favian instantly frowned. "Are you okay?"

There was no chance of her being able to tell him the truth and explain the reason why she was so tired; he was so loyal to her father that he would immediately report back to him, and there would be no more Magic training for her. She could not allow that risk.

She plastered a smile on her face, feeling every muscle ignite as she did so. "Fine, Favian. I am merely feeling under the weather."

"My apologies, Chhaya, but these are your father's orders." The frown was gone, and his face was back to the expressionless canvas she was used to.

"Please, Favian, I really am tired."

But Favian stared blankly at her. She sighed.

An idea struck. She looked up at him and rolled her eyes, feigning acceptance. "I only require a few minutes to dress, and

I will meet you at the entrance," she said before closing the door again.

As quickly as she could handle, she dressed in her tunic before sitting down at her desk, sighing in relief at the slight ease in her muscles.

Dearest Favian,

I was very nervous when I did not immediately see you yesterday. I had been searching for your cloak, but I could not see it anywhere and worried something had happened to you.

Until I spotted your lenses, and I knew you were there.

In a way, I should be grateful. In the brilliant cloak, you were receiving far too many looks from others in the castle. I was finding it difficult to remain calm as I listened to a large proportion of the people in this place talk about you and about how handsome you looked.

At least now I have you all to myself again.

Thank you, Favian.

I heard you were injured yesterday, but you are safe and well again. I am glad you are okay.

I will see you later, dearest Favian, and you will see me too.

You just won't know it.

Until then.

She waited for the ink to dry, blowing on it softly, before folding the parchment neatly and leaving her room, allowing the walls to support her and fighting the fierce fire in her legs.

"I found this inside," she said, exiting the castle with the folded letter in hand and forcing herself to stay standing. "Your name is written on the front."

Favian immediately stopped what he was doing and took the letter. "Inside where?" he demanded.

"Just lying before the door," Chhaya responded innocently, gesturing behind her.

"Did you see anybody on your way here?" he asked seriously.

"No, why? Is somebody bothering you? Because—"

"No," he responded a little too quickly. "Everything is fine."

"Oh, I see. Is it from a... *partner*?"

Favian's cheeks tinged a faint pink. "No."

Chhaya lifted her eyebrows. "Are you certain? This letter—"

"I am not courting anybody," he interrupted.

Chhaya shrugged in response and smiled down at the letter, waiting for him to open it.

"On second thought, Chhaya," he said, "I'm still feeling tired from yesterday. You may return to bed."

"You are sure?"

He nodded, fixing his eyes on the letter. She left immediately.

Chhaya hadn't spoken to Damon since the incident with Shadow the day before but was unsurprised to see him approach her at breakfast the next morning.

"Your Highness," he said with a polite smile and a small bow. "I'm glad to see you this morning. Dinner was not quite the same without your presence last night." He turned quickly to Favian, who was, as usual, standing a few steps behind Chhaya with his hands clasped in front of him. "Favian, have you recovered? I do apologise for what happened."

When Chhaya looked back at Favian, it was clear he wasn't sure how to respond. "Favian is doing a lot better, Damon. Thank you for asking," she said on his behalf. She turned back to see his reaction, and he nodded at Damon. She wasn't sure how, but she had begun to be slightly more aware of his reactions and noticed the slight tension on his jaw ease and his shoulders relax ever so slightly.

Damon cleared his throat in front of her, and she quickly turned back to face him. "Would you like to join me for breakfast?" he asked, gesturing towards a smaller table.

She knew she would have to stop sitting with her friends and start mingling with their guests at some point. She could only hope others joined her and she would not be alone with him. "I would love to," she answered with a forced smile, hoping she had misjudged him the previous afternoon. After all, she could not very well decline his invitation in such a public space.

Trying not to take notice as her friends and the other guests from around the room watched, she sat down with Damon. It was clear to everyone that she had made a choice, but he had also been the only one to ask.

Favian remained standing behind her, and this time Chhaya didn't argue or ask him to sit. He was now officially on duty; she was no longer just having breakfast with her friends. She would order some food for him after breakfast regardless for him to eat in her rooms; they had already agreed on some Magic training before the picnic this afternoon.

"Your Highness," another suitor, whom she recognised as Mark, greeted her with a bow before sitting at the table.

"Mark," she said with a smile. "It's lovely to see you. And how are *you* feeling?" she asked Damon in a hushed voice. "I hope you are not hurt. I should have insisted you see the medic, too."

"Oh, I'm fine," replied Damon with a wave of a hand. "But at least I know I'm not quite cut out for horses."

"Oh, I thought you said you enjoyed it," Chhaya commented, popping a slice of orange into her mouth.

"I've enjoyed it when I've had the opportunity, which hasn't been particularly often, but I much prefer being indoors," he replied with a shrug.

"Even in the Summer?" she asked.

"I suppose I don't really see the appeal of nature."

Chhaya frowned. How could anybody spend all of their time indoors? She would suffocate if she were trapped inside all the time.

"I just feel like in the Summer, it's too hot," Damon continued. "In the Winter, it's too cold. In the Spring, I cannot stop sneezing, and in the Autumn, it's far too windy."

"Good morning," said another suitor, who Chhaya recognised as Aamir—the Duke Favian had tackled to the ground—greeted them. "Princess." He bowed to her before taking his seat. "I heard there was an accident yesterday," he said with a frown. "Is everyone quite alright?"

"We're all fine," replied Damon before Chhaya could speak. "There was just an issue with a horse."

Chhaya fought the urge to glare at him. Shadow had certainly not been the issue; he only frightened in such a way around people he didn't like. And it wasn't often that he was frightened.

"Oh, what a shame," Aamir commented thoughtfully. "I hope the horse is alright?"

"He is fine," Chhaya answered, her voice softening at the concern for Shadow. "Thank you."

"I would be more than happy to take a look at him for you if you would like, princess," he offered before biting into a piece of fruit.

"Why? Are you a stable hand?" asked Damon with a chuckle.

Aamir turned slowly to look at him and raised an eyebrow. "No. But I prefer to look after my own horses."

"So you know how to ride?" asked Chhaya, resisting the urge to react to Damon's comments.

"Absolutely!" he replied. "It's one of my favourite things to do."

"Oh, you must be missing your horses terribly here."

"I suppose I do. It is quite difficult to transition from riding daily to not at all."

"Well, please do feel free to use our stables whenever you wish! Daniel looks after the horses, and I know he would be more than happy to show you where everything is."

"That's very kind of you, princess." Aamir beamed at her. "Thank you."

Chhaya felt a tap on her shoulder and turned around to see Favian leaning closer to her. "If you are finished with breakfast, Chhaya, we should go. We have our training before your picnic," he said into her ear in a hushed voice.

She nodded and stood. "It was lovely seeing you all. Thank you for a pleasant breakfast. Will I see you at the picnic?"

They all nodded, and Chhaya smiled before leaving the breakfast room, with Favian walking just behind her as usual.

"What?" Chhaya asked innocently.

Favian continued to stare silently at her through his dark lenses, his arms crossed and his eggs and coffee abandoned on the table.

Chhaya raised an eyebrow and folded her arms over her chest. "What is it? Why are you staring at me in such a way?"

He uncrossed his arms and leaned forward. "Yesterday, you were happier than you were on your birthday when you were able to hardly even nudge the glass, and today you are suddenly able to lift it into the air as if it were nothing?"

Chhaya swallowed. "Perhaps I needed time for the lesson to sink in. Maybe my Magic needed time to get used to my body, or my body needed time to get used to my Magic."

Favian crossed his arms once again and leaned back in his chair, staring at her in silence.

"Very well," she said with a frustrated sigh. It was clear he wasn't going to believe her. "I may have practised a little last night after I went back into my room."

"A little?"

"Perhaps a little *more* than a little," she mumbled.

"No wonder you were so exhausted this morning. Why did you not tell me? I would not have allowed you even to leave your bed."

Chhaya felt the blush colour her cheeks and neck, feeling foolish. "I thought you would no longer be willing to teach me if you learned that I had continued to practise without you."

Favian stood. "What you did was idiotic, reckless and dangerous." Chhaya's mouth dropped. He had never spoken to her like that before. Granted, he didn't often speak to her very much at all, but she most certainly hadn't expected that. "But nevertheless, I agree with you. You deserve to know how to defend yourself."

"You will still help me?"

He nodded. "But from now on, you must swear to be honest with me."

"I will! No more secret practices."

Favian took a step closer to her. "If that ever happens again," he began in a low voice, "swear that you will tell me."

Chhaya swallowed. "Why? I merely needed a little extra rest this morning."

"You were fortunate this time. But draining your energy in such an uncontrolled way is not safe."

Chhaya nodded. "I will tell you."

Favian exhaled and sat down again. "Using Magic is like using your muscles; you must train it. Lift the glass again."

"Your Highness," Aamir bowed deeply as she emerged from the doors.

Chhaya had decided on a stroll before the picnic and had chosen to visit the rose gardens; they always were beautiful this time of the year, and Chhaya loved to see what the gardeners did with their Magic. Today, the fresh roses were a shimmering baby blue colour that delicately complimented the light crystal colour of the white lehenga she had worn. Her father had asked her to dress more formally today. Perhaps to prevent her from wandering off on horse rides or walks when she was expected to be mingling. She could ride Shadow in her lehenga, of course, but it was not nearly as comfortable as her riding trousers.

"Aamir." She took the hand he offered and allowed him to help her down the stairs. "I didn't expect to see anybody else here."

"Likewise, Your Highness." He smiled at her for a moment before his eyes widened, and he dropped her hand. "My apologies. I did not mean to intrude. I shall leave you to your peace and quiet."

Chhaya laughed and lightly touched his elbow to prevent him from leaving. Suddenly, she felt a prickle on the back of her neck, suddenly very aware of Favian's presence behind her. She removed her hand and cleared her throat. "There's no need to leave, Aamir. Especially not when the roses look so spectacular—they deserve to be admired."

He smiled then, and Chhaya walked to the wooden gazebo in the middle of the garden. The roof gave her a light shelter from the wind and the perfect spot to admire her surroundings. She felt, more than heard, Favian following and positioning himself behind her as she sat on the wooden bench.

"Do you tend to come here very often?" asked Aamir, coming to stand next to her inside the gazebo. He rested his elbow on the ledge and leaned forward.

"As often as I am able," Chhaya replied. "The florists work so hard on these beautiful roses. They are different every day. The way I see it, it would be a shame *not* to come and appreciate them."

"I happen to agree with you, Your Highness."

"What about yourself? Is this your first time in the rose gardens?"

"No, I accidentally found myself here a few days ago. On my first evening, I was unable to sleep and decided to go for a walk. The roses were red on that day, so I thought it was an ordinary rose garden, but I was taken away by the beauty of the garden. I was pleasantly surprised when I came back the following day to find the roses a deep purple colour."

"It is quite easy to lose yourself here," Chhaya commented.

Aamir nodded. "My mother always says I have this bad habit."

"Oh?"

"She claims I spend too much time outdoors. She says it's not right for a Duke, but I cannot help it. I love the fresh air, and I enjoy nature."

"Really?" Chaya raised her eyebrows.

"Wind, snow or shine, you will usually find me outside."

"Well, in that case, I believe it's likely you and I will be running into each other fairly often."

He raised his eyebrows. "Is that so?"

"I spend a lot of my free time with my horse, Shadow."

All of a sudden, the door flung open, and Della ran out into the rose garden. "Chhaya, there you are."

"Is everything okay?" asked Chhaya, suddenly realising she hadn't seen Della all morning.

"It's one of the children. They've been hurt."

Chhaya immediately jumped to her feet. "Infirmary?" she asked, running down the gazebo steps to where Della was standing in front of the door.

"Yes," replied Della, leading the way. "His injuries are not dangerous, but the castle medic is currently out gathering herbs and isn't expected back until this evening."

Chhaya nodded. "Have someone send for Gaia; She's not a medic, but she will know what to do to at least keep him in a safe condition until the medic returns."

Della turned the corner to do just that as Chhaya, with Favian following as usual, entered the castle's infirmary. Fortunately, it seemed to be a quiet day, and Chhaya made her way to the only bed that was occupied.

"Princess!" The small boy exclaimed, tired eyes wide as she approached. His face was pale, and his skin was clammy, but that he was able to speak was a good sign, at least.

"Sebastian," Chhaya said with an attempted warm smile as she sat down next to the boy on his infirmary bed. "I heard you have been hurt."

He nodded, his eyes lowering to his leg.

"Can I see it?" she questioned gently.

He nodded once again, lowering his bed sheet to reveal his leg.

Chhaya sucked in a breath. His leg was covered in deep crimson gashes, and the surrounding skin was stained with blood. Who could do this to an innocent child? "You're being very brave," she said, covering his leg again at the look of horror on his face.

"Isn't he being brave, Favian?" she asked, turning back to look at the man. If he was going to stand there, he might as well be of some help.

Favian looked at Chhaya, who lifted an eyebrow dangerously, then back to Sebastian. "Very brave," he confirmed.

"I remember you," Sebastian said, his voice weak. "You came with the Princess to see us last week."

"I did," Favian replied with a nod.

"You're a bodyguard?" He tilted his head to the side in curiosity.

Chhaya turned back to Favian and motioned for him to keep Sebastian entertained as she filled a bowl with fresh water and grabbed a clean cloth. She gently peeled back the sheet from Sebastian's leg as Favian continued to talk to him.

"I am," she heard Favian reply and fought the urge to smack her forehead into the wall. This was hardly what she had meant by keeping him entertained.

"What does that mean?"

"Well, it means a lot of things."

"Hey," a voice to Chhaya's left whispered, and she turned to see Aamir.

"Aamir? What are you doing here?" she asked, her voice low as she carefully wiped away the dried blood and cleaned the area while Favian and Sebastian continued their strange conversation.

"Your lady's maid said a young boy was hurt, didn't she?" he replied in a voice just as soft, nodding towards Sebastian. "I came to see if there was anything I could do to help."

Chhaya smiled at him gratefully. "Thank you, Aamir, that is very kind of you. But the picnic has likely started by now—you should go and enjoy your afternoon."

Aamir frowned. "Sorry, Princess, but I refuse to go to a picnic while this boy is lying here like this."

Chhaya felt something warm in her heart. "In that case, you can hand me another cloth from that cabinet over there and see if you can find Della and the herbologist Gaia."

She knitted her eyebrows together at the bright red state of the previously-white cloth she had been using as she finished cleaning his leg and tenderly covered it again with the sheet.

"Sebastian, could you tell us how this happened?" she asked after washing her hands and clearing away all signs of any blood.

He nodded and crossed his arms over into a position very similar to Favian's. Chhaya couldn't help the small smile that spread across her face to see Sebastian copying him.

"Me and Kat were playing in the forest, and then there was a lot of shouting." He stopped then and looked nervously up at Favian, who nodded encouragingly at the boy. "We didn't know what was going on, but we hid behind a bush and stayed as quiet as we could, Princess. I promise."

Chhaya smiled reassuringly. "I'm sure you did. You are always the quietest when we play hide and seek."

Sebastian smiled at that. "I'm always the last person to be found," He told Favian proudly.

"Then what happened?"

Sebastian frowned. "I don't remember seeing anybody, but my leg started to hurt really badly. Kat was okay, though."

"You didn't see anyone?" asked Chhaya.

Sebastian shook his head. "No, but there was blood. When we couldn't hear anyone anymore, Kat ran to find help, and she saw Della, who carried me here."

Chhaya sighed and rubbed his head affectionately. "You did a very good job today, Sebastian. I know it must have been very painful, but you're safe now."

It was at that moment that the door opened once again, and Aamir and Della hurried in, followed closely by Gaia.

"I've cleaned his leg as much as possible, but the wounds need to be sealed before he loses too much blood," Chhaya said quietly to Gaia so that Sebastian would not hear.

"You did well," Gaia responded kindly. "I'll take it from here and patch him up, make sure nothing is infected. When the medic returns, he'll be able to speed up the healing process, and with any luck, our brave Sebastian here will be out of here by the end of the day!" she exclaimed, directing the last sentence to the little boy.

"Really?" Sebastian asked excitedly. "Will I be able to play again?"

"Of course you will!" Gaia replied. "But this needs to be reported to your father," she said quietly to Chhaya, who nodded. "I should be done within the hour. He's lucky—whoever did this to him was distracted before they could do any serious damage."

"That's *not* serious damage?" asked Chhaya.

"It looks scarier than it is."

"Please let me know if there's anything I can do."

Gaia nodded. "For now, you should speak to your father. Sebastian and I could do with some quiet."

Chhaya nodded, gesturing for the others to follow her out the door after she said goodbye to Sebastian.

"Hey, bodyguard!" the boy called before they left. Favian turned around. "When the Princess comes to see us again, promise you'll come too?"

Chhaya could have sworn she saw the faint hint of a smile on Favian's lips. "Promise," he responded.

The King sat down at his desk and sighed heavily. "How could this happen?"

"That's exactly my question, papa," Chhaya responded.

"And this far into the kingdom. So close to the castle."

"Your Majesty, if I may make a suggestion?" Favian spoke from where he was standing by the door.

The King looked up at him in surprise. "Favian, there is no need for formality among us. How many times must I ask you to please sit?" He gestured to the seat next to Chhaya, who looked up at him with raised eyebrows. Finally, Favian nodded and sat.

"Sitting before me are the two people I trust most with this Kingdom's fate," Chhaya's father spoke dramatically. "Please, Favian, between us, you must speak freely."

Favian cleared his throat uncomfortably but nodded once more. "I do not believe the boy was attacked on purpose."

Chhaya snapped her head towards him. "You are not suggesting those horrifying gashes in his leg were accidental?"

"That's not what I meant. I mean to say I don't believe the Blood Magicians who created those gashes intended to harm Sebastian. I think they may have sensed Sebastian in their presence and felt drawn to his blood."

"You mean to say the Magician could not stop himself from taking the boy's blood?" asked the King.

"Or *would* not," muttered Chhaya.

"Correct," replied Favian. "He sensed his blood and took advantage. It is only fortunate that he didn't have the opportunity to take any more."

Nausea burned Chhaya's stomach at the word 'more'.

"For now, our only option is to increase security," the King announced. "Not in the castle—I believe we are well enough protected—but bordering the Kingdom."

"And perhaps regular patrols through the woods?" suggested Chhaya.

The King nodded. "It is settled then."

Dearest Bodyguard,

I heard you were injured and could not use your Magic. I was happy to see you well today. Even though I knew you were fine, a little part of me was in such worry.

It pleases me to know that you have been well looked after by the castle medic and the other staff.

Sorry I could not stay to speak to you myself this morning. I could not risk Chhaya seeing me, of course. Then we would no longer be a secret, you and I.

Thinking of you.

Chhaya smiled, exhausted, as Della entered her room with two mugs of hot chocolate. It had been a long day, and even after speaking to the King, Chhaya and Favian had had to attend the picnic. It was times like this that Chhaya appreciated sitting and relaxing with her friend. "I have good news," Della said with a bright, relieved smile. "Sebastian has been taken home already."

Chhaya perked up at that. "Really? That is good to hear. And his pain wasn't too bad?"

"Entirely pain-free," Della responded happily.

"Della, do you think you might spare the time to do me a favour?" Chhaya asked with a cheeky grin, feeling much more relaxed knowing Sebastian was safe.

"Of course, Chhaya," Della replied, setting the mugs down on the coffee table and sitting on one of the armchairs. "As long as the favour isn't to deliver another letter," she joked.

Chhaya sat down beside her and took her hot chocolate in hand, looking at Della with wide, innocent eyes.

Della's jaw dropped. "Really, Chhaya?" she asked in disbelief. "*Another* letter?"

Chhaya took said letter from her pocket and put it on the table in front of them. "It is only a small one."

Della sighed. "Chhaya, are you sure you want to do this? He has already removed the cloak. That is what you wanted, is it not?"

"Della, don't worry. I know what I'm doing. Besides, it's quite amusing to see the confusion on his face when he receives these letters. What harm can it do anyway? Let the man think somebody has fallen for him. It can't hurt him."

Della smiled tightly but with softened eyes. "Okay, Chhaya. I will deliver this one for you."

There was blood everywhere.

It was still dark out when Chhaya awoke, but by the glow of some light somewhere, she could clearly see that the walls, floors and windows had been smeared with scarlet.

She leapt out of bed, terror compelling her into silence. Chhaya looked down and saw that her clothes were red too. She lifted her hands, turning them over and gasping at the smudges of blood on them. Slowly, she backed up and away from the horrifying crime scene, moving slowly until her back hit the door to her room.

A loud scream echoed through the corridors behind her. "Princess!" The small voice called. "Help me, Princess! Please!" There was no doubt about it; that scream belonged to Sebastian. And he was in trouble.

She pulled open the door so hard, she was surprised it hadn't completely come off its hinges, and ran. The corridors were dark, but she didn't need light. All she needed was to follow the sounds of Sebastian's voice.

"I'm coming, Sebastian!" she called.

"Princess!" he screamed in return.

Finally, she turned a corner and found the small boy crouched against the wall, rocking himself, tears dripping down his face. He looked up at her, the terror storming in his eyes, and held up a hand dripping with red.

"Are you hurt?" she asked, taking his hand. He shook his head no. "Then let's go," she whispered, holding his hand and lifting him.

"Ow!" he cried suddenly, dropping back to the floor.

"What is it?" asked Chhaya worriedly, crouching down to him.

"My leg." He lifted the fabric covering it to reveal deep gashes in his skin. "I can't walk."

"That's fine, Sebastian," Chhaya said reassuringly as she got to her feet. "You trust me, don't you?" He nodded. "Well, we need to get out of here, so you'll have to hold me tight, okay?" As gently as possible so as to avoid hurting him any further, she lifted him into her arms.

As soon as his arms were clasped around her neck, she began to run. She ran as fast as she could, stumbling through the corridors, around corners, down some stairs and up others. It was as though, in this darkness, the castle had turned into a maze. She couldn't seem to find the exit, but she knew she had to keep going.

"Princess," Sebastian whispered fearfully in her ear.

"What is it?" asked Chhaya.

"Behind us."

She turned to see a group of figures cloaked in red walking towards them.

"No," she whispered.

She took off again, running even faster this time. But around the next corner was another group of hooded figures.

Waiting.

"No," she said, louder this time.

She turned around, but it was no use. The first group were getting closer.

"No!" she screamed.

Sebastian sobbed into her hair, clinging onto her for dear life.

"What do you want from me?" she asked angrily, holding her arms tightly around Sebastian like a shield. "WHAT DO YOU WANT FROM ME?!"

"Chhaya, wake up!" a voice called, and a pair of hands grabbed her shoulders, shaking her. Chhaya snapped her eyes open to see Della hovering above her. She sat up, breathing heavily and covered in a thin layer of sweat. Della handed her the glass of water from her bedside table and drank the entirety in one go.

"Della? Is everything okay?" she asked once she had finally slowed her breathing. It was just a nightmare. She looked through the window and saw the moon still high in the sky. She couldn't have been asleep for too long.

"I went to deliver the letter," Della responded, lighting the candle on Chhaya's bedside table. "I went a little later because I had some things to do downstairs first. And look!" She waved a sheet of paper in Chhaya's face.

"What is that?" Chhaya was still rubbing the sleep out of her eyes and allowing them to adjust to the brightness of the room.

"A letter. From Favian," Della spoke quickly. "When I went to deliver yours, this one was stuck to his door. It wasn't addressed to anybody, but considering you are the only one who has sent him letters before, I assumed it was for you and took it."

"He wrote back?" Chhaya asked excitedly. "This is even better than I thought it could be. Well, let's read it!" She held her hand out, waiting for Della to hand the letter over to her. She sat up eagerly in her bed.

Who are you?

F

"Is that it?" she laughed. She looked at Della, who was still anxiously wringing her hands at the foot of her bed. "Della, what is the matter?"

"I merely hope he didn't see me, Chhaya. He was awake, and I think he heard me, but I got out of there just in time. What if he followed me or something?"

"Della, please don't worry. If he had followed you, he would have been knocking on that door already. And besides, if he thinks his admirer came back to this room, he would suspect *me,* not you!"

"Of course, Chhaya."

"He won't find out, Della, don't worry. I will just pen a response, and we can return to our beds."

"You are sending another one?" Della exclaimed.

"I need to respond to him, or he'll—"

"Chhaya, I really think this is a bad idea," Della insisted.

Chhaya considered her for a moment. She took in Della's worried eyes and her clenched jaw and sighed. "You're right, Della. Please, do not worry. You go to bed, and we will just forget about this entire ordeal. I'm sure Favian will have forgotten in a few days, as well."

Della instantly relaxed, her shoulders loosening and her jaw unclenching. "Thank you, Chhaya," she said with a grateful smile. "Goodnight." She blew out the candle she had lit and closed the door behind her, leaving Chhaya in her bed.

Chhaya waited a few minutes, not too long, but long enough to be sure Della was far enough away, before jumping out of bed and lighting the candle once again. She wouldn't be able to return to her slumber anytime soon after that nightmare and thought about perhaps having a bath, but instead sat down at her desk to pen another note.

My dearest Favian,

I must say, it was a pleasant surprise to have a response from you.

It was beginning to get frustrating, only imagining what your responses would be. Picturing your face when you received my letters. Visualising your reaction to my words.

To answer your question. Who am I?

What a question to ask, Favian. I am your admirer. I thought I had made this clear already.

But I suppose you can call me...

Aaliya

I look forward to seeing you tomorrow, Favian

Your dearest Aaliya

She smiled in satisfaction at the letter before slipping on her silk gown and her warmest slippers. It only took a few minutes to sneak to Favian's room and back, and with nobody else apart from the guards in the corridor, and outside her room, it was smooth and quick.

She attached the new letter to his door and hurried back into her own room, snuggling back into bed, ignoring the faint pang of guilt in her stomach as she did so. This had turned out to be a most eventful day indeed.

"So do you know what actually happened?" asked Lukas, slathering jam on his generously buttered slice of toast.

"Not yet," replied Chhaya, pouring strawberry syrup over her stack of pancakes. "We are investigating."

"But I'm happy to say little Sebastian is doing just fine," Mia declared as she sat down to join them at the table. "I took him back yesterday evening, and the child was running and jumping all over the place; you would never know he had injured his leg."

Chhaya smiled. "I shall have to go and see him later today. I think I will bring some treats, too."

"Chhaya?" Favian asked, leaning over to talk to her as she drank her coffee.

"Mmm?"

"Do you know of anybody in the castle named Aaliya?"

It was all she could do not to choke on the rich drink or spit it out. She swallowed the coffee slowly, put the mug down on the table and ignored the curious looks around them, plastering an indifferent look on her face. "Aaliya?" she asked, turning towards him and wrinkling her forehead. She rubbed her chin for a moment and pretended to consider the question seriously. She knew there was nobody in the castle named Aaliya; that was why she had chosen the name, to begin with. "I don't believe so." She watched as the glimmers of curiosity and hope turned to shadows of disappointment on his face. He really was very affected by Aaliya. "Why?"

Without even a moment to consider, he began to speak. "I have a message to deliver to her. I have spent a large part of this morning searching for her but cannot seem to find any trace of her at all."

He hadn't quite lied, but he had certainly had his explanation ready for her.

"I see. Well, I cannot tell you the name rings a bell, Favian, but if anything comes to mind, I will be sure to let you know."

"Thank you, Chhaya," he said with a nod before straightening up again and crossing his arms into his usual stance.

"What was that?" asked Mia.

"I have no idea," replied Chhaya with a shrug.

She looked over to see Della frowning at her, but she merely smiled back in response.

My dearest Favian,

I heard you have been looking for me today. I feel ever so flattered to know you are searching so thoroughly for me.

But alas, your efforts are useless. Nobody here knows me as 'Aaliya'. Only you do.

But I will tell you, Favian, that I am closer than you believe. You looked straight into my eyes today, and it was all I could do not to smile. You look so serious all of the time, you know. You would look magnificent if you smiled.

Until tomorrow.

Your dearest Aaliya.

"I was delighted to hear from you," Aamir told Chhaya as they strolled along the river.

"Well, I was happy you accepted my invitation," Chhaya replied.

"How could I reject an invitation from the princess?" he asked jokingly. "I might be beheaded."

Chhaya burst into laughter. "You are joking, I know, but for such a long time, the poor children in the orphanage really did believe that I would send them to be beheaded."

"No way."

"It's true! They were terrified of me for the longest time."

Chhaya heard a snort of laughter and turned around to see Favian clearing his throat. She fought a smile, biting her cheek and turning back around.

"So, I have to ask you something," Aamir told her seriously.

"Please go ahead."

"It's a serious question."

Chhaya folded her eyebrows suspiciously. "Is everything okay?"

"Well, Princess... you tell me."

Chhaya stopped walking and turned towards him. What in the Three Kingdoms was so serious? "Aamir, what is going on?"

"Damon? Really?"

Chhaya frowned. "What?"

"You *truly* thought considering Damon was a good idea?"

She exhaled in relief and released a breath of laughter, giving him a light slap on the arm and continuing to walk ahead. "You scared me, Aamir. But admittedly, I did not know he would turn out to be like that."

"Like what?"

"Umm... an arrogant prat who wanted nothing but my money and the crown and cared only about himself?"

Aamir barked out a short laugh. "I couldn't have described him better myself. But what I meant was that he doesn't seem like your type."

"Oh really?" And just what is my type exactly?" she asked, raising an eyebrow, daring him to answer the question.

"Oh, you know," Aamir replied, dramatically flipping his head and running a hand through his hair. "Dark-haired and strikingly handsome."

"Is it now?" laughed Chhaya.

"Strong, of course," he continued.

"I see."

"And who loves nature. And horses."

"Well, I will have to concede to that one—Shadow must approve of my choice, of course."

"Then perhaps I should meet Shadow so he can approve of me sooner rather than later."

Chhaya hesitated. After Shadow's reaction to Damon, she wasn't sure it was such a good idea.

Aamir picked up on her hesitation and chuckled. "I mean *after* he recovers from Damon, of course."

"Of course," Chhaya laughed.

"This is a lovely view," Aamir commented. It was true; the sun was setting and casting a pink glow on the water and the surrounding rocks and plants.

"It's one of my favourites," Chhaya replied. "I find it so peaceful. No matter what is happening in the castle and in the kingdom, things are always the same here. The sun sets every day, making the water look pink. The frogs hop across the lilies every day. It's just... steady."

She looked at Aamir to find him staring intently at her, his eyes staring into hers as if he could see something she couldn't.

"What?" she asked in a small voice.

Aamir smiled and looked away, watching the river once again. "There is a ball on Saturday."

"Yes, I am aware of that."

Aamir released a short breath of laughter. "Of course you know that. What I meant to ask you is, will you perhaps save your first dance for me?" He had a boyish grin plastered across his face.

"Well... now that depends."

"On...?"

"Can you waltz?" Chhaya asked seriously. "Because I refuse to have my toes trodden on within the first hour. Otherwise, I will be unable to dance for the rest of the evening."

"I can waltz. My mother made sure I knew how. *But* for you, I will practise."

A

I am here because I have a job to do. I do not have time for this.
Reveal yourself.

F

"Good afternoon, Your Highness," Aamir smiled handsomely and offered her an elegant bow as the others began to head inside. With the sun hiding behind the clouds, the icy air, although not as bitter as usual, now chilled her cheeks and hands. They had spent a few hours outside for afternoon tea, under the warmth of the rays and the protection of the gazebos.

Unfortunately, for the duration of the event, Chhaya had been forced to endure the company of a group of high-ranking men whom she had found rather dull and diplomatic, so seeing Aamir's face immediately brought a smile to her lips.

"It is lovely to see you again, Aamir."

Since her first meeting with him, she truly enjoyed each encounter with the charismatic man. It appeared her father also approved of Aamir, with him being a Duke and therefore not after her wealth, as well as being very well-liked across the Kingdoms.

"If you are not too tired, perhaps we could go for a stroll?" he asked, offering out his arm for her to take. Chhaya glanced over at Favian, who appeared indifferent, before nodding at Aamir and taking his hand.

Chhaya led their walk, taking Aamir over the charming cobblestone bridge on the river and around to the lake to see all the little ducks chirping brightly. From their position on this side of the river, they could see the sun setting gracefully behind the castle. It was one of Chhaya's favourite times of the day.

"So, listen," Aamir said in a hushed voice so that Favian would not overhear. "A few of us have arranged to meet this evening after dinner. I think the intensity of all of this," he waved a vague arm towards the castle, "is a little too much for some people. You know, the picnics and the teas and the upcoming balls. I think we'll do something casual tonight. Perhaps have a drink and play some cards."

"Have you, now?"

"Yes, but we all agreed that our evening would be significantly better if you were to join us." He smiled cheekily at her.

"I see."

"So I thought I would invite you, on the chance you perhaps wanted to slip away," he glanced back at Favian, "and join us this evening."

Chhaya grinned. "I'll see what I can do."

My dearest Favian

You worked so hard to learn my name, and yet you do not use it? I live here, in the castle, just as you do.

You have a job to do, of course, but that cannot stop you from living. Have you done a single thing since you arrived in this castle that has not been for Chhaya's sake? Have you taken an evening to yourself?

Probably not. Because the girl is simply a spoilt princess.

You should leave her to it for an evening. Tonight, even. Just rest for once.

Your dearest Aaliya

There was a knock at the door, and Chhaya opened it, glad to see Favian standing nervously on the other side. Hopefully, his appearance meant that he had read the letter.

"Favian, how can I help you?" asked Chhaya, inviting him inside.

"Thank you, Chhaya. This will only take a moment." He stepped into her room apprehensively, using his Magic to close the door as he usually did, but did not move further than that.

"Would you like to sit? Della has already gone to bring tea," she offered, feigning ignorance.

"No, no. I just wanted to ask if perhaps I could take the evening off. If you do not have any plans, of course. I mean to say that if you would like anything, I am available, but otherwise, I will stay in my room and give you some privacy."

"Favian, of course! You have not had a chance to rest since you arrived. Please, have an evening to yourself for once. I am rather tired myself, and will be resting in my room this evening, anyway."

"Thank you, Chhaya." He smiled at her and Chhaya felt her heart clench. He had such a handsome smile that was given out so rarely.

A small part of her felt guilty for tricking him like this, but she shook it away. No matter how he had figured it out, he *did* need some time off.

As soon as Favian left, she removed her gown, adorning a thin cloak over her fitted kurti top instead, and called for Della.

"I will only be downstairs," she told Della. She was in no danger, of course, and would still be inside the castle, but someone needed to be aware of her location. Just in case.

"Chhaya, are you sure this is a good idea?" Della asked, wringing her hands together.

"I will be fine, Della. Thank you for your concern, but I will not be going anywhere, and you know where I am in case I am needed," Chhaya answered reassuringly.

"Okay. But if anything happens, I'll have to tell Favian."

"Of course. But you will not need to."

She left quickly, nodding to the guards outside her room and hurrying down the stairs, actually looking forward to the evening ahead of her. Spending time with some of the suitors in a more relaxed setting would be the change of pace that she needed.

Over the past few days, she had begun to see some of them, such as Mark, as good friends. But she had to admit that the thought of seeing Aamir again made her heart flutter with excitement, particularly in a quieter setting.

"So, the princess has finally come down from her tower!" announced Mark dramatically as Chhaya walked into the dimly lit dining room.

She chuckled. "Finally, the princess was *invited* down from her tower. I didn't take you as one for fairytales, Mark."

"Chhaya," Aamir greeted, standing and walking over to her. "I'm glad you came."

"As am I." Chhaya smiled up at him.

"How did you manage to get rid of Favian?" He pulled out a chair and gestured for her to sit.

"Oh, don't worry about him," Chhaya replied, ignoring the twinge of guilt in her chest. "He needed a break, anyway."

Aamir raised a curious eyebrow but did not press further.

"What are we drinking?" asked Chhaya, feeling a strange and sudden urge to change the topic of conversation away from Favian.

Mark raised his eyebrows. "The type for hard liquor, are we, Princess?"

"It depends on the liquor," she countered.

"Here," said Vex, one of the other suitors, filling a small glass with a golden liquid from an unmarked bottle. "Drink this, and we'll make a move."

Chhaya took the glass from his hand and sniffed the suspicious liquid. It smelt strangely like a mixture of apples and cherries. "Make a move?"

"Well, you don't expect us to sit around all night, do you?" asked Mark with a shrug.

Chhaya folded her arms. "And just where were you planning to go?"

Vex shrugged. "Somewhere in Courtfell. We'll decide exactly when we're in town. Surely some taverns will be open."

"There's a tavern I often frequented when I was in town as an apprentice to the blacksmith," added Mark.

Chhaya turned to Aamir. "You did not mention any of this earlier."

"I didn't know about this."

"Come on. We're only going to have a drink, perhaps some mead. It will be a different evening," insisted Vex.

Chhaya stood up from her chair with a sigh, leaving the untouched glass of alcohol on the table. "You all have a pleasant evening. But I will not be leaving the castle alone, particularly not at this time and with all of you."

Vex scoffed. "Why not?"

"I do not mean this in a bad way," Chhaya began, "but I cannot be seen out in the Kingdom, drinking mead with a group of men I barely know in the middle of the night."

Vex rolled his eyes. "Come on, Chhaya, don't be like that."

"I work very hard for my people and for my Kingdom. And I work very hard to be respected. *This,*" she made a circular motion towards them with her hand, "is not who I am. And it is not who my people expect me to be."

"Chhaya, just relax," Mark said, standing up. "It's not such an issue like you are suggesting."

Chhaya smiled awkwardly at them. "Perhaps not for you, but it is for me. Truly. You all have a nice time, and I will see you all tomorrow."

"Don't be like that, Princess," argued Felix, one of the other suitors at the table.

"Even if I was willing to join you, I am not to leave castle grounds without Favian."

"You don't need a guard!" called another suitor, who had very clearly had too much of the golden liquid. "You've got us to protect ya!"

She walked over to the door without another word. It was no use arguing with them—only a waste of her time. Before she could open the door, she felt two hands grab onto her wrists. "What are you doing?" she exclaimed in disgust, turning around to see Vex holding onto one hand and the drunk suitor grabbing the other.

"Don't leave, Princess. You'll have a great time," the drunk suitor slurred.

"We have just finished a war," she announced angrily, trying to shake them off of her to no avail. "There are Blood Magicians running all over, actively hunting me down, and you think I would leave this castle with you? For what? For a wasted evening?"

Vex suddenly grabbed her by her waist and hauled her onto his shoulders as if she were a sack. She yelped.

"Hey, come on, put her down!" shouted a voice she knew was Aamir.

"Release me," she demanded.

"We'll take you out for a nice evening," Vex laughed. "We can show you exactly what you are missing, being locked up in this place."

"Seriously, Vex, let her go," Aamir insisted.

"Why are you two being so serious about this? We've been cooped up in this place for more than two weeks."

The heavy door creaked open, and Chhaya was jostled as Vex left the room, still carrying her on his shoulders.

There was a sudden bright flash of light, and before she knew it, Vex was on the ground, and Chhaya was being held upright by two strong hands around her waist.

"What is going on here?" demanded Favian, his voice vibrating through her as he kept a tight hold of her to prevent her from falling.

Chhaya widened her eyes, along with the others, as they stared fearfully at Favian. He had moved so swiftly that Chhaya hadn't even noticed his presence until he was holding onto her. He had knocked Vex off his feet with his Magic and caught Chhaya in the process so she wouldn't be dropped onto the ground.

He looked at her with a worried frown before turning back to the others, letting go of Chhaya only when he was certain she was steady on her feet, before moving to stand over Vex. "Were you attempting to kidnap the princess?" A dangerous tone painted his voice.

"Uhh," Vex stammered. He gulped. "Not really."

"If you have not left by the morning, I will report it to the King." He turned around and gestured for Chhaya to go ahead of him, and together they walked up the stairs.

Chapter Ten

A aliya

    Please do not talk about Chhaya in such a way. It is my duty and honour to guard her and my reason for being here.

    I still believe it to be unfair that you know who I am while I have no way of identifying you.

    Tell me something about yourself, at least.

    F

My dearest Favian

    You would like to know something about me? Let me think. What is there to tell?

    Perhaps you would like to know my eye colour? Or my hair colour? Or my favourite colour? But no. Those are all fairly mundane facts, are they not?

    Instead, I will tell you this: I love your eyes. They are beautiful. Is this enough information for you? Your stormy grey eyes could hold me in a trance forever.

Perhaps I should demand a fact about you now. Share a secret, and I shall do the same.

I look forward to seeing you. Even though you will not see me.

Your dearest Aaliya

Chhaya sat with her friends for dinner that evening craving their familiarity after the events of the previous evening.

"Chhaya?" her heart stopped when he whispered in her ear.

She cleared her throat. "Yes, Favian?" she asked him.

"If you accept, I will walk around the perimeter. Normally I would go in between your afternoon activity and dinner, but there was no break today."

"Of course, Favian. I will be here." She frowned as soon as the words had left her lips. She had told him the same thing the day before, but that had been a lie.

The moment Favian left, Mia leaned over to her. "He seems different lately." Together, they watched as he left the dining room.

"Do you think?" Chhaya asked, cutting her potatoes and pretending to be unknowing. Nobody else knew of the letters—even Della was unaware she had continued to pen them.

"Absolutely," Mia replied enthusiastically. "He seems much more relaxed."

"Oh, I am not sure about that." She let out a hesitant laugh that sounded strange even to her own ears.

"What was that sound you just made?" Mia asked with a laugh.

"No, nothing," she answered a little too quickly. "He is the same Favian as usual. Just... without a cloak, I suppose."

"I don't know about that, Chhaya. Something about him has changed. He doesn't seem as stiff and as tense all the time as he was when he first arrived. You never know—perhaps I was right, and he needed a little love in his life."

Chhaya almost choked on the potato she had been chewing but took a steadying sip of wine and cleared her throat.

"Perhaps."

"But I would like to discuss the important things. What in the Three Kingdoms is happening over there?" she asked slyly, looking over at Aamir, who kept glancing over at Chhaya.

"Not much." Chhaya shrugged, but she could feel the traitorous blush creeping its way across her cheeks.

"Why, Chhaya! Do you *fancy* him?"

"You sound like a child," Chhaya commented but laughed all the same.

"It is a rather big change!" exclaimed Mia. "You have never taken an interest in anybody in such a way before, and now you are expected to marry one."

"Well, I am expected to consider. I am not necessarily required to *marry* one."

"Della, did you hear that?" asked Mia as Della came and took the seat on the other side of Chhaya. "Chhaya is considering marrying Aamir."

"You are?"

"Oh, do not be ridiculous, Mia," laughed Chhaya. "No, I am certainly not considering marriage," she replied to Della.

"He would hardly be the worst choice," Mia continued, looking over at him while Chhaya fought the urge to hide under the table in shame. "He is, after all, *very* cute."

"I know, but—" Chhaya began.

"I know what happened yesterday was... far from ideal, shall we say," Mia interrupted. "*But* I truly don't believe he meant any harm. From what I overheard earlier today, it was the others that decided on this plan without telling Aamir about it. You cannot hold it against him, surely."

"I suppose not," Chhaya replied, biting her lip.

"And he is a magnificent conversationalist," added Della. "I overheard the two of you talking the other day." She raised her eyebrows at Chhaya.

"When did you hear us talking?"

"Chhaya, in all seriousness, I realise you decided you would never love anyone after what happened with your mother, but don't you think it's time to move on?" asked Mia.

The smile dropped from Chhaya's face. "*Move on*?"

"That's not what I meant—"

"Then what exactly did you mean, Mia? Because I do not think my mother's death will ever stop being a part of me."

"Chhaya, I run an orphanage. If anybody is aware of that, it's me."

"Then you will also know the heartbreak one goes through when one loses somebody they love. My heart broke when my mother was brutally murdered in front of my eyes. I thought my life was over. I had no idea what I would do without her. But my father... a part of him *died* that day, Mia. He has never been the same since, and he never will. So excuse me for not wanting that for myself."

Della placed a comforting hand on Chhaya's shoulder. "Chhaya, Mia knows this. We all do. And we understand. But your mother wouldn't have wanted this for you. A life without love—"

"A life without love is better than a life filled with loss," Chhaya stated, standing and leaving the room.

"Chhaya, is everything okay?" asked Favian, almost colliding with her as he turned the corner to return to the dining room.

Chhaya quickly wiped the stray tears from her cheeks before he could see them. "Fine, Favian, thank you. I think I'll spend the rest of the evening in my room."

Chapter Eleven

Aaliya

You must know I will discover your identity eventually. It is what I am trained to do.

Besides, I do not have much to share with you. I grew up in this Kingdom and began my training to become a soldier at the age of five. Will that suffice?

F

"I am glad finally there is some time to visit Gaia," Chhaya said, content as she strolled along the cobblestoned streets to the apothecary. She glanced back at Favian, who was walking ever so slightly behind her and seemed to be off in his own world, a small, subconscious smile painted on his lips. Chhaya couldn't help but smile then, seeing him so serene. It was a significant change since he had first arrived.

"Favian?" she asked him sweetly.

"Yes, Chhaya?" he asked, startling out of his reverie.

"May I ask you something?"

"Of course, Chhaya."

She slowed down so that she was next to him rather than in front of him. "You seem very happy lately, Favian."

The blush instantly appeared on his face. She didn't bother to fight against the smile that appeared each time she turned his cheeks that intriguing shade of pink.

"I did not intend to embarrass you, Favian," she said innocently. "I am happy for you, actually." She watched him for a moment, smiling at the way his lips twitched upwards ever so slightly. "Whatever or... *whoever* is making you so happy has my gratitude."

Favian's blush grew even deeper, and a small smile twitched the corners of his lips. "There—" he stopped suddenly, and all traces of happiness vanished from his face. "Wait here," he ordered in a low voice.

Chhaya frowned at him. What had caused this sudden change of mood? "Favian, what—" He quickly put his finger over her lips to stop her from speaking, looking from her to the apothecary.

Gaia's door was open, hanging on the hinges and creaking in the wind.

"Wait out here while I check inside," he whispered, removing his hand from her face.

Chhaya nodded silently.

She watched as he opened his palms, and she saw the sparks of Magic flying across his hands. He walked into the apothecary and, after a few minutes, walked out again, marching over to her and grabbing her by the arm. "It is empty."

"Not even Gaia...?" Chhaya asked, her eyes frantic and her arms fighting his grasp, as Favian started to lead her back towards the castle.

Favian shook his head.

"We have to do something! What if something has happened? What if Gaia is in danger?" she cried, shaking off his hand.

Favian stopped and looked at her. "We need to get you back to the castle."

"I cannot leave Gaia!"

"Chhaya, please!" Favian shouted, surprising Chhaya into silence. "I do not want to leave Gaia either, but you are my first priority. I cannot come back and locate her until I know you are safe."

She gulped. His lenses had slipped, and she looked into his honest grey eyes, sparkling silver with the Magic he was prepared to use. She nodded. "Let us go, and then you can—"

"Princess!" a voice called from behind them.

They turned to see a merchant waving frantically at them from the other side of the small stone bridge.

Chhaya looked at Favian before they both hurried to the merchant. "Is everything okay?" Chhaya demanded.

The merchant shook their head. "You should both come this way."

Favian looked at Chhaya hesitantly but eventually nodded. "Stay behind me," he ordered in a low voice.

The two were led over to a small cottage behind the first row of shops. The door was open, and crowds of people stood outside, some weeping, some comforting them, and others standing in complete shock.

Chhaya caught sight of Sebastian standing defeatedly, alone on the other side of the crowd, and hurried over to him without a second glance at Favian. "Sebastian?" she whispered, crouching down and holding his arms. He looked so lost, staring up at her with empty eyes and a blank face.

Almost immediately, she pulled him into a hug. "It's okay," she whispered.

A hand touched her shoulder, and she looked up to see Favian. He instantly pulled his hand back but nodded towards Sebastian.

"I don't know," she mouthed at him. "Sebastian?" she asked again, but the boy remained silent. She released him, sat him down on a bench and turned back to Favian. "We need to find out what is going on."

Favian pressed his lips together and met her eyes with his, removing his lenses entirely. "Chhaya, you could stay with him," he offered gently. "There may be distressing—"

"You do not think I am not going in there with you?" she asked with a scoff, storming past him.

"I merely wanted you to have the option," he replied.

The moment they entered the building, it was clear what had happened. Drops of blood trailed along the floor, and bloody handprints marked the walls. To her short-lived relief, Chhaya could hear Gaia speaking from another room.

"Fill this basin with fresh water," Gaia instructed somebody as Chhaya entered. She gasped as she saw the pale and lifeless face of Kat, one of the children from the orphanage, on one of the makeshift beds in the small room.

Gaia turned to her then, but her eyes were not warm and welcoming as usual; instead, they were defeated.

"What happened?" Favian asked when Chhaya found herself unable to speak.

Gaia sighed heavily. "There was another attack."

"Where?"

"Near the market. There were children playing, and it was very busy."

"Is she going to be alright?" asked Chhaya in a shaky voice.

Gaia looked solemn but had no answer for them. "It was mostly internal damage, but she had coughed up a lot of blood when we found her. A *lot* of blood."

"But... but the potion you were brewing? The Moon Orchard Potion?"

Gaia held up an empty vial. "This was the last of it. We never expected to use it at all, let alone not have enough of it."

"What about the others?" she asked, gesturing around at the surrounding beds and people on top of them. There must have been at least fifteen patients in this room alone.

"We arrived quickly. That is a small mercy. Their chances of survival are higher, but not guaranteed."

Chhaya felt the tears pricking the corners of her eyes as she looked around her. On one bed lay an elderly man she recognised from the market—the florist. Every week she attended the market, and each week he told her all about his granddaughter, who was training to be a soldier. He was so proud of her.

On another bed was a pregnant woman, her arms covered in deep gashes and her face contorted in agony, even in her state of unconsciousness.

On another, another child looked to be no more than two years of age. He was yet to be able to speak properly, but across his face was a deep gash that would definitely scar and stay for the entirety of his life.

Chhaya refused to cry here. She had no right to do so. She had no right to grieve, mourn, or feel sorry for anyone right now. She needed to help. "What can we do?" she asked, forcing her voice to be steady.

"There's nothing left to do. All we can do now is wait," Gaia replied.

"We can bring food to those waiting outside," Chhaya suggested determinedly. "Can we, Favian?" she asked, turning to him. But even he, the person who rarely showed any emotion at all, seemed dejected. "Favian?" she asked him again.

"Yes, Chhaya."

"Let us bring some hot tea for everyone. Gaia, may we use your teas and apothecary? I will reimburse you for everything, of course."

"Of course you can."

Chhaya didn't wait to leave the house with Favian behind her. She stopped in front of Sebastian and crouched down again. "Sebastian, I need your help. You will help, won't you?" Finally, there was a reaction from the boy. He looked up at her and blinked a couple of times before nodding. She held out a hand for him to hold and took him with her to Gaia's apothecary.

There, Chhaya and Favian got to work. She settled Sebastian down on a chair and draped a blanket over him. She hadn't needed his help but couldn't bear to leave him alone. He had nobody in his life but the other children, some of whom had been lying in that house.

First, Chhaya set lavender tea to steep and then filled one cup, adding extra honey and giving it to Sebastian. His hands were freezing, and his face was still pale. She had hoped the heat from the drink, and the sweetness of the honey would help somehow.

She instructed Favian to bring more water from the spring while she set chamomile tea to steep next. When Favian returned, he put the water over the fire.

While they waited for it to boil, Chhaya turned to Favian. "There must be something we can do," she whispered.

"Gaia is the most experienced herbologist I have ever met."

"But still. Favian, your Magic. Is there anything you can do?"

He hesitated then. "Well..."

"What is it?"

"Some can heal with their Magic, but I have never been able to do so."

"What if I can do it?" asked Chhaya desperately. "Teach me. Perhaps I can do it."

"Chhaya, it's very rare," Favian replied. "I have only ever seen one medic who was capable of healing Magic to the extent these people would require. And even that was when I was a child. Healing bones and wounds, even with elixirs, is difficult enough, hence the vigorous training our Healers and Medics must endure. But to heal somebody who is unconscious and has such severe injuries would be far too difficult."

"But we have to *try,* Favian!" she cried, grabbing his arm.

He stopped and looked calmly at her before looking down at where her fingers were crumpling his clothes. She let go as soon as she realised where his gaze had landed.

Before he could answer, the water began to bubble over, and Chhaya quickly took the teapot from the fire, adding in passionflower and lemon balm to steep.

"We do not have time. We should return," Favian said in a low voice, standing right behind her.

Chhaya nodded. She walked over to Sebastian and took the empty cup from him, glad to see that he had, in fact, drank it all and regained some colour to his face. She made one more cup for him and handed it to him while Favian gathered everything else.

It was not a Magical elixir or potion, but Gaia had taught her the power of calming teas during their time together. And if that was all she could do to help right now, that was all she would do.

"Thank you, Chhaya," Gaia said gratefully as Chhaya passed her a cup of tea.

While they had been gone, most people in the room had awoken. A large number were still in a terrible amount of pain and being given pain-easing elixirs, and still needed to be treated for some of their wounds, but they would live.

Only Kat remained unconscious. She had been in the most critical condition, according to Gaia, and had almost suffocated in her own blood. They had given her immediate attention, having found her in a pool of hot and sticky red liquid. Even still, there were traces of the blood staining her face and clumped in her hair.

There was a groan, and everybody in the room immediately turned to look at the small bed by the door.

Kat.

She coughed—lightly at first, then more forcibly. Gaia hurried over and helped her sit up, guiding her to drink some water.

"What happened?" Kat rasped out.

"Try not to speak for now," Gaia responded gently. Chhaya handed over a cup of tea, and Kat sipped on it gratefully, relaxing as it soothed her throat.

"This is a good sign?" asked Chhaya.

The corners of Gaia's mouth twisted upwards, hopefully. "An excellent sign. Kat should be fine. And it seems everybody else will, too."

Chhaya's heart filled with relief. "Then we will stop distracting you. I will take Sebastian with me to the castle. I will have him seen by the medic for his shock, and then he will stay in the guest room."

"That sounds like a wonderful idea, Chhaya," Gaia told her proudly.

"We will return tomorrow with Sebastian."

Chhaya certainly felt much more at ease that evening.

While she had taken Sebastian to the infirmary to be seen by the medic, Favian had left to discuss the attack with her father. The medic had said that Sebastian was simply recovering from the shock and needed some rest after seeing such horrific events earlier, particularly as they were against his best friend. Gaia had also sent word that Kat and the other patients were recovering remarkably well and that bringing Sebastian the next day would be a good idea.

Her father had arranged for more patrols in the Kingdom, and Chhaya and Favian had spent the evening with Sebastian. They had played games, read books and eaten plenty of strawberry cheesecake, which happened to be Sebastian's favourite.

"Are you feeling any better, Sebastian?" Chhaya asked warmly as the boy came and sat down next to her on the sofa, leaving Favian the armchair opposite them. He nodded, still seeming slightly distracted but looking much more present than he had earlier.

"Would you like some hot chocolate?" she suggested temptingly. He nodded eagerly at that, his eyes lighting up ever so slightly. It was rare for them to experience delicacies such as cheesecake and hot chocolate in the orphanage unless Chhaya arranged for them herself. "Let me go and fetch some for us then, shall I?" She stood, but Sebastian gripped tightly onto her hand. She looked at him in surprise.

"Please don't go, Princess," he whispered.

Chhaya's heart clenched, and she sat back down again, pulling him closer to her. She glanced at Favian with a raised eyebrow, and he nodded, getting up and leaving the room to ask for the drinks.

"Princess?"

"Yes, Sebastian?"

"There were bad people today."

"I know, Sebastian. I am sorry you had to see all that," Chhaya responded sincerely.

"They were talking about you."

Chhaya straightened. "About me? What do you mean?"

"The reason why they did those bad things was because nobody would tell them where you were."

Nausea churned in Chhaya'sstomach.

"Did they say anything else?"

"They said they knew you weren't in the castle. But then there was a loud bang, and they ran away."

"We are very happy to see you're feeling better, Kat," Chhaya told her with a wide smile. "Gaia even said you were well enough for some of this." She presented a bowl of fresh blackberries, a rare find in the Khiona Kingdom. Even in the castle, they did not have the luxury of blackberries very often. It was pure luck that some had been brought by traders from the Peleia Kingdom that very morning.

Kat gasped, bringing her hands up to her cheeks. "Wow! Thank you, Chhaya! Blackberries are my favourite," exclaimed Kat.

"Thank Sebastian—he suggested you might like them."

"Hi, Kat," Sebastian spoke hesitantly, his eyes fixed down on the ground as he fiddled with the bottom of his tunic with one hand. He poked his head around Chhaya's leg but kept hold of her hand.

"Hi, Sebastian!" Kat responded eagerly, her enthusiasm giving Sebastian the confidence to release his tight grip on Chhaya's hand and sit in front of Kat on her bed. He put a puzzle that Chhaya had given him that morning down between them.

Chhaya then turned to Gaia, allowing the kids to play. "I am glad to see that most of the others have been sent home."

"It was a miracle that we had the Moon Orchard Potion on hand. None of them would have survived without it," Gaia replied in a hushed voice.

"If there's anything else we can do, please do send word."

"Of course."

Chapter Twelve

"It is a relief that Gaia had that Potion prepared," Chhaya spoke as she and Favian walked back to the castle after having visited Gaia and Kat, as well as a trip to the orphanage.

"It is a shame she felt the need to prepare it at all, but I agree. I am thankful she did," replied Favian, surprising Chhaya. She was still acclimating to his more frequent sharing of opinions.

"Sebastian told me something interesting yesterday evening while you were gone," Chhaya commented, changing the subject.

Favian raised an eyebrow but remained silent.

"According to him, the Blood Magicians that attacked yesterday were searching for me."

Favian immediately snapped his head up and looked at her. "Why did you not mention this earlier? I would not have allowed you to come today." He began looking around them as if a threat could appear at any moment.

"*That* is why, Favian. You would have all but fought me to prevent me from coming today, which I could not allow. And just who told you you have the ability to '*allow*' me to do anything? You are aware you work for me and not the other way around?"

"This is serious, Chhaya." Favian stopped to look at her. Through the dark lenses of his sunglasses, Chhaya could not see his eyes, but she recognised the lines of concern on his forehead, the wrinkled eyebrows and the tension in his shoulders. "You could be in severe danger at any given moment."

Chhaya rolled her eyes and continued to walk. "That is not even the interesting piece of information I was referring to, Favian. Sebastian told me the Blood Magicians knew I was not in the castle. How could they possibly have known that?"

Favian's face instantly paled, and his jaw tensed. "Chhaya, please listen to me. We are going to cancel today's events, and you will be required to remain in your room—at least until the guards finish their sweep of the Kingdom and the surrounding forests. Until yesterday, we were under the misconception that the Blood Magicians had been taken care of, and none were remaining, other than a stray here and there. But now we know for certain that there are more. There are too many.

"If they have left, you may be safe for the time being. But if they knew you were not in the castle, someone must be helping them."

"Favian, do you not think you may be acting slightly rashly? I have you with me, do I not? I this circumstance not precisely why my father hired you?"

"Chhaya, did you not see what happened yesterday? Did you not see Kat? Do you truly believe the Blood Magicians would hesitate to do something like that to you? And Gaia has no more of that potion in her stores. We cannot risk it."

"Favian, you fail to remember that my own mother was murdered by those monsters in front of my very eyes. If anybody is aware of the dangers, it is me."

They walked in silence for a few moments before Favian spoke again. "Chhaya, I did not mean to speak to you as if you did not understand the risks. Of course you do. I merely mean to say that if somebody within the castle is helping the Blood Magicians, we are in more danger than any of us could have imagined."

That evening, when Chhaya returned from dinner, she collapsed straight onto her bed. Finally, after waiting for the entirety of the afternoon and a large proportion of the evening, the guards had reported back to say there were no Blood Magicians in the area, and Chhaya had been allowed to leave her room and eat with her friends and her guests.

She had sat with Aamir that evening, during which they had had an intriguing conversation about a book he had read recently. Still, Chhaya had not been able to stop thinking about what Favian had said. Someone in the castle had been helping the Blood Magicians.

But who?

Something crumbled under her hand, and she lifted it to see the last letter Favian had written to her. She had completely forgotten about it. Her heart warmed when she reread it, knowing he had really shared something personal about himself with her.

She brought the letter over to her desk to write her response.

My dearest Favian,

You began your training at age five? That is rather young, is it not?

I did promise some information of my own, so here it is. My mother passed away when I was very young.

Your dearest Aaliya

Chhaya had felt a strange mixture of ease and discomfort when she had delivered the latest letter. It had warmed her heart that Favian had shared something about himself with her, but she wondered if she had done the right thing in telling him something so personal, something he might identify with her.

But as she read his latest reply, all traces of regrets or worry vanished. A warmth spread through her stomach as she read the note from the comfort of her bed. She had spotted and taken his response from his door after their training session, while he was in the shower, and was now taking the time to savour each word.

Aaliya

I am sorry.

I wish I could understand your pain and loss, but my family died when I was only a few days old and I cannot remember them, let alone miss or grieve them. I suppose that is an answer to your question, also, in a way.

My family was murdered by Blood Magicians. It was by chance that they did not find me; I suppose my mother had hidden me away in a wardrobe. Again by pure chance, I was found by soldiers who brought me to His Majesty, the King, to whom I owe everything.

The King gave me a life by allowing me to stay in the palace as a baby so that I would have care. He placed me in an orphanage when I was able to walk. When I was old enough, he put me into a boarding school in which I trained to hone my Magic and become a soldier. It is only thanks to him that I am here today.

I have shared even more information with you, Aaliya. Does this mean I will receive another piece in return?

F

Her heart hurt for him. To not have known his family, to have felt alone all his life. She had her papa, at least, even if she did not have her mother any longer.

But to have nobody? She couldn't imagine it.

She wanted to write to him again, to tell him it was okay and that he wouldn't be alone anymore because he had her, but before she could reach her writing desk, there was a sharp rap at the door. Quickly, she hid the letter under her pillow before calling out to whoever was on the other side to come into the room.

"Chhaya." It was Favian. The sight of him caused an unusual fluttering feeling in her stomach that disoriented her.

It was only when Favian lifted an eyebrow that Chhaya realised she had been staring at him without saying a word. "Yes... Favian... How can I help?" she spluttered.

His forehead creased. "You are due for breakfast in around five minutes, I believe?"

"Oh yes, of course!" Chhaya hopped off her bed, shaking herself mentally for being so flustered and in her own world. "Yes, I will just put on my cloak, and we can go." She put on a thin cloak, as she was not planning to leave the castle that morning, and walked over to Favian. She nodded awkwardly and walked out the door, narrowly stopping herself from slamming her head against the wall in embarrassment.

"So," Favian said, breaking the silence as they walked, "today is a one-on-one breakfast?"

"It is," replied Chhaya. "With Aamir."

Favian nodded. "I will remain in the room at all times, but I will remain at the door so as not to intrude on your meal."

"That is rather different," Chhaya said suspiciously. He usually stayed within two metres of her at all times. Even during her birthday ball, he had stayed uncomfortably close to her.

"Your father's orders."

Chhaya felt a little twinge in her heart.

"Great. That is great. Thank you."

Favian held the door open for her when they arrived and entered the room after her, closing the door with a flick of his hand and taking his position in front of it.

"Good morning," Aamir said brightly, standing to greet her with a small bow before pulling out her chair.

"Good morning Aamir," Chhaya greeted him just as warmly before taking her seat. From where she sat, Chhaya had the perfect view of Favian guarding the door. She wondered how he could stay so still for so long without getting a cramp.

A server delivered Chhaya's usual chai and the orange juice Aamir must have requested before asking what they each wanted to eat.

"I must apologise again about the other evening," he said suddenly. "I did not realise the others would try to force you out of the castle and it was entirely inappropriate of them. I hope you know that I would never purposefully bring you any harm?"

"There is nothing to apologise for." And Chhaya truly meant it. "I understand for them, it was entirely fun and games. And that is fine. Except I cannot be with somebody who does not understand my limitations, as the Princess of Khiona. I cannot be with anybody who wants to run around in the middle of the night, who wants to behave irresponsibly."

Aamir sat in silence for a few minutes, and Chhaya couldn't help but glance over at Favian to gauge his reaction to what she had just said. To most, it would seem as though he had not heard her, but Chhaya knew him well enough to spot the tiny but revealing curl of lips. He was happy with what she had said.

"I agree." Chhaya almost jumped at the sound of Aamir's voice breaking her reverie. She looked back at him.

"With what?" she asked.

"Everything you said," replied Aamir sincerely. "You should not—no, you *cannot* be with somebody who is willing to risk your life for some fun. Or someone will risk you getting hurt for some mere entertainment."

Chhaya raised an eyebrow. One problem with being the Princess of Khiona was that it could be difficult to tell when a person agreed with you genuinely or simply because you were the Princess of Khiona.

Subconsciously, she glanced over at Favian to see if he had a reaction to Aamir's words, but his face was as blank as ever. She couldn't even identify any subtle changes in his expression.

"No, really," Aamir said, obviously noticing her hesitation at believing him. "I think what they did was ridiculous. As you know, I told them to stop. Leaving the castle in the middle of the night, without any protection, and especially during a time like this, so soon after the war with attacks still occurring, is just stupid."

"You really think so?"

"Of course. I wouldn't lie to you. Besides, as a Duke, I don't have to be quite as careful as you do, but certainly more so than the average person."

He did have a point. Most of the men that were here had no titles, and even though Chhaya could not care less about any titles, if there were any one person who was to understand her limitations when it came to freedom, apart from Favian, of course, it would be a Duke.

"I suppose you are right, Aamir. Anyway, my speech was not to put the blame on you in any way. I merely want to make it clear that I have certain limitations in my life, limitations that I am fine with but with which you may *not* be. And I understand if you are not. I do not blame you in any way whatsoever."

"Well, it is a good thing that breakfast is not one of your limitations. Because that is one thing I really could not live without." Aamir grinned handsomely at her, taking a sip of his juice and putting a helping of scrambled eggs on his plate.

Chhaya beamed back at him and chose toast for herself, slathering the slices with golden honey. "A good thing for me or for you?"

"I'll have you know I am a wonderful breakfast companion," Aamir huffed in fake indignation.

"You say that, but so far, you have been very boring," Chhaya teased.

Aamir grabbed his chest dramatically. "You wound me, princess."

Chhaya chuckled and flung a grape at him, laughing even harder when he caught the grape in his mouth without even blinking an eye. She felt her heart warm just looking at him, but the stoic, blank expression on Favian's face behind him made her feel something else entirely.

Lost.

Dearest Favian

I am sorry your family were taken away from you so brutally. My mother was also attacked by a group of Blood Magicians.

How do you practise Magic so easily, knowing it was Magic that took your family?

Your Aaliya

Aaliya,

Knowing all remaining Blood Magicians are practising forbidden forms of Magic makes using my own Magic easier.

To access their Magic, they chose to exchange a part of themselves. They are no longer whole.

Their Magic is horrid, while ours is beauty. Where they use their blood Magic to hurt, we use our energy to protect.

I am sorry to hear about your mother. The Blood Magicians are vile, and their Magic is rotten to the core.

One day, we will have to worry about them no longer.

F

Chapter Thirteen

C hhaya walked into the ballroom in a beautiful blue-grey floor-length dress adorned with tiny sparkling jewels, which she had chosen to pair with long diamond earrings and a matching necklace. Her hair cascaded in gentle waves down her back as she walked.

She felt beautiful.

Today marked the first ball of the season. It was two weeks late, given that her father had promised to hold one every Saturday, and today was the third Saturday since the guests had arrived, but Chhaya was happy nonetheless.

To celebrate the first ball, her father had invited almost every family in the kingdom to come along and have a festive evening, another way to help them feel more at ease in the kingdom after the war.

Chhaya adored hosting huge balls like this, with little children running around and their parents and grandparents dancing. There was something about such a happy and joyful environment that made Chhaya's heart swell.

"You look very nice tonight, Favian," she told him as they walked down the stairs together, her arm on his elbow. She had always feared falling down those very stairs in a crowd and had all but forced him to escort her down. "I do not believe I mentioned it earlier."

This evening, he was wearing a red cloak over a white kurta—a significant change from his usual black trousers and tunic combo or his previous cloaks. And he certainly looked good in red.

"Thank you, Chhaya," Favian responded, a hint of surprise colouring his voice. "You look beautiful. As you always do."

"Beta, you look lovely," her father said, approaching her with outstretched arms.

"Papa!" Chhaya kissed her father on the cheek. "I feel as though I haven't seen you in an age."

"I know beta, I'm sorry, There has been some... *upset* on the Northern border. But there is no need to worry about that this evening. You just have a wonderful time tonight, will you? And I will have a chat with Aamir as well when I see him." He smiled knowingly at her, and she felt a blush rise to her cheeks.

"Papa!" she complained, but he only laughed in return.

"Ah, Favian. It's nice to see you dressed up for the occasion. I trust all is well?"

"Perfect, your Majesty." Favian bowed.

"No, no, Favian. How many times must I tell you? There is no need for any of that. Now, even though you are on duty tonight, I expect you to have a nice time. Eat the lovely feast our chefs have spent so much time preparing and perhaps even dance once or twice?" he said with a wink.

Favian began to redden, and Chhaya smiled, jumping in to save him, "On that note, I think I will find a drink. Favian, will you join me?" He nodded wordlessly and followed behind. "Would you like anything?" she asked him, taking a flute of champagne for herself. She sighed when he shook his head. "My father is right, you know. Even though you are working, you should try and enjoy the evening."

"It is difficult to do so when I am so focused on you, Chhaya."

Chhaya's breath caught in her throat before she realised what he meant.

"Well, there is one workaround," she said, putting her still-full flute of champagne on a table. Favian raised an inquisitive eyebrow, and she raised hers in return. "We can dance *together*."

Immediately, Favian began shaking his head.

"Why not?"

"It is not appropriate, Chhaya," Favian responded seriously, offended she had even suggested such a thing.

"What is not appropriate?" Chhaya asked, folding her arms. "You cannot let me out of your sight. Well, what better place to keep me in your sights than during a waltz?"

"I do not think your father would approve."

"My father will be absolutely fine. He only encouraged you minutes before to dance. All I want is for you to have a nice time tonight."

"That is very kind of you, Chhaya, but what will people say if they see you dancing with someone like me? It is just not proper."

"What will people say? Who cares what people will say?" Chhaya asked him.

"You are the Princess of Khiona. You care what people will say. *I* care what people will say."

"Well, I hate to tell you, Favian, but I am expected to dance with many of the people in this room tonight. Children, elderly, in fact, it would come as a surprise to me if there was a single dance where I remained off the dance floor tonight. So, truly, nobody will say a thing about us dancing together."

Favian stood stiffly and awkwardly, not saying a word.

"Come on, please?" she asked softly, placing a hand on his elbow. He turned his head to look at her then, and she could sense him relax. His eyes were still covered by those wretched sunglasses, but his shoulders dropped and his fists unclenched. She was certain he was going to say yes.

Finally.

He would say yes, and they would dance, and he would finally unwind and have a nice evening.

Favian opened his mouth to speak but before he could, Chhaya felt a light hand on the small of her back.

"Your Highness. What a coincidence seeing you here." Chhaya turned around to see Aamir looking rather dashing in his own dress cloak.

"Aamir. Wh—"

"You look magnificent, Chhaya," he said in a low tone, his eyes soft and intimate. "Favian," he said suddenly, holding out a hand to greet the bodyguard. Favian, of course, did not respond but shook his hand in silence. Chhaya looked between the two of them anxiously, but neither of them seemed to notice any discomfort.

"Well, Chhaya, I believe I was promised the first dance of this evening?" Aamir asked, holding out a hand.

"Oh yes, of course," Chhaya stammered. She had entirely forgotten he had asked her.

Aamir chuckled. "Well, they are preparing now to start the first dance."

"Yes, of course." Chhaya looked over at Favian and felt her heart sink ever so slightly. She didn't want him to be alone. Not again. She wanted to say something, but no words seemed to be coming out.

"I will be here, but I will not get in the way," Favian said reassuringly with a nod. Her heart hurt to know that he believed she was worried about him getting in her way.

"Yes, of course," she repeated awkwardly. "Okay then." She took Aamir's hand and allowed him to lead her to the dance floor.

When Chhaya was younger, she would dance with her father in this very same ballroom, counting the steps in her head. One, two, three. One, two, three. She would repeat the sequence over and over again, paying attention to nothing else around her other than the numbers and her feet. Today, she could not concentrate on the numbers, no matter how hard she tried.

As Aamir led her around the ballroom, Chhaya could only keep her eyes on Favian. He watched her steadily, keeping to the side of the ballroom this time rather than following her and her dance partner.

As he watched her, Chhaya couldn't help but wonder what was going through his head. Was he upset Aamir had arrived when he did? Was he happy? Would Favian have even been a good dancer in the first place? Would he even know how to waltz at all? Did soldiers waltz? Were they allowed?

She had no idea.

She did, however, find herself looking forward to writing to him again later that evening. However, she had no idea what she was going to say to him, especially after his last letter had been so intense and angry about the Blood Magicians. But she understood.

"Chhaya?" Aamir's voice broke her reverie, startling her gaze away from Favian and back to Aamir. She gasped as she felt her foot hit something and tripped. Luckily, Aamir caught her arms in his hands, narrowly stopping her from falling entirely on top of him and humiliating them both. "Are you okay?" he asked, frowning down at her as they continued to move around the ballroom.

"Fine, sorry," she replied with an embarrassed giggle. "I made such a fuss about your waltzing ability and here I am stumbling."

He smiled. "I happen to think you are rather spectacular at the waltz. But you seemed to be lost in thought."

"Is that your way of asking me what was so prominently on my mind that I almost sent us tumbling to the ground?"

"I wouldn't be so forward, but since you are offering up the information?"

Chhaya huffed out a laugh. "I was thinking about when I was still learning to dance as a child." It wasn't entirely untrue.

"You were?"

"Yes. My papa taught me." She smiled fondly at the memories. "Believe it or not, I was rather bad at dancing when I was a child. I loved it, but nobody loved being my partner."

Aamir laughed. "Are you claiming to have improved?"

She hit him lightly on the shoulder and glared jokingly. "Whether or not I have, I'll have you know I'm much better than you are."

"Well, if there's one thing we can agree on, it's that we're nowhere near your father's level of skill," he commented, nodding his head towards where the King was dancing with Gaia, spinning her elegantly across the floor and smiling handsomely as he did so.

Chhaya smiled and rolled her eyes. "He is such a lady's man. I promise you he will not spend a single dance this evening sat to the side. Look." She gestured to the side, where a group of people were watching him and Gaia move gracefully around the room, eagerly awaiting their own turns.

"Well it appears like you have your own band of admirers," Aamir commented, indicating to a small group behind her where Sebastian and some other children from the Kingdom were watching her with bright, excited eyes. Chhaya smiled brightly and removed her hand from Aamir's shoulder to wave at them. "I'll consider myself lucky that I asked you first. Otherwise, I might not have seen you for the rest of the evening!"

Chhaya forced a laugh. If he had arrived mere seconds later, she would be talking to and dancing with Favian instead. She glanced over to the corner of the room he had been standing at but knitted her eyebrows together when she saw him missing. Where had he gone? He had promised to stay and to be there.

"Are you looking for someone?" asked Aamir, one eyebrow raised.

"Just Della!" Chhaya blurted. "I arrived before her, so I just wanted to make sure she got here, too. She works far too hard."

"Ah, your Lady's maid?"

"She is more than that—she is a friend to me. My closest friend, in fact. I have known her for as long as I can remember and spend more time with her than I do anybody else."

"It's nice to have somebody like that in a life like this."

"A life like this?"

Aamir shrugged. "As I said, I'm no royalty, only a Duke, but even in my position, I encounter many people who like my title and not me. You can never really know if somebody is in your life because they want to be or because they want something."

Chhaya nodded. "I am very lucky to have Della." Out of the corner of her eye, she caught sight of a dark tint that she knew was Favian's sunglasses and exhaled in relief. He was there, just hidden behind the array of people.

"Can I be honest with you?" she asked suddenly.

"Of course," Aamir replied, intrigued.

"When all of this started... well, I never truly intended to get married."

He raised an eyebrow. "Oh? Then why—"

"Well, that's the thing," she interrupted, already knowing what his next question would be. "I made a deal with my father. I told him I would seriously consider everyone that arrived as a marriage candidate and give everyone a fair chance. I promised to seriously consider marriage. But in the interest of honesty, I never imagined myself meeting anybody I would want to marry. I never *wanted* to meet somebody I wanted to marry."

"And what did you receive in exchange?"

"Exchange?"

"You said it was a deal."

" Oh. Nothing, I suppose. I merely did it because it was what the Kingdom needed."

Aamir smiled, a glimmer of hope in his eyes. "You're using the past tense. Are you telling me this because you've changed your mind?"

Chhaya swallowed. "I didn't think I ever wanted to marry. I was sure of it, in fact." As they moved, Favian came into Chhaya's line of view behind Aamir. She stayed silent.

"Okay," Aamir said finally, realising Chhaya wasn't planning to speak again. "So why are you telling me all of this?"

Chhaya looked up at him, meeting his eyes. "I just wanted to be honest with you. Because I still don't know if I will ever marry."

Aamir nodded with an understanding smile. "I understand. Thank you for being honest. But I hope you don't think this means I will be leaving."

"No?"

Aamir shook his head as the song ended, bowing to her as she curtsied to him. "Not at all, princess."

"Princess!"

Chhaya turned to see Sebastian running towards her, dressed in one of the formal tunics she had made for the kids in the orphanage. She had also sent an array of dresses and was happy to see Kat wearing a red one, looking much healthier now and energetic on her feet.

"Good evening, Sebastian. You look very nice!"

Sebastian smiled shyly. "Thank you."

"Sebastian, this is Aamir," Chhaya introduced. "You have both met once before, but I am not sure if you remember."

Sebastian nodded. "You were there in the infirmary."

"I was," agreed Aamir. "But it's nice to meet you properly this time, Sebastian. And in nicer circumstances." He held out a hand.

"Where's Favian?" Sebastian asked, turning to Chhaya after shaking Aamir's hand.

She smiled. Sebastian had become so attached to Favian since their first meeting and Chhaya felt her heart warm. "He is just over there."

Sebastian frowned. "Doesn't he want to dance?"

She took a breath. If only he did. "I'm sure we can convince him to dance eventually. And what about you, Sebastian? Do you plan to dance tonight?"

Sebastian beamed brightly, showing all of his teeth. "That's what I came to ask you, princess!"

"Oh really?" asked Chhaya, feigning surprise. "Well, I am undoubtedly honoured."

The two of them walked over to the dance floor, and Chhaya exchanged a glance with Aamir, raising her eyebrows at him in amusement.

"Have you at least eaten anything?" Chhaya asked Favian, approaching him after dancing with Sebastian, her father, Lukas, two of the other children and a few others from the Kingdom.

"I will eat after the ball," Favian replied.

She sighed. "You are surrounded by all of this amazing food and you're determined not to eat any of it?"

"I am on duty."

Chhaya smiled. He was so persistently frustrating that it was beginning to feel familiar to her.

"Very well. But I believe I am owed a dance?" she asked, holding out a hand for him to take. Favian looked at it warily. It had taken her so long to get him to almost agree earlier; she couldn't go through that again. "Surely you will not decline a dance from the princess, will you? I can assure you that nobody, including my father, will think twice if you dance with me, but everyone *will* be discussing it if you reject me. I do not ask people to dance very often," she leaned in and spoke the last sentence in a whisper.

Finally, Favian nodded and took her hand, leading her over to the dance floor.

The musicians started playing, and Chhaya, recognising a Waltz, placed her hand on Favian's shoulder. Once again, he hesitated. Chhaya grabbed his hand and placed it on her waist for him.

They began smoothly, and Chhaya smiled up at him. "See, it is not so bad dancing with me, is it? Were you afraid I would step on your toes?"

But Favian was not looking at her. Instead, he was nervously looking around them at the people watching. Chhaya's eyes softened. As the princess, she was used to having the attention on her, particularly at an event such as this one, but poor Favian was certainly not. He was accustomed to observing everybody else, not being observed *by* others.

Gently, Chhaya lifted a hand to his chin and turned his head down to face her.

"Do not pay attention to them," she said softly. "If anybody is looking at us, it is in appreciation. I promise, Favian."

He nodded, and after a moment, a small smile spread on his lips. "I am honoured you forced me to dance with you," he said.

"Forced?" Chhaya laughed. "Nobody forced you to do anything."

"You would not leave me alone," he joked. "Was your dance with Aamir really so bad that you needed me?"

Chhaya felt a blush rise to her cheeks. "*Needed* you?"

Favian's eyes widened ever so slightly, and a faint pink touched his cheeks. He cleared his throat. "As a dance partner and conversationalist, of course."

"Of course."

The rest of the dance passed in silence, and Chhaya smiled at the fact that Favian didn't look around but instead kept his eyes on her.

"Chaand," Favian said suddenly. She raised a questioning eyebrow. "You look like Chaand."

"Like the moon?"

He nodded. "Radiant."

It was certainly the most unusual compliment Chhaya had ever received, but it touched her heart. He thought she looked radiant. And he truly *meant* it. It wasn't one of the obliged or half-hearted compliments she usually received because she was the princess.

She smiled shyly up at him. "I—"

There was a loud blast. A scream pierced the air. And then everything happened so quickly.

People began to run, and Favian instantly jumped into defence mode, pulling Chhaya behind him and pulling her with him through the crowds to the nearest exit.

There were loud and frightened cries, and blood spilled quickly across the floor, painting it a deep, crimson red. "We cannot leave them!" Chhaya cried, pulling on Favian's shirt as he tried to usher her through a hidden exit behind a wooden panel in the wall.

"Chhaya, my duty—"

"Screw your duty, Favian!" She tightened her hands around the fabric covering his chest, tears cascading down her cheeks. "These people will die. These vile and rotten Magicians have robbed so many innocent lives already; they cannot be allowed to take any more!"

It took only a moment for Favian to consider her words. "Stay here." He threw off his lenses, turned and ran towards the cries of agony. He raced through the crowds of people, his hands outstretched and the Magic glowing on the tips of his fingers, ready to be used.

Chhaya helped people to clamber out of the room, all the while keeping an eye on Favian. Watching him in this moment was like watching a dancer. Every movement he made was so graceful and elegant, and purposeful.

One Blood Magician spotted him and his glowing hands as he hurried across the room. She stood and pricked her finger, pointing her hand at him.

But Favian was too fast. He swirled his hands, and a strange rope-like light shot towards her from his palms, constraining her and throwing her, unconscious, into the corner. Another Magician approached him from behind, but Favian seemed to sense him and spun around, throwing him back just as forcefully and knocking him unconscious.

Favian looked in her direction for a split second, his stormy grey eyes glistening silver from the power pulsing through him. From his hands exploded pink, blue and purple bursts of colour and in one swift movement, another attacker on his left was down.

Favian had distracted them long enough for all of the visitors to have escaped the room, but now that the room was clear, Chhaya had a clear view of what was going on. How they had managed to get into the castle, let alone the ballroom, she had no idea. But there were a lot of them. And they had just as clear a view of her.

Already, Favian and the other soldiers that had come rushing in had taken care of a handful of the Blood Magicians, leaving them tied or unconscious in the corner, but there were still so many left. The floor was stained with blood, and Chhaya fought to stop herself from searching the area to find where, or who, the blood was coming from.

Still, Favian did not give up. In one swift movement, the Magician on his left was restrained, and quickly after, so was the attacker on his right. Chhaya watched in horror as another attacker in front of him used a shard of glass to create a gash across his entire hand, not just the tip of his finger. "Favian, watch out!" she screamed.

The Magician began to speak under his breath, his mouth moving so quickly that Chhaya could not identify the words. But before he could finish, Favian moved his arms in a great sweeping motion, lifting them from the ground to the sky, causing a cluster of roots to burst through the marble floor and wrap themselves around him. The Magician cried out in anguish, in a rough voice, and tried aggressively to break through the plants that held him tight. But even more roots emerged, wrapping themselves around his mouth.

Chhaya felt a brief moment of relief before three more Magicians sliced deeply into their hands. She looked at Favian, who was panting now. Sweat dripped down his forehead, and his shirt was torn in more than one place. She could even see bursts of dark red staining the white kurta, where some of the Magicians had managed to cut him.

He looked exhausted.

She knew firsthand how tiring it was to use Magic; even at Favian's level of experience, this much Magic was far more than he was accustomed to. He looked around the room desperately, searching for something or somebody who could help him, but there was nothing. The soldiers that had rushed into the room were either fighting other Blood Magicians, unconscious, or worse.

The remaining Magicians advanced, surrounding him and chanting under their breath in unison. Chhaya held her breath, her limbs frozen with fear, and her voice stuck in her throat. Any moment now, Favian would suffer a blood-curdling, horrifying, agonising death. And there was nothing she could do about it.

The thought almost made Chhaya vomit. She had to do *something*. *Anything*. She could not stand around watching, waiting for it to happen. She had to distract them.

Desperately, she looked around for something she could see. And then she saw it; one lit candle. She lunged towards the candle, grabbing it from the holder and keeping a hand around the flame, making sure it stayed alive as she ran.

She moved as quickly as she could towards the curtain. If she could set the curtain alight, the entire room would be surrounded by a ring of fire, and the Blood Magicians would have no choice but to leave to save their lives.

Just before she reached the curtain, an agonised groan echoed from behind her. She turned to see Favian on the floor, his face contorted in pain and his chest covered in slashes of red. She was too late. They had already reached him.

Nausea, panic, terror and pain all curdled together in the pit of her stomach. She felt it rise and build. She allowed the horror inside of her to travel to the palms of her hands, making them burn with sensation, a more intense replication of the tingling she had felt in her Magic lessons with Favian.

And she screamed.

Chhaya screamed for Favian, for the fallen soldiers in front of her, and for the others that had not escaped the ballroom in time. She screamed for Favian's family. She screamed for her own mother.

Finally, when she felt the last of the fear drain from her, she collapsed, falling to her knees and gasping for breath. She had no strength left in her. What had she done?

Chhaya raised her head, tears already falling as she expected to see Favian's lifeless body lying in front of her.

But instead, her eyes met his, filled with life and sparkling with curiosity towards her. The red gashes in his chest were gone, the only evidence they had been there at all being the blood still staining his white kurta. The three attackers lay on the ground around him. Dead or unconscious, she didn't want to know.

Still breathing heavily, she locked eyes with Favian, who stared deeply back at her. His intense gaze trapped her, and she was unable to tear her eyes away. There was an emotion behind his that she couldn't identify, but it was curious, calculating, and understanding. Urgent.

Suddenly, she realised. His eyes. His stormy grey eyes. She had mentioned them in the letter, but he had never removed his sunglasses in the castle in front of anybody other than her the night that he had been injured. He must have realised; he must have made the connection. He knew she was writing the letters.

Slowly, he took a step towards her.

"Favian," she said in a whispered voice, unable to gather the strength to do much more. He took another step. "Favian, I—"

He took another step and held his hand out, both to silence and help her up. Chhaya felt the tears well in her eyes as she exhaled in relief. He was not upset.

She placed her hand in his, allowing him to support her, lifting her onto her feet and keeping her steady on her still shaky legs. "Favian," she whispered once again, holding his hand in her own and looking up at him through her eyelashes. But he wasn't looking at her. As soon as she was on her feet, he wrapped one arm around her and moved her to the side, behind him and out of harm's way.

"Favian?" she asked, confused but still gripping tightly onto him in order to stay standing.

"Stay back," he whispered.

In front of them was one last Blood Magician slicing through his hand.

Chhaya felt her heart deflate as Favian extended his arm and struck down the Magician, sending him to the ground with a simple flick of the wrist.

His arm was only around her to keep her standing. He had looked at her so emotionally because there had been a murderer standing behind her. He did not know the truth. She was still only the princess to him—just his job.

She let go of his arm in horror.

He turned back to her. "Are you okay?"

"I—" the word came out weakly, and her legs wobbled beneath her. She stumbled towards him, and he caught her in his arms just as her knees buckled under her. "How—" She allowed herself to collapse completely in his arms, letting him take her weight as she struggled to keep her eyes pried open.

"Let go," whispered Favian, placing her gently down on the floor but keeping his arms around her. "I've got you."

Chapter Fourteen

When Chhaya awoke, she felt as though her head had been smashed open with a rock.

A sharp burst of pain shot through her skull the moment she opened her eyes, and she winced, her eyes unadjusted to the bright light surrounding her. She turned her head to the left and lifted her arm, reaching for the glass of water on her bedside table. A searing pain immediately shot down her arm and through her neck.

"Careful!" Della cried, hurrying over to her and gently helping her into a seated position. Every movement she made resulted in a pain so intense that Chhaya was unable to even cry out. Della sat next to her, keeping one hand on Chhaya's back and using the other to lift the glass to Chhaya's lips, allowing her to take small sips that simultaneously burned and soothed her throat.

Chhaya took a deep breath. With every passing moment, the pain was lessening. She continued to breathe in silence, still squinting as her eyes adjusted to the light until finally, she was able to speak. "What happened?"

"You don't remember?" asked Della.

Chhaya tried to recall the previous evening but winced when another sharp pain pierced her head. She could remember a pair of stormy, grey eyes with slivers of silver glistening in them looking at her with concern.

"Where is Favian?" she asked, snapping her eyes open.

"Resting," replied Della, the corners of her lips twitching upwards as she glanced knowingly at Chhaya.

"Why are you looking at me like that?" Chhaya questioned, narrowing her eyes as much as she could without pain.

"Why are you so worried about Favian?"

Chhaya felt a blush rise to her cheeks. Why *was* she so worried about Favian? "You asked me if. I remembered anything from yesterday; the last thing I could remember was Favian," she insisted.

Della raised her eyebrows. "Oh really?" she teased.

Chhaya rolled her eyes and instantly regretted it as more blinding pain coursed through her skull. "Are you going to tell me or not?" she asked, rubbing the palms of her hands into her eyes in an attempt to soothe the pain.

"I sent him to his room," Della replied finally, gesturing towards the leather chair beside her bed that was usually in front of the fireplace and not her bed.

"He sat there all night?" A strange and unfamiliar warm feeling tingled in Chhaya's stomach.

Della nodded, helping Chhaya to have another sip of water before getting up and fluffing the stray pillow that had been left on the chair. "He kept talking about his duty. You know what he is like."

The warm feeling instantly vanished.

"Oh, right. Of course."

"He was worried about you, though," Della added. "He tries not to show it, but I think you may have grown on him, Chhaya."

Della glanced at her with a knowing gaze. "Almost as much as he has grown on you."

Chhaya looked down to avoid Della's eyes and gasped at the sight of her dress and even her hands. The entire right half of her pale ballgown was stained a deep red colour that matched her right hand and arm, and it had also apparently seeped into her bedsheets. She looked up, eyes wide with fear. "Whose blood is this?" her voice trembled.

Della swallowed. "I should let Favian update you. He will want to know you are awake anyway."

Chhaya's face paled. "Whose blood is this, Della?"

There was a sudden jolt in her memory as she caught glimpses of the dark, red liquid spilling across the floor. "There was so much blood."

"It is not yours," Favian spoke from the doorway. Chhaya's immediate reaction was to pull up her blanket. The idea of Favian seeing her drenched in blood like she was made her feel nauseous. She tried not to think about the fact that he had been the one to carry her here in the first place, looking like she did.

"There were a few civilians injured and more than a few soldiers, but fortunately, no casualties," he continued, stepping into the room and closing the door firmly behind him. "Thanks to you."

"Thanks to *me*?" asked Chhaya. But it was true. She remembered now that Favian had tried to leave, to get her to safety when everything had begun, but instead, she had forced him to stay. She had forced him to risk his life and fight. She had asked him to put himself in danger, to risk dying a brutally violent and painful death, and he had.

How could she have asked him to do something like that? And how could he have listened to her?

"I'm so sorry," she choked out, fighting the sob that threatened to escape her throat.

"*Sorry*?" He removed his sunglasses.

"I am the reason why you were there." A flash of Favian lying on the floor, crying out in agony as blood bloomed across his skin flashed in her eyes. "I sent you—"

"No, Chhaya," Favian interrupted. "I am a soldier. Fighting was my duty. I would have been murdered if you had not been there." His tone was expressionless and matter-of-fact, but Chhaya could see the slight twinge of his eyebrow and the glisten in his eyes. "You saved my life."

All of a sudden, the full memory of the previous night opened up in her mind. Chhaya's eyes widened at the image of Favian looking at her with so much emotion in his eyes. Her breath caught in her throat. Favian. Favian, who would do anything for her because it was his duty. Favian, who was so clearly in love with Aaliya. Favian, who was going to get his heart broken. Favian, who would hate her forever.

"Favian, there is chai ready on the table," Della said, likely having sensed Chhaya's discomfort. "Why don't you help yourself while I help Chhaya get cleaned up so she feels a little bit fresher? Then I will leave the two of you to discuss what happened last night."

Favian looked with concern at Chhaya, the emotion barely visible on his face, but nodded compliantly and made his way over to the fireplace.

"Chhaya, are you ready?" asked Della in a hushed voice, offering a hand to help Chhaya up. Chhaya nodded, accepting Della's help to emerge from the duvet and stand on her legs. She leaned heavily on Della as they made their way to the bathing room, Chhaya's legs trembling with every step.

She allowed herself to collapse onto the floor, leaning against the bathtub as Della filled it with warm water and added some relaxing bath salts and fresh-smelling soap. With difficulty, Chhaya got herself into the bath and stared silently as Della gently cleaned her face with a washcloth. The water turned red, and Chhaya closed her eyes.

She didn't want to see any more blood.

The combination of fresh clothes, clean skin, hot water and the aroma of her bath had done wonders for Chhaya. Her head felt clearer, no longer feeling clouded with grey fog as it had felt earlier. Her limbs were feeling stronger, and she didn't feel so drained of energy anymore.

She had also had the chance to think after Della had rinsed the bath and run a second one for her to soak in once the blood had been scrubbed off.

She didn't know what she was going to do about Favian, but she did know that she would have to deal with it later. More importantly, for now, there had been an attack. People had been injured, and their lives had been put at risk. That was her first priority; her people.

"Are you feeling better?" Favian asked, the slightest hint of hesitance in his voice as Chhaya sat next to him on the sofa. She cursed inwardly at herself for having paid so much attention to him that she was able to recognise it so easily.

She took a breath, forcing herself to put thoughts of Favian aside for the moment, and nodded. "I apologise for the state I was in before," she spoke calmly. "I suspect I may have been in a state of shock."

Favian turned towards her ever so slightly before responding. "It is to be expected, Chhaya. There is no reason to apologise. As long as you are feeling better now."

"I would also like to thank you," she added with a smile, "for worrying about me and staying here to make sure I was okay."

The blush appeared almost immediately on Favian's cheeks and made Chhaya smile even more. "It is my duty," he responded awkwardly.

"Duty or not, I want you to know that I appreciate your caring for me."

Favian cleared his throat uncomfortably, and Chhaya decided to end his discomfort.

"Please, update me on what has been happening and what we know so far."

Favian nodded. "I will begin with the blood. As I have already mentioned, nobody was killed. There were a few severe injuries, but none proved fatal. Most of the guests at the ball last night managed to escape relatively unharmed. A few children and merchants from the Kingdom were injured, as well as some of the staff and the soldiers, but it seems that most of the blood in the ballroom, including what you were covered in, had come from the Blood Magicians themselves."

Chhaya nodded. "As far as I remember, they have to offer up their own blood in order to use and control the blood of others?"

"That's correct."

"And did you and the other soldiers manage to capture all of the Blood Magicians?"

Favian raised an eyebrow. "We... a handful escaped, but the majority were captured. But that is likely something we should discuss."

"Oh?"

"*You* captured them."

Chhaya watched, stunned, as Favian stared at her expectantly. "Oh?"

"Chhaya, you still do not remember?" he asked with a frown. "Your Magic..."

"What about my Magic?" she asked. "You know as well as I do that I can do barely more than lift a glass with my Magic."

Favian shook his head. "Chhaya, yesterday I was surrounded by multiple Blood Magicians. I could feel them creating cuts into my skin. My torso was covered in deep gashes that were oozing out blood." Chhaya swallowed, biting her cheek to prevent the tears from falling at the imagery. "I was certain it was the end. I knew I was going to die, and it was okay. I turned around to tell you to leave, to tell you to run. But you screamed."

"Yes, I remember I screamed," Chhaya responded.

Favian huffed out a breath of air, shaking his head with the corners of his lips upturned in bewilderment. "You mistake my meaning, Chhaya. You didn't just... *scream*. Your scream rendered them all unconscious."

Chhaya's eyes widened. She had felt the power coursing through her, but had she truly been able to do all of that?

"Not only did you render them all unconscious, but you completely healed me. Not only were my cuts gone, but my energy was restored. After fighting the way I had, using as much Magic as I had, I should not have been able to walk, let alone use my Magic against yet another Blood Magician and carry you to the infirmary and then back here afterwards."

"But how is that possible?"

"I have never seen anything like it before," Favian replied.

"But... but what—"

"As far as my research has revealed and my experience goes, it could mean one of two things. Either you felt a very strong emotion that caused your Magic to react in such a way, *or* you have the blood of a very powerful Magician running through you."

Chhaya watched Favian, her face expressionless. Was it possible that her fear for Favian had caused her Magic to react like this? "I was scared," she said when it was clear Favian was waiting for a response. Something fluttered in her stomach to know that he was purposefully explaining and sharing things slowly so as not to overwhelm her. He either cared about her or was still horrified by her state that morning.

Favian nodded. "Expectedly. I understand why your first instinct would be to blame it on emotions. But in my years as a soldier, I have been in horrifying positions. And not once have I witnessed fear so strong it could knock out five powerful Blood Magicians the way you did yesterday evening."

"What if it wasn't fear for my life, but fear for yours?"

Favian was silent for a moment but kept his eyes on her. "I understand it may have been frightening, but it's simply not possible you felt so fearful for my life that your Magic was unleashed in such a manner. Perhaps if it had been your father in my position, it could have been considered, but no. I don't think that's the case."

Chhaya considered his words. There was no way she had powerful blood running through her that she was unaware of; each and every member of the royal family of Khiona were recorded and available to the public. "What if it was not fear?"

"The only emotion that could cause such a reaction is love."

Chhaya scoffed. "That is a little cliché, wouldn't you say?"

"It is a cliché for a reason," Favian responded seriously. "All those fairy tales and children's tales are stories, but they are based on reality in one way or another."

Chhaya raised an eyebrow. "I did not take you as one for fairy-tales, Favian."

Favian stared blankly in return, neither reacting nor explaining himself. "Chhaya," he said suddenly, leaning forward on the sofa towards her, his elbows on his knees and his hands clasped, "either way, no matter the origin, your Magic is clearly more potent than either of us had expected or suspected."

Chhaya nodded in response. She didn't feel as though her Magic was anything spectacular, she didn't feel spectacular at all today, but if she had done what Favian said she had done, there was definitely something going on.

"Well, what do we do now?" she asked as Favian stood from the sofa, apparently finished with the conversation.

"We train your Magic."

Chhaya could feel her eyelids beginning to droop as she and Favian walked through the corridors. Her legs wobbled ever so slightly with every other step, and she struggled to keep her head up, sheer will keeping her from collapsing then and there.

Favian had been so determinedly convinced that they needed to start training and honing her Magic immediately that he had only given her a moment's break all afternoon. It was with a sense of urgency that he had instructed her to move objects across the room or lift them into the air, each new object heavier than the last. But the most surprising part of the training had been the ease with which she had actually managed to move the objects.

"I will wait for you here," Favian said, stopping outside of her father's office with a nod of his head.

"Thank you," Chhaya replied, her voice shaky.

She moved forward, reaching for the doorknob in front of her, but yelped as her knee buckled below her, sending her towards the ground. She closed her eyes, bracing herself to hit the hard ground below her, without enough energy to even put her hands out to protect her face.

But rather than feel the impact of the stone under her, she felt two large, strong hands tightly grab her waist. She cracked open her eyes to see Favian's face mere inches away from her own, his dark lenses missing and his stormy eyes slightly wide in alarm as he continued to hold her in a dip. Slowly, Favian lifted her up into a standing position, keeping his arms around her to keep her stable.

Chhaya swallowed. "Favian," she whispered, looking deeply into his eyes with her own, placing one hand on his shoulder to keep herself stable. He continued to look down at her in silence. His eyebrows folded into a barely visible line of concern. Chhaya fought not to reach out and smooth them with her hand. His eyes flicked down at her lips for the briefest of seconds, and Chhaya let out a shaky breath.

"Are you okay?" he asked in a tone just above a whisper, his deep voice vibrating in her ear.

Her breathing was heavy, but she nodded, and as soon as she did, he let go of her, taking a step backwards but staying close enough to support her again if she needed it. Chhaya took a deep breath and stumbled back into the wall. Favian stepped towards her again, his hands reaching for her, but she shook her head and held out an arm to stop him.

"I am fine," she said. "I am fine."

The door opened next to her, where she was leaning against the wall, and her father emerged. "Chhaya?"

"Your Majesty," Favian greeted with a short bow.

"Favian," the King replied. "Please, both of you, come in." He put an arm on Chhaya's right shoulder and ushered her in ahead of him before gesturing for Favian to follow.

"I can wait outside, your Majesty," Favian told him hesitantly, lingering in the doorway.

Chhaya looked behind at him after sitting in her seat and felt her heart melt at the sight of him, finding herself fighting between laughing and crying as she watched him pick up his lenses from the floor where they had fallen in his rush to catch her. "Oh, come in, Favian," she chuckled.

He stood up straight and made a half-bowing, half-nodding motion before entering the room and closing the door behind him. He sat in the seat next to Chhaya and looked at her, his eyes meeting hers and his lips curving into the briefest of smiles before he put his sunglasses back on and turned to the King.

It was difficult to pay attention to what her father was saying when Favian was sitting so close to her. All she could focus on were the letters.

If she had known before writing the first one that he would have fallen in love with her—with Aaliya—she would never have done it. She had thought it was harmless. She thought he would detest the attention of an admirer and do anything to stop them, not to write back.

But now she was ruining everything. The longer she let this continue, the longer she let him believe there was an Aaliya, the longer she continued with this wretched charade, the more hurt he would feel upon discovering the real truth.

"Chhaya, are you alright?" She looked up when Favian spoke softly to her, his lips closer to her ear than they should have been, and the frown once again etched into his eyebrows. Both he and her father were watching her worriedly.

"I'm fine," she replied, leaning away from him as subtly as possible, trying to put as much space as possible between them. The closer he was, the more difficult it was to think logically.

"You are looking pale, beta," her father said, reaching across the table and placing the back of his hand against her forehead, feeling for a temperature.

"I am fine, papa, really," she insisted, forcing her lips into a reassuring smile. "Just tired." And confused.

It was time to end this all. It was time to come clean. She needed to tell Favian the truth.

Chapter Fifteen

My dearest Favian

I understand everything now.

I'm sorry for everything I have said about your duty and about Chhaya. I saw everything that happened.

I understand it all.

I think it is time we meet. I will be waiting by the river at midnight tonight. I hope to see you there.

Your dearest Aaliya

She sealed the letter and pressed it to her heart, closing her eyes and taking a deep and steadying breath. It was time.

No longer was she able to act normally around Favian, knowing he was in love with her even though he didn't know it, knowing he was being deceived, knowing she was the one lying to him. She could no longer concentrate on the matters at hand, the issues which mattered most to her – her people, her kingdom.

Chhaya was consumed with the thought of Favian. And she couldn't take it anymore.

She was almost always with him, and yet he didn't truly know who she was. He didn't know she was the one he was in love with him. And it hurt.

"Della, I am feeling rather tired today," she said in what she hoped was a nonchalant tone. "I think the effects of last night may still be lingering. If you do not mind, I would like to postpone our hot chocolate. I think perhaps I will simply read in bed and have an early night." She smiled at Della, who nodded in return.

"Of course, Chhaya. Would you still like me to bring you something to drink before I leave you to your privacy?"

Chhaya looked at the time. It was only 9. "I could do with some peppermint tea if you do not mind."

"Not at all," Della smiled brightly. She returned a few moments later with a steaming mug, and Chhaya wrapped her hands around it, absorbing its warmth. She took a deep breath, inhaling the sweetness of the drink. Della had added two sugars, just as she liked it.

Chhaya had actually intended to practise her Magic a little more before heading out to meet Favian, having felt a lot better after eating, but suddenly found herself feeling very tired. The business and excitement of the last few days were finally taking their toll on her. She put down her tea and decided to close her eyes for a few minutes.

By the time she woke up again, the fire in front of her had died, and the tea on the table had cooled before she could even drink any. She checked the time in a panic. It was 11.45. She jumped up and put on her thickest winter cloak, heading out the door and through the corridors as quietly as possible.

A burst of cool air hit her when she emerged from the main door, instantly freezing her face and her hands. It was refreshingly icy, and she breathed it in like she was drinking water for the first time in days. She was so used to spending time outdoors in nature, alone in the fresh air, that a serene sense of comfort and peace settled over her, easing her anxiety ever so slightly. Even the dark and the icy air did not faze her.

As she turned around the corner of the stone castle, Chhaya saw the shadow's movement ahead of her out of the corner of her eye. She immediately ducked behind a short wall, dropping to the floor and keeping her head lowered. Until she was sure that whoever it had been in the area was either gone or too far to spot her, she stayed in the shadows, not even risking a shuffle in movement in case she was heard. Finally, she lifted her head slowly, peeking over the small wall. She was in the clear.

But she stayed in the darkness granted to her by the shadows of the building, keeping her eyes peeled for her bodyguard.

Finally, the river and the majestic cobblestone bridge sitting over it were in sight, and Chhaya prepared to wait. Even with the unusual and unpleasant mixture of anxiety and anticipation coursing through her, the view before her took her breath away.

The moon was bright, glowing in the inky black sky, even brighter than usual on a night like tonight with no stars in the sky. The light bounced off the dark water in the river, creating a peaceful blue glow that lit up the bridge in the most Magical way.

It was as she watched the moon and the ethereal sight before her that a figure walked onto the bridge, stopping at the top and looking up into the sky. Just like her, Favian was admiring the moon in all her glory above them.

Chaand. That was how he had described her the previous evening. As beautiful as the moon.

As Chhaya watched, Favian turned around. He looked to the left and then to the right, spreading his arms out and reaching across the stone railing as he waited. As he waited for *her*.

It was a surprise for Chhaya to feel a tear trickle down her cheek. She hadn't realised she was crying.

For as long as she could remember, Chhaya had sworn not to care for another like her father had her mother, not to love somebody as more than a friend or a family member. But never could she have imagined this heart-wrenching, devastating, overwhelming and yet simultaneously glorious and freeing feeling. Never could she have imagined feeling such a way for another person. This was not love. This was more than love. This was everything.

And yet, her legs remained frozen in place as she continued to watch him from afar. No matter how much she wanted to, she couldn't move. She really had intended to tell him the truth, but she couldn't. She couldn't bare the thought of his sadness upon seeing her. She couldn't face his disappointment at finding out she was Aaliya. She couldn't face him.

Yet she stayed. She waited. She watched.

A few minutes turned into ten, then half an hour and then a full hour had gone by that Favian had been waiting. His hands must have been frozen because Chhaya's certainly were, even through her leather gloves. But she could hardly feel them. All she could feel was the overwhelming hurt that she had caused him.

Her dearest Favian.

She could see the dismay on his face, still lit up by the beautiful glowing light of the moon. The time ticked by as Favian continued to wait, every passing minute breaking Chhaya's heart more. And still, she couldn't move.

She couldn't do this any longer. She couldn't, and wouldn't, continue to watch him suffer like he was. To not understand why he had been left out in the cold without an explanation. It was time to face the truth and accept its consequences.

Suddenly, just as Chhaya was about to stand up, there was a loud cry from behind her. Favian instantly turned in her direction, and even though she knew he couldn't see her, Chhaya dropped to the ground.

As lights flickered on in the castle, it quickly became clear that was where the scream had come from. Each window lit up, and there was movement, loud and urgent, as soldiers ran to investigate and workers began to dart about.

Chhaya quickly jumped to her feet, still careful to remain in the shadows, and hurried around the walls of the castle to the side entrance that led into the rose garden. As she entered the main hall, she caught a glimpse of Favian running in through the other door and rushing to talk to one of the soldiers marching through the corridor towards the stairs. She watched anxiously as a flash of fear crossed his eyes, and his face twisted into one of panic. He looked around the room in distress before catching her eye and visibly exhaling in relief.

Chhaya gulped as he marched over to her, unable to do much more than wait for him. "Favian—" she began, but he wrapped his fingers around her wrist and pulled her with him through the corridors.

"Favian, what are you—?"

"Hurry," he cut her off in a hushed yet urgent voice as they continued to run.

Confused and afraid, Chhaya had no choice but to follow as Favian pulled her through the corridors. "Favian, slow down!" she exclaimed, stumbling along the stone floors, her own legs unable to keep up with Favian's longer and faster legs.

Favian either did not hear her or did not want to listen as he sped up, all but dragging her behind him. They were moving far too fast for her to keep track of where they were going. They ran through corridors, up a set of stairs, through another corridor and down another set of stairs. Finally, after entering another corridor, Favian stopped, looking around him as Chhaya gasped for breath but refused to let go of her. Before she could finish catching her breath, Chhaya felt a tug on her arm as Favian lifted a tapestry concealing a door hidden in the stone corridor and pulled her through.

"Favian," she said his name breathlessly, her back pushed against the cold stone wall in the tiny space, freezing her skin even through her clothes, and her wrist still clasped tightly in Favian's grip. "What is going on?"

Finally, Favian released her, allowing her hand to drop down by her side as he stepped back, as far away from her as he could be in this compact area. The sudden lack of heat from Favian's hand around hers and closeness to her body was immediately felt by Chhaya, who rubbed her arms in an attempt to keep warm.

"It is still unsafe," Favian responded, his voice hushed yet seemingly loud in the small space.

Chhaya took one step backwards and gasped as the floor beneath her vanished. Favian immediately grabbed her arm and pulled her towards him again. "Be careful. That's a long staircase you wouldn't want to fall down."

She swallowed and nodded, stepping back into the wall the moment he let her go again.

"At the bottom of this staircase will be the door to a safe room. Once we are inside, we'll be fine."

After so many years of exploring the castle and identifying every nook and crevice, or so she had thought, Chhaya was surprised to learn there were safe rooms. She had never heard of them or seen them. But this hidden staircase was concealed by a tapestry Chhaya had never even glanced at twice, and at the bottom was a secret room that she didn't even know existed before this moment.

Chhaya took one step at a time to get to the bottom of the staircase, one hand resting on the wall to use as a guide and the other outstretched to balance herself. She could feel Favian behind her, never more than one step away and constantly vigilant. In the rush and flurry of the shouting and running, Chhaya hadn't even had the chance to think. But now it was silent, and there was nothing preventing the thoughts from bombarding her.

What was happening? Had the Blood Magicians returned? Would her father be safe? Especially if the Blood Magicians were searching for her. Or would they attempt to use him in an effort to get to her? Would they succeed? And what of anybody else in the palace? Where had that scream come from? Were they hurt?

What would have happened if she had been in her room as she had been expected to be? What would have happened if Favian had not come to her rescue?

Favian.

She hadn't turned up. She had been weak. Favian had waited for her, nervous and excited, thinking he would finally meet the woman he was in love with, see her face for the first time, speak with her, hug her. Maybe even kiss her. And she had let him down.

He had risked everything for her on countless occasions; he had jumped to her aide as often as he could; he had hunted for her as soon as he had heard the cries. And in return, she had lied to him.

"This is it." Favian's whisper broke her train of thought. He twisted the handle of a large wooden door in front of them and held out a hand, requesting silence, before he pushed it open with a loud creak that cut through the silence like a blade. He stepped across the threshold first, making sure it was empty before inviting her in and shutting the door behind them.

Finally, after crossing two doorways, Chhaya emerged in a bedroom that looked very much like Favian's. She turned to see Favian close one door, the door that led to the staircase and a second, the door to a wardrobe that concealed the first.

"Where are we?" she demanded, crossing her arms over her chest. How could it be that Favian knew about this room when she, the *princess* and the next in line to the throne had been completely oblivious?

Favian turned towards her with a straight face. He wasn't wearing his tinted lenses, and his eyes seemed duller than usual, another reminder of the evening that made her heart shatter. "There has been an attack."

Chhaya sat in an armchair on the edge of the room and gestured for him to do the same. He sat in front of her and clasped his hands together, staring blankly at the wall.

"An attack on who?"

Favian snapped his head towards her, his eyes boring into hers and his jaw tense. "On you."

For the last thirty minutes, Chhaya and Favian had been sitting in silence.

Chhaya had listened while Favian explained there had been an attack on her rooms during the night, her entire rooms ransacked. When she was declared missing, it had been assumed she had been taken by the attackers, so when Favian saw her, he knew it was imperative to get her out of harm's way immediately.

Chhaya felt a mixture between guilt and relief, thinking about how she had not been there.

If she hadn't decided to see Favian, not only would she have been in her room, but the likelihood was that Della would have been, too. What would have happened to them? Either way, Chhaya was glad neither of them needed to find out.

But on the other hand, Favian was looking so dejected in front of her that she couldn't even bear to look at him. Anybody who wasn't so used to the subtle changes in his face would likely have assumed that he was simply waiting for somebody to tell them it was clear to come out, but Chhaya could tell otherwise.

The tension in his jaw, his clenched fists, the furrow of his eyebrow. He felt guilty for not being present. He felt angry at himself for being distracted. He felt frustrated that whoever had done this had gone free.

But his eyes were also downcast. No matter how hard he was trying to ignore the distraction that was his feelings, he felt hurt. Hurt because of Aaliya. Hurt because of Chhaya.

"Where were you?" he had asked her. "You should not be leaving the castle without me, and someone should always know where you are. Even Della did not know."

"I only went for a walk in the rose gardens. I could not sleep," she had replied lamely.

Favian had stared at her for a moment longer than necessary but said no more on the subject. "We have more important matters to worry about now." And that was the last thing he had said.

While Favian's silence seemed a mixture of calculated and pensive, Chhaya's was a guilty silence, the kind of silence that occurs when one doesn't know what to say or do.

Although Favian still didn't know it was her that had stood him up, she didn't know how to act around him. Every silent, heavy sigh, every tense of his muscles, every frown on his brow. They each made the guilt heavier.

She knew this was the time to tell him the truth. She knew it. But she couldn't. With no idea how long they would have to stay in this room, Chhaya couldn't handle the thought of having to remain after his rejection.

Every so often, Favian would stand, walk over to the door, press his ear against the wood for a few moments, and then sit back down in silence. Each time he stood, Chhaya felt a flutter of hope, assuming he had heard something she had not and they were getting out of this small room. But each time, she was disappointed.

Finally, Favian's head shot up from where he had been staring distractedly at the wall. He looked at her with an urgency in his eyes and pressed a finger to his lips, urging her to be quiet. Chhaya swallowed but nodded, watching as Favian got up and walked silently to the wardrobe, pressing his ear against it.

Three soft taps came from the other side of the door, and Favian immediately straightened. He lifted his hands, the Magic already sparking across his fingertips. Glancing over his shoulder, he motioned for Chhaya to duck behind the table, which she did as quietly as possible, taking care not to stare too long into his eyes which were sparkling with silver once again.

She could not see from her position, but she heard the door creak open and soft voices travelled through the gap before it closed again.

"You can stop hiding," Favian spoke. "The castle is clear."

She stood to see Favian's downcast expression as he waited for her.

"I am sure you have questions," he said, quickly focusing his gaze back on her. "As do I. But I think it is best you try to sleep tonight; we will not learn anything concrete until the morning."

Chhaya nodded. As much as she would have liked to argue, to insist he tell her everything he knew, she did not have the mental or the physical energy. All she wanted was to collapse into a bed and forget everything.

"You cannot return to your personal rooms tonight, but I have been told a spare room has been set up for you."

She nodded awkwardly once more, making Favian look at her strangely before nodding in return and holding the door open for her.

It didn't take them long to reach the room, where a guard already stood at the door.

"I assume the bedroom is through that door," said Favian once they were inside, and the door was closed behind them. "I will sleep out here on the sofa, and there will be a guard on duty at all times outside."

Chhaya sighed but agreed, unwilling to argue with him.

"Please stay here while I ensure the room is clear."

Chhaya kept her eyes on the ground as he completed his checks and continued to look down as he walked past her, confirming the room was, in fact, empty.

"Favian?" she said suddenly, turning back to him from the doorway to the bedroom.

"Yes, Chhaya?"

She swallowed. "Thank you."

Chapter Sixteen

It was 8 o'clock when Chhaya woke up the following day, feeling surprisingly unhappy to learn that her training session with Favian had been cancelled. At first, the mere thought of their early morning training sessions had made her want to scream into a pillow and pound her head against the wall, but over the course of their time together, she had grown rather fond of them.

She especially appreciated the Magic training that came along with the sessions, enjoying the freedom that was exercising and learning to use her own Magic, an energy that had been locked away inside her for so many years, not allowed to be released.

Simultaneously, she was grateful she didn't have to spend that time with Favian; although sleep had helped to clear her mind, she wasn't looking forward to facing him after the events of the previous evening, the guilt eating away at her like acid.

It was not long after she woke up that she discovered the reason for her awakening. Someone was knocking on her door. She slipped out of bed and hurried over to the door. On the other side, Favian was wearing a fresh change of clothes and his sunglasses once again.

He entered the room without invitation and closed the door behind him. "Your father would like to see us."

Chhaya blinked. "Okay. I would just like to change."

Favian nodded. "Della brought you a change of clothes." He gestured to the sofa, where a small bag was sitting neatly. "She was not permitted to stay, and so you will have to dress yourself. I will wait here for you."

"Ready?" asked Favian, standing from his position on the sofa when Chhaya reemerged a few moments later.

"Ready."

"Let's go."

"Chai, I am very glad to see you." Her father immediately pulled her into a warm hug as soon as she entered the room.

"Me too, papa," she responded, hugging him back just as tightly.

"Favian," the King said, placing a hand on his back after letting go of Chhaya. "I am forever grateful to you."

"Not at all, Your Majesty," Favian replied with a small bow. "I am just as glad as you are that Chhaya is safe."

And because it was his job. She knew this, and yet Favian's words created a warm feeling in her stomach.

"Take a seat, please. Both of you," the King said, gesturing to the two leather chairs on the opposite side of his desk, food and coffee already waiting for them and the scent making Chhaya's mouth water. Her stomach grumbled, and she blushed.

"Sorry. I haven't eaten in a while."

The King chuckled. "I didn't think either of you would have had the opportunity, so I took the liberty of having breakfast prepared. Please, help yourself."

To Chhaya's surprise, Favian needed no convincing, taking a huge sip of coffee before her father had even finished speaking. She took a sip of her own coffee before a bite of generously buttered toast slathered with honey as she waited for her father to continue.

He sat at his chair on the other side of the desk, resting his arms on the surface and leaning in seriously. "That is two attacks now in the castle. Not only that, but two attacks in the space of *two days*."

"Do we know how they entered the castle last night?" asked Chhaya.

"No," he replied. "But we suspect they had help from inside the castle."

Chhaya widened her eyes. Favian had been right. She looked over at him, but he continued to stare at the King as blankly as usual.

"Now, at first glance, the sensible thing to do here would be to cancel all of this. One of the boys must be responsible for all of this; everything was fine before they arrived, and now *everybody* is in danger."

"That sounds like the right thing to do," replied Chhaya. "So what are we waiting for?"

"If it *is* one of them, we are putting the entire Kingdom and the other guests at risk just by keeping them here," Favian added.

"But we have a problem," the King countered. "After all that has happened, not only these two attacks but also the other attacks on our people, there has been talk in the Kingdom. Our people are saying one of our guests is responsible, and even though I agree, if we send them back, it announces distrust. We have dukes and lords here as well as ordinary men. Sending them back as though they are guilty will insult the other Kingdoms. We live in harmony now, but I refuse to light the flame that could spark another war so soon after the previous."

"We cannot risk that," Chhaya said. "But what are we going to do?"

"If we can identify the culprit and prove it is their fault, we can punish them without starting any wars," Favian stated. "And solve our problems."

"Precisely," agreed the King. "So, for now, we must continue with the events. The number of guards on patrol in the castle and in the kingdom will, of course, be increased, and Favian, you are to remain with Chhaya at all times. She is not to be alone with anybody else, and you are to stay in the same guest suite at night. Anything you require will be brought to you. It is twice now that you have saved my daughter's life. I trust it with nobody else."

"Yes, your Majesty."

"But papa—"

"I will have no arguments, Chhaya," her father interrupted. "This is for your safety. I know you did not take us seriously at first, but surely you now understand the gravity of the situation. These Blood Magicians came for your mother first, and now they are after you. I refuse to let them take you."

"Chhaya," Favian began in a hesitant tone when they arrived back at the suite. "I know you are not happy with me invading your space and your privacy in this way, but it really is for your own safety. I vow to stay out of your way unless truly necessary."

Chhaya shook her head and looked at him in disbelief. "Really, Favian? With all of this happening, do you really believe I am so distressed to have you around? You think I am worried about you invading my space?"

Favian's eyebrows lifted slightly, the only sign of surprise on his face, but he stayed silent.

"I happen to like your company," she told him, ignoring the slight blush colouring his cheeks. "What I *am* concerned about, however, is the fact that these awful Magicians will kill and injure anybody they must, just to get to me. And for what? What do they want with me?" And how was she going to spend so much time with Favian without telling him the truth?

A small smile ghosted Favian's lips, and Chhaya knew if he wasn't wearing his lenses, she would have seen that familiar little sparkle in his eyes that she so enjoyed catching. "Yes, Chhaya," he replied.

"That is settled then," she said, forcing an upbeat tone to her voice. "So now what?"

"What do you mean?" Favian's left eyebrow lowered by mere millimetres in confusion.

"How are we going to find whoever is responsible for all of this?" She collapsed onto the sofa, slouching back into the cosy cushions.

Favian stared at her silently, frozen in his place like one of the stone figures of previous rulers that were placed creepily in front of the castle. Whether that was because she had shocked him or he truly didn't know how to respond, Chhaya had no idea.

Finally, he moved forward, taking a seat on the sofa beside her. Chhaya had to fight the urge to move further away from him, his closeness making the emotions inside of her surge once again. He removed his sunglasses and looked at her openly and somewhat vulnerably, further intensifying the rotten ball of guilt in the pit of her stomach. "I am likely going to have to carry out my investigations in the early afternoons and late evenings when there are no events to escort you to."

"No," replied Chhaya, much to Favian's surprise.

His eyebrows sank, but his eyes lit up. "No?"

"Favian, do you truly believe I am ready to sit here and do nothing? That I will allow everybody but myself to investigate? That I will be the only person to sit silent and obedient?" She stood up, glowering down at Favian, where he was still sitting.

"You think I will sit happily while there are people—monsters—who are attacking my home, my people, my loved ones? Who apparently will stop at nothing to kill me?" She took a step closer, their knees almost touching.

"I may be a princess, but I'm nothing like the princesses in those Mountains-forsaken fairytales, Favian. I am the next Queen and ruler of this Kingdom." She was leaning over him ever so slightly, their faces only a few inches apart. "And you will treat me as such."

Favian stared up at her, his face as stoic as usual, but his eyes... his eyes were practically beaming at her. No wonder he insisted on wearing his sunglasses so often; his eyes betrayed every inch of his emotions.

"Chhaya, I understand, but—"

"Favian," Chhaya whispered. "If anybody understands my position at all, it's you. Your family were killed by Blood Magicians just as my mother was. Can't you understand?"

The glimmer in Favian's eyes turned dark. "How did you know of my family?"

Chhaya widened her eyes, having realised what she had just done, what she had just revealed. She swallowed and stood straight, suddenly extremely aware of how close she had gotten to him, walking backwards until the backs of her legs hit the table behind her.

She opened her mouth with no idea what to say or how to say it, but fortunately, Favian got there first. He stood with a tight-lipped smile. "My apologies Chhaya—of course you knew about my family. Your father must have told you."

She could hardly believe it. She released a shuddering breath and licked her dry lips. "Yes. Papa told me."

"Well, I just so happen to agree with you," Favian said, taking a step towards her. Chhaya swallowed as he took another step closer and pressed herself as far back against the table as she could. If he took one more step, he would be pressed flush against Chhaya. "All I was going to say is that we must not tell anybody we are investigating," he told her, looking honestly into her eyes as he walked around her to where coffee had been laid out on the table for them. Chhaya had not noticed that before. "Would you like a cup?"

Chhaya shook her head. She was nervous enough as it was. The last thing she needed in her system was caffeine.

"So I suppose we should begin as soon as possible?" she asked after taking a steadying breath.

Favian nodded. "As far as I am aware, the upcoming days are free from any events, as your father has cancelled them due to security reasons."

"Yes, but if you truly consider the situation, it may be in our best interest to continue these events, such as the teas and dinners?" Chhaya commented.

"How so?"

"If we are right and one of the suitors is responsible for all of this, chances are they will say or do something that will reveal themselves."

Favian considered her statement. "It's true, but that could be dangerous."

Chhaya shrugged. "We do not have to actively seek out the information. We merely keep our ears open for any information that could be relevant."

Favian sighed. "You are right. Besides, even though we cannot share it, the likelihood is that it *is* one of them."

"So we start tomorrow?" asked Chhaya.

"We start tomorrow."

Chapter Seventeen

My dearest Favian

She wrote the words and then immediately crossed them out.

Dearest Favian

She tried again. After staring at the words for a moment, she slashed through them.

Favian

It felt wrong. She crossed that one out, too, scrunching up the sheet of parchment and throwing it across the room into the fireplace.

She could not send him another letter. Not now.

Even if he forgave Aaliya, he wouldn't forgive *Chhaya* and she couldn't keep lying to him. It would be wrong to continue. It would be wrong to keep deceiving him. It was all wrong.

But a truth struck Chhaya in that moment, a truth she was deeply ashamed of. A truth she could not escape.

She was a coward.

She threw the quill across the room into the wall in frustration and groaned loudly, throwing her head onto the table with a dull thump. Tears pricked the corners of her eyes, and she blinked fiercely in an attempt to clear them. She had taken this too far. She had allowed her emotions to become involved and ruined everything.

It was her own fault. If she had done what she had always promised herself she would do, if she had not fallen in love, none of this would have happened.

All she wanted to do in this moment was get out of the suffocating room she was stuck in and go for a ride, or see Shadow, just get out of there. But she couldn't. Because Favian was in a meeting with her father and she was not permitted to leave the room without him.

As if spending so much time with him was helping matters at all.

She lifted her head to look out of the window; if she couldn't go outside, at least she could imagine it. Finally giving up on holding them back, Chhaya allowed the tears to fall down her cheeks, leaving wet streaks down her face.

It was raining. How poetic.

The lack of people out there felt bizarre to her, even in the rain. But then, everything felt odd at the moment; the castle and the grounds had been so busy and filled with people, laughter and conversations, which had all vanished very suddenly.

For the past three days since the attempted attack, all events had been cancelled, and everybody been encouraged to stay in the castle for protective measures while they ensured the grounds were secure. At least, that was what her father had announced. The protective measures had been part of the reason, that was for sure, but the main goal of the three-day period was investigation. Her father had told her that every entrance and exit in the castle was being observed to see if anybody would attempt to sneak out and give them a lead.

He had also announced that anybody who wanted to leave was, of course, welcome to, and the Kingdom would not take offence. Unsurprisingly, more than half of the remaining suitors had left the following morning. Chhaya couldn't even attempt to blame them; if she had the choice, she might have left too.

Nevertheless, the silence was strange. Where she normally found comfort and peace in the quiet, it was now eery and somewhat disturbing. Over the past weeks, she had become used to the constant hustle and bustle. Now it was all empty.

And then, of course, there was the matter of Favian. Because of the tightly controlled measures, Chhaya had spent almost every waking moment of the last three days with him. They would train in the mornings and investigate or exercise her Magic in the afternoons.

Every morning Favian had greeted her with a small smile, and every morning, when he thought she was no longer looking, his smile turned into a blank gaze, empty and lost. And every morning, Chhaya's heart sank into her stomach, knowing she was the reason.

The tears streamed harder down her face as she watched the rain outside become heavier until all she could see was a blur.

"Chhaya?" Della's voice made her jump and turn around, startled.

"Oh, Della!" she exclaimed in a stuffy voice. She quickly turned back around to the window and wiped away the tears. But there was nothing she could do about her puffy eyes and her red nose. "Come in."

"Are you crying?" asked Della carefully, taking a small step towards her.

"I suppose I am," Chhaya replied, her voice unsteady no matter how hard she tried to control it.

"What has happened?" Della asked gently, perching on the arm of Chhaya's chair.

And just like that, Chhaya could no longer fight the tears. "I have made a horrible mistake," she cried between sobs, weeping on her friend's shoulder.

"It's okay," whispered Della comfortingly, stroking her hair with a gentle hand. "It's okay. Just breathe. Here, have some water."

Chhaya accepted the glass Della offered her and took small sips of water, breathing deeply in between.

"Why don't I go and get some tea and we can really discuss what has happened?"

Chhaya nodded, wiping the tears from her face. Waiting for Della to return, she sat on the sofa and counted the bricks in the fireplace, feeling herself calm further with each brick.

"Lavender tea," Della announced, returning to the room with two large steaming mugs. Chhaya took one of the mugs in her grasp, gratefully absorbing the heat and allowing it to warm her red hands, cooled from being pressed against the icy glass of the window. She inhaled the steam with a deep sigh, as though it alone would solve everything or take her back in time and give her the ability to do everything again. But for now, she settled for the small amount of comfort and familiarity she received.

"So," said Della expectantly, "would you like to start from the beginning?"

Chhaya sighed heavily, her shoulders slumping and her face drooping down to her knees, unable to look at her friend, knowing Della herself had warned her against what she had done. "I made a mistake, Della."

"Oh, Chhaya," Della said in a tone that was consoling with a touch of condescension that made Chhaya frown. "It surely cannot be *that* bad." She rubbed her shoulder comfortingly and Chhaya knew she had only imagined the condescension.

"I would not be so certain of that, Della." She looked up at her friend then. "You remember those letters? The letters I had written to Favian?" Della nodded, but the wrinkle of her brow and slight widening of her eyes told Chhaya that Della knew now what she had done. "I lied when I told you I had stopped writing them. I have still been sending them to him."

"What?" The shock was more than evident on Della's face and in her voice.

"I know," Chhaya sniffed. "It is really bad. I do not know why I continued. I just couldn't help myself! It was all so innocent and fine until... well, until it was not."

Della stared at her in silence for a few moments, her mouth stuck open. Finally, her brain began to catch up with her and she opened and closed her mouth a few times, unsure of what to say. "Okay," she finally blurted. "Okay. So you continued writing the letters. What did you say? Did he write back?"

"I said so much," Chhaya groaned, smacking her face into her hands. "And yes, he certainly did write back. In fact, a few days ago, the night of the attack, I had arranged to meet him to tell him the truth about Aaliya."

"Who is Aaliya?"

"That is the name I used in the letters. But it does not matter; I could not do it. The sight of him standing there, waiting for me, knowing he would be disappointed to see me was too much." She looked up at her friend, pain scratching at her heart. "I think I love him."

Della's eyes widened again. "Chhaya, think about this. You cannot love Favian."

"You think I do not know that?" exclaimed Chhaya, jumping to her feet.

"Chhaya, he worships your father! He will never feel the same way about you, no matter how he feels about Aaliya."

"But what can I do? I never intended to fall in love with Favian—I never intended to fall in love at all!"

Della sighed, looking thoughtfully at the ground, trying to come up with a solution. "I think there's only one thing you can do," she said finally when Chhaya sat down once again. "You have to tell him the truth. Before either one of you is hurt any further."

Chhaya slumped her head. "When I didn't turn up that night, I stopped writing to him. I hoped he would forget about me —about Aaliya—but he has not. He is so down and distracted all of the time, even though he tries to hide it. I suppose you're right. But how can I tell him? How can I break his heart like that?"

Della opened her mouth to reply, but the door flung open with a large gust of wind before she was able to speak.

"Chhaya," Favian announced, marching into the room with an excited gleam in his eyes that Chhaya hadn't seen in too long. It warmed her heart to know that he was finally comfortable enough to stop wearing his lenses around her. "We must go."

"Go where?" asked Chhaya, her voice not quite as steady as she had hoped it would be.

Favian looked over her and cleared his throat, quickly straightening up as if he had only just noticed Della's presence. "Your father is expecting us," he replied, his voice and face now clear of any enthusiasm.

Chhaya frowned. Why was her father expecting them? What could that mean? And why in the Kingdoms was Favian so excited about it? "Of course. We had better go then."

Della stood. "I will see you later, Chhaya. Favian." She left the room, shooting one last knowing look at Chhaya before closing the door behind her.

Favian quickly moved over to sit on the sofa next to her. "I lied," he stated suddenly.

"What?"

"I lied," he repeated. "Your father is not expecting us."

Chhaya narrowed her eyes at him. "Then why did you say that?"

"I did not want to tell the truth in front of Della, but there has been an attack on the Western border."

"Is anyone hurt?"

"Everybody is fine. But it was an attack by Blood Magicians."

"Okay." She wrinkled her forehead. Why had Favian come in so excited about an attack?

"At the moment, we can assume that everybody involved in the attack will be hiding, staying low, and trying not to be noticed."

"I still do not understand your point."

"Today, with nobody around, would be the perfect time to visit the library."

"The library?"

"I told you I would keep you informed if I discovered any information. Today, your father shared a fact about the library that I believe will be very useful to us."

"What did he tell you?"

The glimmer was back in Favian's eyes as he turned to her. "There is a hidden section."

A hidden section. For her entire life, she had lived in this castle, and not once had anybody mentioned a hidden section.

"Your father mentioned it because he believes it may be helpful."

Chhaya sighed. "Very well. What are we waiting for?"

Why Favian had led her from her room and into the suite across the corridor, Chhaya had no idea. They were supposed to be going to the library, but at this point, Chhaya knew not to be surprised. There were hidden doors behind tapestries and in wardrobes that she never knew existed, hidden rooms and staircases that she had never even heard about. And sure enough, in the suite, Favian walked casually over to a painting and swung it open as if it were entirely normal for there to be entire doors behind artwork.

It hurt Chaya that her father had decided to share these mysteries with Favian rather than her, given she was the heir to the Kingdom, but there was no use bringing it up now.

On the other side of the door, Chhaya found a dark stone hallway and, at the end of the hallway, another door.

"I will check that the library is empty," he whispered. A small stream of light flooded the corridor when the door was cracked open, and Chhaya hurried out when Favian confirmed it was safe to leave.

"Wow," Chhaya murmured, emerging into a corner of the library. "That was a lot faster. How did you even know about that shortcut?"

"I was given a map when I arrived on your birthday," Favian replied, closing the door behind them. "Your father gave me access to all the hidden corridors in the castle in case of any danger. They were designed for this very reason."

"Then why do I not know of them?" Chhaya asked, her voice vibrating with frustration.

"I think your father hoped you would never have to use them. But you have a good point. I will give you the map."

Chhaya blinked. She hadn't expected that response from him. "Th—"

The creaking sound of a door being opened echoed in the otherwise silent library, and before she knew it, Favian had pushed Chhaya against the wall.

Her back was flat against the wood behind her, and Favian's hands were on her waist. He looked down at them and suddenly reddened, immediately letting go. He lifted one finger to his lips, urging her to be quiet.

But even if she had wanted to, Chhaya couldn't make a sound. She could feel Favian's breath on her cheek and heard the steady rhythm of his inhale and exhale. She could smell the smooth, musky smell of sandalwood that she hadn't detected before. Was he wearing some sort of scent, or just him? Perhaps the soap he had been using? She could practically feel the heat radiating from him—he wasn't touching her, but he was close enough that he may as well have been, his arms on either side of her head on the wall to steady himself.

A minute passed in silence, then another. At the sound of light footsteps, Favian poked his head around the wall that was concealing them. The footsteps stopped, then continued. The familiar sound of the door creaking open and then closing again made Chhaya exhale in relief.

"Sorry," Favian said, removing his hands from the wall and stepping away from her.

Chhaya waved her hand.

Even though he had taken a few steps away from her, she was certain the distinct smell of sandalwood had lingered in the air. Or perhaps she was simply more aware of it, *too* aware not to notice.

"Who was it?" She followed Favian, who led her through the shelves as though nothing had happened. Perhaps, to him, nothing had.

"I did not see their face, only the back of their head—dark hair tied into a bun. But it looked as though whoever it was took a book from a shelf and left again."

"That was close."

"We should make a move," Favian responded, his tone smooth and even as he increased his pace through the familiar wooden shelves.

After rows and rows of thick and heavy tomes, they came to Chhaya's favourite section of the library—the shelves filled with fairytales. "This was my favourite place when I was younger," Chhaya recalled with a warm smile, her fingers brushing against the shelves and across the familiar titles that had filled her childhood. "I would beg papa to bring me every night to choose a new story and then force him to read it to me."

She chuckled softly at the memory of her father reading the story of the princess and the pea. For weeks afterwards, she had made him check under her mattress, afraid she would find stray vegetables around her room that would prove she wasn't a princess at all.

When they reached the final shelf of fairytales at the end of the row, Favian turned towards the right, scanning the old and dusty titles with expressionless eyes. They looked so fragile, Chhaya was convinced any one of them would fall apart at the slightest of touches.

"What are you looking for?" She whispered.

"A book of fairytales," he answered in a low tone. "It's called 'The Kingdoms of Talia'."

Chhaya crinkled her forehead. She had read so many children's stories and fairytales growing up but had never even heard of that one before. Nevertheless, she scanned the titles along with him until, finally, her eyes landed on a short, thin black volume sandwiched between two rather large ones.

"Here." She indicated to the book, and Favian nodded at her before pulling on the book. The moment he did, a whirring noise began, sounding as though it was coming from all around them in every direction. Slowly, a group of tiles in the ground slid open, revealing a long marble staircase below. "What is it with this place and secret staircases?" she whispered.

The two exchanged a glance of bewilderment. "You can go first," Chhaya told him seriously.

Favian's mask cracked as his lips curved in amusement. "Of course." It was only a few seconds later that Favian called back up the stairs to inform Chhaya it was safe to come down.

The moment she walked from the staircase into the dimly lit room, Favian pulled a lever on the wall, and the whirring sounded again, closing the hole above them. Simultaneously, a light flicked on above them, and the entire room lit up.

Chhaya gasped when she turned around. When Favian had told her about a hidden library, she had assumed it would have been a few shelves. But this... "This is an entire library," she whispered in awe. Every time she had come to the library with her father, this spectacular collection of books had been right under her feet. "Where in the Kingdoms are we to start?"

Favian huffed out a short breath. "It is fortunate you do not have any events to attend this evening." Even his eyes were wide as he took in the numerous amounts of shelves and stacks upon stacks upon stacks of books. "This is going to take us a while."

They walked methodically through the rows, taking note of how things were organised—they seemed to be organised by topic—and trying to decide which sections would be the most useful to look at first. Some shelves seemed to be completely irrelevant to them, while some were overwhelmingly full. There was an entire section solely focused on the history of the Khiona Kingdom that they collectively decided to return to.

Finally, after all of their searching, they compiled a pile of twelve books to take with them to read. There was a mixture of history books, ranging from the history of Khiona to the history of Magic itself. Favian had even found a book about ancient artefacts they thought might be useful.

"I'll go up first," he told her when they were finally ready to leave.

Chhaya waited quietly as Favian pulled the lever and climbed the stairs, leaving the pile at the bottom just in case there was anybody out there. Chhaya paced as she waited for him to return; they had decided he would check the entire library to make sure they were alone so nobody would see the books, so Chhaya knew she would be waiting for a while. She ran her fingers over book spines on a shelf they had determined as 'miscellaneous' and reread the titles.

'The Magicians Cookbook' was the first title, a large, green, leather-bound book that had an illustration of a large cauldron on the front of it. The next was a book of spells, although Chhaya knew spells no longer worked in the Three Kingdoms, so there was no point in even considering it. And then her fingers landed on a small, thin black book that looked extremely familiar.

The Kingdoms of Talia.

That was the title of the book they had used to get down to the hidden library in the first place. Chhaya's eyebrows collapsed as she pulled the tiny tome out of the shelf. It didn't seem to open anything. So why were two copies of the same book? And why was this one hidden down here? Especially if it was simply a collection of fairytales.

"We are clear," Favian said, appearing once again from the stairs and lifting the stack of books. "Are you ready to go?"

On a whim, she decided to bring the book with her. "I am ready." She walked over to him and took half of the books from the stack he was carrying. Favian made to protest, but Chhaya simply raised an eyebrow.

He pressed his lips into a tight line but nodded and waited for her to go up before him.

"Concentrate," said Favian smoothly, sounding almost unbothered now as Chhaya inhaled deeply. It was understandable that he had given up; Chhaya had been attempting to light the candle in front of her with her Magic for almost an hour already.

She exhaled a short breath of irritation before shaking herself loose and closing her eyes. She absorbed the oxygen in deep gulps as she breathed in through her nose and exhaled through her mouth. With every breath, her shoulders relaxed, and the tension in her jaw eased. She allowed the frustration to float away until she felt lighter than a feather.

Feeling calm once again, she opened her eyes, keeping her focus on the steady and even pace of her breathing. She anchored her eyes onto the thin white candle before her, concentrating on the tip of the wick and ignoring everything else in the picture. As far as she was concerned, she and the candle were alone in an empty room.

With a deep inhale, she imagined the tip of the candle twinkling with flames.

Nothing happened.

Another inhale, and she pictured the candle bursting alight.

Nothing happened.

On the third inhale, she willed it to burn, she *forced* it to burn, but still, nothing happened.

She stood up so quickly from her chair that it collapsed backwards behind her, toppling onto the floor with a noisy clatter. "It is useless," she grumbled, running a hand through her hair as she walked away from the table with the candle and over to the window to stare out into the gloomy grey sky.

"It is not useless, Chhaya," Favian spoke in a tone she hadn't heard him use before, a tone with rough edges that made her turn to him in surprise. "You are just not working hard enough."

Chhaya's eyes widened, and she stared at him, her jaw slack and her mouth ever so slightly open in surprise. Favian had never spoken to her like that before. In fact, he had never spoken to her in a way even remotely close to that before.

His own eyes widened almost immediately, and he took a step back. "Sorry. I should not have spoken to you like that, Chhaya." His stiff and tense tone of voice reminded her of when she had first met him when he had first started working as her bodyguard. He had seemed so arrogant then, irritatingly emotionless with his suit and sunglasses and taking his job entirely too seriously. So much had changed since then.

Since the letters had stopped, he had been different. His eyes, no longer so bright and sparkling, glazed over when he thought nobody would notice. He drifted away in the evenings when he thought Chhaya wasn't looking. His formerly powerful march was now a forced walk.

And it was entirely her fault.

Chhaya forced her lips into a smile and looked up at him with understanding eyes, guilt gnawing away at her like a dark cloud devouring anything it touched. "I know you are just as frustrated as I am," she said kindly. It wasn't quite a lie, but it wasn't quite the truth. If only she could gather up the courage to tell him the truth, this would have been resolved. For better or for worse, she was unsure. But nevertheless, resolved it would be. The guilt in the pit of her stomach would be gone, and the heartbreak that graced Favian's face would, at the very least, be lessened.

But her heart already ached heavily at the thought of his rejection, at the thought of his horror at discovering it was her all along, that she was Aaliya. No. She couldn't do it. She simply couldn't do it.

"Still, please accept my humble apology. It was not my place to speak to you in such a way," Favian replied earnestly, his voice thick but steady.

His humble apology. Not his place. He didn't even see himself as on the same level as her. Even if he accepted that she was Aaliya, even if he felt the same way, he would never accept their relationship. He would never allow himself to love her the same way she loved him.

"There is nothing to apologise for, Favian. Truly," she said in a strained voice, turning around to pour tea as she blinked away the tears that threatened to fall. "I am very well aware I must be able to defend myself if I am to have any chance against the Blood Magicians."

She heard movements as Favian shifted on the seat. "It would be an advantage, that is certain, but it is not necessarily essential. I am with you, after all."

Chhaya turned back to smile at him. If only he *was* with her. "It is my job."

Chapter Eighteen

C hhaya fidgeted with the seam of her kurta top as she walked down the stairs with Favian, her breathing faster than usual and her jaw aching from grinding her teeth. She had been forced to tie up her hair after Favian commented twice that she wouldn't stop playing with it and had made herself drink a calming cup of peppermint tea already this morning.

"Stop," Favian suddenly announced, stepping in front of her just before she reached the door to the breakfast room. He looked down at her with calm eyes, the slight glimmer she missed flashing across it ever so briefly, and placed both hands on either of her shoulders.

Chhaya swallowed. He was standing so close to her that she could smell the lavender soap he had used that morning. His deep eyes bore into her own, and if she was not careful, she could have easily lost herself in them. A shiver coursed through her as he rubbed one thumb comfortingly over her shoulder, and she felt her breath catch in her throat.

"Remember what we discussed," he said, his voice low and his words careful. He raised in eyebrows, seeking confirmation, and Chhaya nodded hastily in response. He smiled, tight-lipped, and let go, apparently satisfied, and opened the door for her.

Taking a deep breath, Chhaya dropped her top and straightened her shoulders, relaxing her jaw as she entered the room.

"Chhaya!" Aamir called, walking over to her almost immediately and greeting her with a bow and the handsome smile she had now become familiar with. He straightened up quickly and clasped his hands together, his eyes dancing with relief as he looked at her. "I am glad to see you. We were told you were unharmed, but none of us had seen you in days and... all I mean to say is that... I am glad to see you."

Chhaya returned his smile in earnest, feeling her nerves calm at the sight of him, at the feeling of familiarity. "I apologise for worrying you, Aamir. I am glad you are also well."

Aamir nodded, rubbing his hands together anxiously. "It is terrible, all of this." His eyes lowered then. "I'm sorry you were targeted in such a way."

Chhaya pressed her lips together. "I am sorry all of you were put in harm's way because of me," she replied, addressing the entire room, now significantly smaller since many had chosen to leave.

Aamir's eyebrows furrowed ever so slightly, a tiny crease appearing in the middle of his forehead before it smoothed out again. "You shouldn't be apologising for being attacked, Chhaya," he told her in a low voice.

"Nonetheless, as the Princess and your host, I cannot help but carry some portion of the blame," Chhaya replied evenly. Before Aamir could say any more, she smiled. "I was going to have some breakfast. You're more than welcome to join me if you're otherwise unoccupied." She glanced over her shoulder at Favian, who, to any other, would have appeared to be uninterested, but Chhaya caught the smallest of nods directed at her.

"I would love to," Aamir replied with a smile. They walked over to an empty table with Favian following no less than two steps behind. He moved silently, but Chhaya could feel him and smell the faint hint of lavender in the air following her.

"You must have been terrified," Aamir uttered, buttering a slice of toast. When he looked at her, his eyes seemed so open and honest that Chhaya refused to believe he could have had anything to do with this. He was one person she could rule out, at least.

"It all happened so fast," Chhaya replied, pouring another cup of peppermint tea for herself, then one for Favian, which she offered out to him. His eyebrows quirked up by a fraction of an inch, but he took the cup with a nod. "But it was quite frightening. I was more worried for my father than anything else."

"These Blood Magicians," Aamir grumbled, his lips turned upwards in disgust. "When will they ever leave us alone?"

Chhaya could only sip her tea and wish she knew.

Suddenly, Aamir put down the piece of toast in his hands and turned his head towards her. "What do you think they want?" he asked.

What did they want? It was a good question. At first, Chhaya had thought it obvious that they wanted to kill her and her father, but why? To take control of the Kingdom? But things did not work that way. Even if they had managed to kill them, there was a line of succession. A member of the court would take over. Perhaps it was that member of the court orchestrating all of this? But why only attack Chhaya? She had been targeted at the ball, and her bedroom had been targeted that night. What did she have that they could possibly want?

"Your Highness," spoke a deep and heavy voice from behind her. Chhaya turned to see Mark standing before her in a bow.

"Mark?" Chhaya stood.

"It was an honour being here," he said, exhaustion evident in his voice. "Thank you for inviting me." He stood again, and Chhaya understood. He carried a packed trunk by his side and wore a thick cloak and riding boots. "I apologise, but I must go. My family have been injured, and I must return to them."

His family? "Are your family okay?" Chhaya was prepared to offer any medicine or assistance they required.

Mark only lowered his eyes, his shoulders sinking. "I hope to see you soon," he replied, ignoring her question in a way that told more than any words could have before bowing once again and leaving.

Chapter Nineteen

"Is it at all possible that you could get any information on Mark's family?" Chhaya asked Favian as they walked back to their shared quarters after lunch.

"I will see what I can learn," Favian responded with a nod.

"Thank you," Chhaya said softly. "I want to make sure they are alright. And if not, I want to be sure we provide as much support and aid as possible."

Again, Favian nodded, his gaze distant and his eyes lowered. Chhaya felt a pang in her heart—this was all because of her.

She took a deep breath. "Favian, there is something I—"

Before Chhaya could finish her sentence, Favian wrapped a hand around her small wrist, pulling her against the wall and startling her into silence.

"Wh—" she tried again, but Favian placed his finger on her lips, stunning her into silence. Removing his finger when he was sure she would stay quiet, he leaned in closer, one hand braced against the wall next to her head and the other on her arm.

His stormy eyes locked onto hers, and Chhaya felt her breath catch in her throat, her head tilted back so she could face him. He truly was tall. There was a hint of a sparkle in his grey irises as they bore into hers. He got closer, so close that she could smell the lavender, so close that her heart stopped breathing.

She swallowed.

Just when his face was mere millimetres away from hers, when he couldn't come any closer without their lips colliding, he leaned in. His lips brushed her ear, and a shiver ran through her, her eyes closing in the comfort of his warmth. "Listen," he whispered.

Listen? She snapped her eyes open and turned her head to face him, her teeth digging into her bottom lip. He flicked his head to the corridor, to the corner that had been about to turn and stepped closer, removing himself from her completely.

Chhaya swallowed, feeling his loss more intensely than she had expected, but followed him nonetheless. There were voices on the other end of the corridor, deep voices.

"—you think?" asked a hushed voice that Chhaya couldn't identify. She glanced at Favian to see if he had recognised the voice, but his eyes were fixed on the stone floor in front of him. Frowning, she turned her attention back to the voices.

"It's a shame," another voice, this one Chhaya recognised as Aamir, said with a heavy sigh.

"But what will happen now? Will people be able to go home?" the first voice asked, their words carrying the faintest tremble.

"The Bone Magicians are like the Blood Magicians," Aamir explained. "In the same way the Khiona soldiers were forced to... *remove* the Blood Magicians, the Peleia soldiers will likely have to do the same."

Chhaya felt ice travel down her spine as she listened. Bone Magicians? She had never before heard of such a thing. She had thought only the Blood Magicians plagued the Three Kingdoms with their horrors. But Bone Magicians? She shuddered.

The effects of the Blood Magicians were enough for the worst blood-curdling nightmares. She couldn't imagine what Bone Magicians would do.

The first voice gulped so loudly they could hear it. "I suppose we must be grateful there have only been a handful of attacks. Let's hope the Peleia soldiers will resolve the matter."

"And let's hope Mark's family have survived," Aamir added.

Their footsteps clattered along the stone flooring as they walked away. The moment their steps were no longer audible, Chhaya turned to Favian. "What in the Kingdoms are Bone Magicians?" her voice was venomous, and her eyes filled with fire.

But Favian, slowly, shook his head, his eyes distant as he looked at her. His forehead creased, and his chin scrunched. "I do not know."

"Chai! This is a surprise," her father said with a smile as he rose up from his chair and removed his small glasses as Chhaya entered his office. She entered alone, Favian waiting outside the room. This was a conversation she needed to have without him.

The sun had already set, and the moon cast an eerie glow through the room. Shadows danced along his desk, fluttering with the flames of the candles lit and placed around the room.

Chhaya looked sadly at her papa, her eyes empty and her stomach filled with a dark pit. "You have been keeping things from me," she said, her voice quiet.

Her father frowned, his eyes filled with genuine confusion as he rubbed his head with one hand. The pit in her stomach grew. "What things?" he asked.

Chhaya walked closer until she stood on the opposite side of his desk. "The Bone Magicians."

The moment she uttered the words, her father's eyes widened before he sighed heavily and sank down into his chair once more. "Sit down, beta." He waved his hand towards the chair next to her and ran it through his hair. The dim yellow flicker of the candles accentuated the dark silhouettes under his eyes. How had she not noticed them before?

"Chhaya," he began in a thick voice, pinching his lips into a thin smile, "before I begin, I must tell you that I have not kept anything from you for any reason other than to protect you." She opened her mouth to reply, but he raised a hand before she could speak. "I need you to know that."

Chhaya's eyes softened. "I understand, papa."

Her father's eyes glimmered with something Chhaya hoped was recognition. Recognition that it was time to be honest with her. Recognition that it was time to share everything with her. Recognition that it was time to start treating her as who she truly was, as the heir and the future ruler of the Khiona Kingdom.

"I suppose I had better start from the beginning. As you know, Chai, the Khiona Kingdom is at the head of the Three Kingdoms."

Chaaya nodded. Of course she knew that. Even if she had not been forced to sit through those gruelling history lessons she had sat through as a child, it was common knowledge across the Three Kingdoms.

"Well, Chhaya, what you do not know is how we came to be in this position."

Chhaya cocked an eyebrow, tilting her head to the side. "Yes, I do, papa. It was agreed upon by the Council of Old because we had the most land and the most resources."

But her father shook his head, pinching his lips together. "That is the story told to the public. It is even the story recorded in our official history books. But it is not true."

Chhaya leaned back in her chair, hugging her arms around herself.

"There was once a time in which the Three Kingdoms ruled in harmony. Each of the kingdoms' leaders respected the others and their kingdoms and all were expected to work together. If one kingdom was short in food, the others would provide as much of their extra wheat and grains as they could. If another was short in land for their people, the other kingdoms would welcome them in with open arms."

Chhaya's stomach warmed at the thought—three kingdoms that lived in peace. No wars, no gruesome death, no attacks. It sounded like something achievable only in dreams.

"Everything was... well, in a word, perfect," her father told her. "Until one day, there was an attack."

"What sort of attack?" asked Chhaya, her brows knitted together.

Her father rubbed his chin with his hand. "An unusual one," he replied. "You see before there were three monarchies in the kingdoms, there was only one ruler, an emperor. The Emperor Escara."

Chhaya sucked in a breath. She had never even heard mention of an emperor before—perhaps in a far-off land, but not in these kingdoms.

"He was a beloved man," her father continued. "Beloved by *most*, I should say. Because one day his body was discovered, along with those of his wife and his two sons, on the south-most border of the Three Kingdoms, the border of Khiona."

Chhaya inhaled sharply. "His wife and sons, too?" Her stomach churned.

With twisted lips, her father nodded. "There was great upheaval, not only because the Emperor and his family had died, but because they had been slaughtered in such a brutal manner."

Chhaya swallowed, knowing already what must have happened to them.

Her father looked straight into her eyes, his own open and honest but creased with deep sadness. "Their blood had sizzled through their skin like acid." Just like her mother. "Their bones were bent in unnatural ways, cracked where they should never be cracked."

Chhaya's eyes widened. *That,* at least, had never happened to her mother.

"And, the most disturbing fact for many in those times, they had been found at the bottom of a cliff."

"A cliff? How could that have been the most disturbing fact?"

"Because it seemed they had jumped themselves."

She pursed her lips. "But surely they could not have done that to themselves? Papa, it is clear they had been attacked by Blood Magicians, and I assume from what you told me by Bone Magicians, also, but how could anybody assume they willingly jumped from the cliff after all of that? Surely they would not have been able to move in such conditions!"

"That was the same conclusion the council members arrived at then, beta. They had clearly been attacked. By creatures who could control blood, who could control bones. And, it appeared, who could control minds."

Chhaya's mouth gaped. "Control minds? But I thought—I only overheard talk of *Bone* Magicians."

Her father's face turned grim as he lowered his eyes to the table. "Understandably, there was great fear that spread quickly among the people. Their emperor, their ruler, had been barbarically murdered, as had his heirs.

"Under the emperor, each kingdom had a council of sorts, made of ministers that took over as acting rulers. But the attacks continued. At first, the deaths had appeared accidental. A young boy was found in a lake, having drowned. Of course, an unfortunate and tragic accident. Then an elderly farmer was discovered on their land with deep gashes all across their body. And then an entire family was discovered with their bones twisted and snapped. Finally, they realised these were no accidents at all. It became clear whoever had killed these people had also killed the emperor and his family. They all knew something had to be done about it."

"So many lives lost," muttered Chhaya, "all because they couldn't see what was plainly in front of their eyes?"

Her father shook his head. "Not so plain, Chhaya. Not when you have never seen, or even heard of, Magicians before. Not when the facts are telling you the complete opposite of reality."

"Never heard of Magicians before?"

He took a deep breath, his shoulders moving heavily with him and his eyes closing tiredly for a moment. "It was only then that the Three Kingdoms were introduced to the Magicians. The Blood Magicians, the Bone Magicians and the Soul Magicians."

"Soul Magicians," Chhaya repeated with a quiver. She had thought Blood Magicians the worst possible evil to exist, but she shuddered to think of what Soul Magicians could do.

"A council member from Khiona went to the Sacred Mountains." Looking out of the window in her father's office, Chhaya could barely see the outlines of the mountains under the dim light of the moon, but they were there. The Sacred Mountains that overlooked all three kingdoms, the only spot that connected all three of them in one place. "She begged the Goddess for help. She prayed and promised anything, offering whatever she could to be rid of these monsters. And it was there that the Goddess graced us, and she discovered Magic. A new sort of Magic, the kind used by Favian, for example."

Chhaya felt her heart flutter at the mention of him, but she lowered her eyes and forced the feeling away. She had no right to feel anything of that sort for him after what she had done.

"It was a Magic of light, a Magic of protection, of defence. It was hope," her father resumed. "And so the other two kingdoms came to us for help. They came to learn and with the kingdoms united in war, the Khiona Council member led the way to success. With what started as a group of volunteers, they sought out the Blood Magicians, the Bone Magicians and the Soul Magicians. And they killed every last one of them. Or so they had thought.

"The Khiona Council member became the first Monarch of the Khiona Kingdom, the very first queen."

"But they hadn't been killed? The Magicians?" Chhaya asked, leaning forward to rest her elbows and arms on the desk.

"No. At first, everything seemed well. But slowly, the attacks started again. Once again, they appeared entirely unprovoked. But that was much later."

Chhaya held her breath. "How much later?"

Her father exhaled a heavy sigh. "When you were young. When your mother was killed by the Blood Magicians."

Bile rose in her throat, but she choked it back down.

"Only recently have we discovered the Blood Magicians are not the only threat to return. In the West, in the Kingdom of Peleia, there have been reports of Bone Magicians, reports of vicious and violent attacks."

"How recently?" asked Chhaya, her eyes hard.

"Beta, it doesn't matter—"

"How recently?" Chhaya repeated through gritted teeth.

"A few months ago," her father finally responded.

She exhaled a single, sharp puff of air. "This is why you had me invite all of these people to the castle? This is why you tried to force me into a life of unhappiness? A life you know I have never wanted. As a distraction."

Suddenly, her father stood. "How could you say that? How could you accuse me of drowning you in unhappiness when all I have ever wished for you was to be happy and live a good life?"

"Actions speak louder than words, papa," Chhaya whispered, tears threatening to spill.

"Chai, I never intended—"

"Whether or not you intended, that is what happened, papa."

"No, I would never allow that to happen to you, Chhaya. I merely thought an event like this would be a way to lift spirits."

"You used me as a pawn, father." His eyes flashed with hurt at the last word. "A pawn, rather than a queen. Quite literally. You see me as old enough to marry but not old enough to know the truth. You even told Favian of the secret passageways, the hidden room, the locked library. But you did not think to tell your own daughter."

"I only meant—"

"To protect me, I know," Chhaya interrupted. "And yet I am being targeted. It seems your *protection* was for nothing." Unable to stop the tears from flowing any longer, Chhaya stood, her legs shaking, and walked to the door. She twisted the handle but turned back before leaving. "I will never be a good ruler if you do not allow it."

Chapter Twenty

C hhaya slumped heavily on top of her bed, not bothering to get under the covers. It was still early in the evening, and yet she was exhausted. Her limbs ached from the continuous training. Her Magic was drained, tired from the neverending practice. Her brain was foggy, clouded by the intense hours of research and emotion.

Between her feelings towards Favian and the argument she had had with her father, Chhaya had barely had a chance to breathe. Every waking moment had been consumed, by either the Blood Magicians or the Bone Magicians or, more lately, by the possibility of Soul Magicians.

And when her thoughts were not filled with those threats, her mind wandered to her papa, to his betrayal. Had she been too harsh on him? Had she misunderstood? As much as she wished she was wrong, as much as she prayed to the Goddesses of Old, she had not. Her father had been willing to marry her off to cover up the attacks, or at least to draw attention away from them. Her own papa.

Chhaya blinked back the tears that threatened to fall. She had cried enough already. With a deep sigh, she pressed her fingers into her temples, easing away the dull ache that refused to let her be.

Even her dreams were no salvation from the endless churning in her mind, the ongoing spiral of images that spun her into nausea.

She dreamed of Favian discovering the truth, the disappointment and rejection on his face that would be inescapable. She dreamt of him leaning in close, his lips close enough for her to reach before he hissed his dismissal, disgust raw in his upturned mouth and narrowed eyes.

She dreamed of Gaia lying with deep gashes across her frail body, her bones contorted in ways that could only be described as inhuman, her eyes wide in panic as the life drained away from her.

She dreamed of the devastation the Soul Magicians could cause if they so wished, the utter destruction they could reap.

She dreamed of that night, of her mother. Of seeing her being torn apart by the deep gashes that appeared seemingly by themselves across her torso. Of hearing her beg for mercy, crying out in pain as the blood turned to acid in her very veins, dissolving her from the inside. Of hearing her father sob for weeks afterwards when he thought she could not hear him.

A light tap on her door broke her from her painful reverie. Clearing her throat, Chhaya wiped the traces of tears from her eyes and swung her legs over the side of the bed to sit up. "Come in," she called out, knowing it could only be Favian or Della on the other side.

"Chhaya." It was Favian. He stepped in cautiously, his analysing eyes fixed on her face. Her nose was likely still red, and it was possible her eyes had puffed, but hopefully, Favian would attribute the tears to her argument with her father. It had happened a few days prior, but it still felt fresh. And Favian had seemed to have picked up on it, treating her as delicately as if she was a feather.

"How may I help you, Favian?" she asked, standing from where she had been perched on the edge of her bed and wrapping her arms around herself in a sort of hug.

Favian's eyes shifted downwards. "I have been summoned to a meeting," he looked up at her then, meeting her eyes with his own, "with your father."

Chhaya swallowed but nodded. "I will not leave the room until you return," she told him evenly. "I was planning to read through some more of those history books we found, besides. I do not feel up to doing much else as it is."

Favian's shoulder's dropped, his jaw unclenching as he took three steps further into the room towards her. Chhaya inhaled sharply and took a small step back, causing the briefest frown to flash across Favian's face, his eyebrows sinking.

"I was going to suggest you take this evening to rest," he spoke finally, taking a small step away from her. "You have been working very hard, and I know it must be very difficult for you."

Chhaya scoffed. She *had* been working hard, but if she stopped, she would be alone with her thoughts, and that was one thing she couldn't handle. "You, of all people, cannot tell others to stop working so hard, Favian," she told him with a raised eyebrow and a small smile playing on her lips.

He pressed his lips together. "I am your bodyguard."

Chhaya rolled her eyes, unable to resist the short burst of laughter that escaped her lips. "It is your job. I know, Favian. That does not change the fact that you need some time off."

He shifted his eyes to the side. "I should go. Your father will be waiting." He did not wait for a response before leaving the room, closing the door behind him.

With a loud exhale, she looked around the room. There was a stack of history books by her bed, but Favian was right—she needed a break. Just the sight of the books was creating a dizzying throb at the back of her skull. No, the history books were out of the question.

A thin, black, leather-bound book on her bedside table caught her eye, and she lifted it, running her fingers over the lettering on the front.

The Kingdoms of Talia.

Perhaps a story was the distraction she needed.

Gathering a cloak, as it was still cold in their quarters, even with the warm fire roaring in the fireplace, Chhaya took the small book and headed into the living room, settling into the chair closest to the flames.

The small, makeshift bed in the corner of the room made her heart twinge. It was hardly the most glamorous sleeping arrangement and didn't look comfortable at all, but Favian had insisted on sleeping there rather than in the second bedroom. He was certain that if something were to happen, he would hear first if he were sleeping in the living room rather than behind another closed door.

Draping her cloak over herself, Chhaya opened the book, stopping at the first page. The words 'The Three Tales of the Kingdoms of Talia' were written in a curly but smooth and precise style with flourishes on the first letters of each word.

The first story was entitled 'The Sword of Souls', and Chhaya furrowed her eyebrows. She truly had not heard of these stories before. Not even a whiff of a memory was brought to the surface.

The second was entitled 'The Crown of Bones'. Again, nothing came to Chhaya's mind. But the third tale piqued her interest. 'The Stone of Essence'. It sounded familiar somehow as if she had heard of it before.

With barely more than a glance at either of the other two stories, she went straight for the third and began to read.

Chapter Twenty One

T he Stone of Essence.

A tale of two siblings; Anjali and her brother Viraj.

In a far and mystical land, a girl named Anjali and a boy named Viraj were born. They were born in the Kingdom of Snow, the largest of the Three Kingdoms of Thalia.

Their family was very poor, and as soon as they were old enough, their mother sent the two of them out to forage and earn money.

Every day, Anjali and Viraj would walk through the forest, gathering mushrooms, fruits, edible plants, and any herbs growing in the wild.

For years, they searched the forest every morning. For years, they lived in poverty, barely having enough food to eat. For years, they wore only clothes they could make themselves, clothes that did not fit them properly. For years, they could not go to school.

One morning, on their walk, Anjali stumbled upon a bush overflowing with ripe blackberries. Overjoyed to see such ripe and rare fruits, she and Viraj picked every juicy berry they could find and carried two full baskets home to their mother.

Blackberries were extremely hard to find in the Kingdom of Snow; they did not like to grow in such cold climates, so their mother took a handful to bake into a pie before exchanging the rest for a very large amount of gold.

Every morning for two weeks, Anjali and Viraj took their empty baskets to the blackberry bush. And every day, just like Magic, the bush was filled with fresh, ripe blackberries. They carried their baskets home proudly to their mother, who would take a handful to bake into a pie for the three of them and sell the rest.

Then, one day, Anjali and Viraj arrived at the blackberry bush to find it empty. They couldn't even find any unripe or baby blackberries growing on the bush. Anjali and Viraj searched high and low for the blackberries, thinking they had missed a turn in their journey or had stopped at the wrong bush.

But it was no use. The blackberries were gone.

When they came back home with empty baskets, their mother was furious. She demanded they return to the woods and return home when they found the blackberries.

Anjali and Viraj searched for the tasty blackberries for three days and three nights. They walked as far into the deep trees as they could during the day and checked the far edges at night.

On the fourth morning, Anjali and Viraj were exhausted. They had eaten nothing but wild fruits and had drunk water only when they stumbled across a fresh stream. Still, their baskets remained empty.

Viraj, so tired that he could no longer walk properly, tripped over a tree trunk. He hit his head on a sharp rock, and Anjali cried as blood streamed from her brother's skull, pooling onto a strange stone slab beneath him and creating strange red patterns. She cradled his head on her lap and tried to bandage his wound with a strip of cloth from her dress, but she, too, was weak and soon collapsed from exhaustion.

On the morning of the fifth day, Viraj awoke, surprised to find his head was healed, and surrounded by a sweet and musky scent.

Blackberry bushes.

They were everywhere, and they were filled with ripe and juicy fruits. He woke his sister, and together, they filled their baskets. Even then, more than enough blackberries were waiting for them to return.

When they were leaving this strange clearing they had somehow stumbled into, Viraj saw the strange stone slab he had fallen onto. It was stained dark red with his blood swirling and zigzagging across it. But the rich colour was fading.

Viraj knew, at that moment, that this stone was why the blackberry bushes had appeared. He showed the slab to Anjali, and they decided to carry it home with them.

When Anjali and Viraj arrived home with the two baskets filled with blackberries, their mother gave them each a big hug. As usual, she put aside a handful to bake into a pie and traded away the rest for gold.

That evening, when his mother and sister were asleep, Viraj crept into the garden with the mysterious stone slab. He traces his finger over the lines his blood had created, but by now, they were almost too faint to see. He found a sharp stick and poked it into his finger until he felt a prick.

Viraj pressed his pointer finger, with one drop of blood on the tip of it, to the centre of the slab. Almost immediately, the blood spread out, making the fading lines and spirals vibrant once again. Viraj smiled proudly.

I want blackberry bushes, he thought.

But nothing happened.

Viraj waited and waited until finally, he fell asleep, lying in the grass.

When he woke up the next morning, Viraj smelt the sweet and familiar smell of blackberries. It had worked.

Every night, Viraj wished for more blackberries, and they continued to appear every morning.

Anjali and Viraj no longer needed to make the dangerous journey through the woods each day, and their mother was happy. Every day, she made a fresh blackberry pie, and every day she took two baskets of blackberries to the merchants to trade.

One day, Viraj decided he did not want to wish for blackberries anymore. He was bored of picking blackberries and eating blackberry pies. Instead, Viraj pressed his blood to the slab that night and wished for gold. With gold, they could eat whatever they wanted and could do whatever they wanted.

The next morning, the blackberry bushes had been replaced with big pots filled with gold.

Anjali, Viraj and their mother used the gold Viraj had wished for to buy a new house with a bigger garden and a roof that did not leak.

But Viraj had become greedy. He knew it was not enough for him. He wanted more.

He wanted a castle.

So that night, Viraj wished for more gold, more gold, and even more gold.

Finally, Viraj had enough gold.

So Anjali, Viraj and their mother bought a castle.

But it was not enough for Viraj. No, he had only a small castle. But he had power. He deserved a big castle. He deserved a castle bigger than the Prince of the Three Kingdoms. He deserved a palace bigger than the Emperor of the Three Kingdoms.

And so, that night, Viraj took the stone slab with him once again. He cut himself and bled, but it was not enough. He bled more and more until, finally, the slab was full and vibrant with his essence once again.

The next day, Viraj used the gold he had wished for to buy an army. He bought the biggest and strongest army he could find and sent them to retrieve his palace.

But then came another problem for Viraj. The army would not fight against their Prince. They would not charge against their King.

Viraj was very angry. He had an army, but they would not fight for him. In his anger, he retrieved the stone slab. He slashed his palm and pressed it against the cool material. He wished for the soldiers to be punished for disobeying him.

But the stone would not listen.

No matter how much blood he volunteered, no matter how hard he wished, the stone would not hurt the soldiers.

Finally, Viraj became so angry that he threw the stone, shattering it into three jagged pieces, each sparkling brightly like jewels in the sun, rich with the colour of the stored blood.

The ground began to rumble.

At once, the soldiers began to scream in agony.

Viraj watched as the blood boiled in their bodies, spilt out of every orifice, and drowned them from the inside. Their blood turned to poison, causing blisters to burst from their skin. Their blood clawed its way out of them, tearing them apart.

Finally, when the destruction was over, Viraj smiled.

Anjali ran out of the castle and looked in horror at the hundreds of dead soldiers, brutally sliced and mauled in pieces before her.

"What have you done?" she asked her little brother—the boy who, only a few days ago, had only been wishing for blackberries.

He tried to explain that they wouldn't listen to him and needed to be punished, but she continued to stare at him in fear.

He told her not to look at him like that, but she wouldn't look away. Again, he told her, but she did not stop.

Viraj closed his eyes. He wished she would stop looking at him like that.

He heard a sound and opened his eyes to see Anjali's eyes closed.

He told her to open them, but she didn't. He told her again, angry. She opened her eyes, and they were filled with blood. She cried crimson tears that flooded her eyes and begged her brother for mercy.

He wished that the bleeding would stop. It did. Her eyes cleared up even though her cheeks were still stained scarlet.

She looked at him in terror. He wished she would stop feeling scared, and she clutched her heart, her face in pain. She couldn't breathe. He didn't know how he knew, but he could feel the blood pooling around her heart, suffocating it, drowning it. There was horror in her eyes, but the feeling of her blood was too strong. He felt powerful.

He felt hungry.

He wished the blood would pool faster, and it did. The energy surged through him like lightning.

And then it stopped.

Her sister crumpled to the ground before his eyes.

She was dead.

He had killed her. He had killed his sister.

Chapter Twenty Two

T he moment Favian returned from his meeting with her father, Chhaya jumped up from her seat. "Favian, look at this." She held out the book, propped open on the story of The Stone of Essence.

"I thought we agreed you needed a break and—"

"Just read this," Chhaya interrupted him, keeping the book outstretched before him.

Favian looked at her with a slight quirk of his eyebrow but took the book in his hands. "This is a book of fairytales?" he asked, examining the cover and the title.

"Yes, but it is the last fairytale that you need to read."

Favian nodded and sat down to read, leaving Chhaya to pace as he did.

Finally, he cleared his throat, looking back up at Chhaya who hurried over to sit beside him. "Well?" she asked him, her eyes wide and her hands clenched in an attempt to stop the trembling.

"I thought fairytales were supposed to have happy endings," he replied, handing the book back to her.

"That's not what I was showing you, Favian." She pinched the bridge of her nose between her finger and thumb. "Is none of the story ringing a bell at all? Viraj controlling the blood of the soldiers and his sister?"

Favian knitted his eyebrows together. "You think this is a story about a Blood Magician?"

"Not just any Blood Magician," Chhaya replied, flicking through the pages. She opened it again onto a page with an illustration of the boy holding the stone in wonder. "The *first* Blood Magician."

Favian leaned closer. "But that would mean..." He turned the pages, stopping on an image of the stone, broken into three. "The stone was not intended for harm. But when he broke it..."

"He must have done something to it to make it violent," finished Chhaya.

"He gave the stone so much of his own blood that it eventually broke under the pressure." Favian turned to her.

"So it could no longer resist the darkness?" Chhaya asked, twisting her head to face him.

Favian looked at Chhaya with a brightness in his eyes that she hadn't seen since the first night he had removed his sunglasses in her presence. She was glad he didn't keep them on around her anymore. "Do you know what this is?" he asked, leaning closer.

Chhaya swallowed, glancing down at his lips which were far too close for it to be considered appropriate.

"The story of the first Blood Magician?" Chhaya asked, her voice breathy. They had already established this.

"The key. The key to everything, Chhaya." Favian leapt up, walking to the fireplace and leaning against the bricks. Chhaya inhaled, able to breathe once more. Still, his lavender scent lingered in the air, and it was all she could do not to gasp it in like a thirst-ridden cat sipping at milk.

"How? It's intriguing, of course, but there is hardly much we can do with a story," she muttered. "Even if the Stone was used peacefully at first, it no longer is. It is being used to tear people apart, to control them, to destroy."

Favian frowned, pursing his lips. "We need to find it."

"Find what?"

"The Stone."

Chhaya scoffed. "Just like that, Favian? We simply locate an ancient object that we had not even heard of before today? One we are unsure still exists? And if it does, it will likely be one of the most protected objects in the entirety of the Three Kingdoms!"

"I did not claim it would be easy, but it is the key nonetheless."

She sighed. But there was no doubt about it; Favian was right. Still, something bothered her.

"Favian..."

"Yes, Chhaya?"

"This book has three stories. This tale, The Stone of Essence, is the story of the Blood Magicians. So perhaps the other stories are of the other Magicians. The Crown of Bones surely refers to the Bone Magicians, so the Sword of Souls..."

"Must be the Soul Magicians," Favian finished.

"If the rumours are true," Chhaya began, "and the Bone Magicians have returned, we must share this information with the Peleia Kingdom."

Favian nodded. "And if the Bone Magicians were able to return..."

"The Soul Magicians could, also. Favian, we must share the tale with the Kaura Kingdom, too."

Favian pressed his lips together. "I shall arrange it. But for the moment, we need more information on the Stone."

"Chhaya. Chhaya! Wake up, Chhaya! Wake up!" She awoke to Favian's hands on her shoulders, shaking her urgently. Favian had never come into her room alone like this before. Let alone in the middle of the night while she was sleeping.

"Chhaya, we need to leave," he whispered, hoisting her up into a seated position by her arms.

"Favian, what—" Her voice was raspy and her eyes heavy with sleep, but Favian didn't care.

"There is no time," he interrupted, grabbing her hand and pulling her out from her thick, warm bedding, the cold air instantly chilling her through her pyjamas. "We need to go."

Just as Chhaya was about to speak, about to ask him again what was happening, there was a sound from the living room. A muffled clattering sound that seemed louder than an explosion in the dead of night. Favian and Chhaya looked at each other, his eyes hard and hers creased with fear. Who in the Kingdoms was in their room at this time of night?

Quickly but somehow gently, Favian pushed her against the wall and put his finger to his lip, urging her with his eyes to be silent. He put his lips against her ear and whispered, "stay here."

Chhaya nodded, holding her breath and pressing herself back against the wall, the cool, smooth stone somehow reassuring against her back. She watched, teeth digging into her lips, as Favian crept over to the door. Slowly, he twisted the door knob and paused, taking a deep breath. It opened with a creak, and Chhaya watched in horror as Favian disappeared behind it. There was silence, then another sound and a flash of light before Favian appeared again, running over to her and taking her hand in his.

"We need to go," he said, pulling her along with him through the door and into the living room. Together, they ran to the door, Chhaya landing in Favian's arms after tripping over something in the dark. He steadied her but didn't stop to ask what had happened or if she was okay, continuing to pull her along after him instead.

"What was that?" she whispered in a trembling voice. But when she turned around, she gasped. There was a dark silhouette on the floor that she was almost completely convinced was a person.

"Come on," Favian murmured.

She swallowed but allowed him to pull her to the door. He opened it ever so slightly and stuck his head out before opening it fully and pulling Chhaya along with him across the hall and into another room, closing the door firmly behind him. Somewhere, a window was open; Chhaya felt the breeze through her thin clothes.

Footsteps clamoured outside in the hallway, the sounds of people running through the corridors. Then, the swinging sound of a door being opened. She looked at Favian in panic. Was that the door to their quarters that had just been opened? Without a word, Favian clenched his teeth and led her over to a large bookshelf that took up an entire wall.

"Check in here!" a deep voice called from outside of the room they were in. Any second now, they would come in and find them.

Favian quickly scanned the titles until he found a large green book and pulled it, and the entire bookshelf slid open. Favian grabbed hold of Chhaya's hand once again and dragged her inside with him, closing the shelf just in time to hear the door being slammed open behind them.

Chhaya gripped Favian's hand tighter when they heard foot-steps march in and towards the bookshelf which was keeping them hidden. She tried to look at Favian, but it was far too dark to see anything. They sank down to the cold ground.

They stayed silent while they listened to what was going on behind them. Footsteps, things were being knocked over, and there was rummaging. "That blasted bodyguard!" a female voice complained.

Finally, the footsteps faded away and the door shut again; they had left.

Chhaya exhaled. "Favian—"

"Shh," Favian interrupted. He stood from where he had been sitting and leaning against the back of the bookshelf on the cold floor and grabbed Chhaya's hand to help her up, too. He placed his hands on her shoulders and his lips to her ear. "Be careful," he whispered so quietly it was barely audible. "There are no lights in this passage, but we need to make it down a set of stairs. We need to move slowly."

Chhaya felt a pang when he let go of her but was grateful when he took her hand with his. She was shaking so much that she was sure she would have fallen if she didn't have him steadying her. Slowly and carefully, the two of them walked down about thirty steps. The stairway was just big enough for both of them to walk side by side and for Chhaya to keep one steadying hand against the wall. The stone was freezing under her bare feet, making her shiver violently.

When they reached the bottom of the stairs, Chhaya waited patiently as Favian felt along the wall. Finally, there was a small clicking sound, and a panel slid open in front of her, allowing a dim glimmer of light into the passage. Chhaya squinted, her eyes having adjusted to the darkness, and allowed Favian to help her into the room.

"What is this, Favian?" She rubbed her arms in an attempt to keep herself warm. They had landed in what seemed to be a bedroom without any doors or windows and only one candle burning. There was a thin blanket draped over the duvet on the bed, and Chhaya wrapped it around her shoulders and torso.

Favian walked over to the table and picked up a small candle that was already burning. "This room is maintained regularly. There is food, water, matches and spare clothes hidden in compartments around."

"Okay, but what has happened?"

Favian sat on the chair and gestured for Chhaya to sit opposite him. "After you went to sleep, I kept reading the books I had taken out from the library. In one of them, there was mention of an ancient artefact that came from the Scarlet Mountain. It was found split into two pieces. Apparently, there were many attempts to fix it using different types of technology, herbs and Magic. When it became clear that it could not be put together again, they settled on reserving it."

"But in the story, Viraj broke the stone into three pieces."

"Exactly. But they only found the two, not realising a third piece was missing. One day, the pieces were stolen and shortly after that, Blood Magicians began to attack."

Chhaya gasped. "So they have it again? That is why this entire war started?"

"They must have it," Favian agreed. "But that's not all. It seems an astrologer predicted that the stone could only be healed with the blood of a true royal heir."

Chhaya's mouth dropped open. A true royal heir. "They could not go after my father because he married into the royal family. That was why they killed my mother?"

Favian nodded. "I am sorry."

"But... why did my mother's blood not work?"

Favian bit his bottom lip. "I do not know."

"And why tonight?"

"What?"

"Why tonight? Why have they come for me tonight?"

"The astrologer also declared the stone could only be healed on the night of a full moon."

"And tonight is the full moon." She stared at him in silence for a few moments, toying with the frills on the blanket around her. "Favian, what would happen if they got my blood and fixed the stone?"

"We cannot let that happen."

"There is one thing that doesn't make sense to me; how have they become so strong recently? How have they become strong enough to get into the castle on three separate occasions?"

Favian sighed. "If I am correct, somebody in the castle is helping them get around. We need to send a message to your father and get him to safety, but we cannot trust anybody, and I cannot leave you here alone."

"I do not require a babysitter," Chhaya told him seriously.

Favian knitted his eyebrows. "You cannot surely believe that is what I mean?" he asked disbelievingly. "Surely you see this is a matter of your safety and not—"

"Favian, how many people know of this room?" Chhaya interrupted.

"Aside from your father and the two of us, only the footman who maintains it and replenishes supplies."

"And does anybody, other than you, know of my location at this very moment?"

"No."

"Then surely you can see I do not require protection," she insisted.

Favian pressed his lips into a thin line, clearly hesitant to leave her.

"Favian, please. My father may be in danger. If they cannot find me, I am afraid of what they will do to him." Tears welled in her eyes. If only she had understood him, if only she had forgiven him. But now, there was a possibility she would not see him again.

"I understand, but your safety is my priority. I cannot leave you for so long."

"So do not! Send Della to my father with the information to find a safe place to stay. And then you can return immediately."

He looked consideringly at her but nodded finally. "Fine. But you must promise you will not leave this room."

"I promise."

With a final hesitant glance towards her and a crinkle of his eyebrows, Favian left through the same door they had entered.

A loud thud startled Chhaya and she turned from where she had paced along the room to face the entrance with wide, alert eyes.

It had been a while since Favian had left; it should not have taken this long for him to find Della and send a message to her father.

"Favian?" she asked in a hushed voice, wrapping the blanket tighter around her shoulders. "Favian, is that you?"

Only silence followed.

Chhaya frowned, taking a step closer to the panel Favian had left through. Leaning forward, she pressed her ear against it. But there was nothing. Perhaps the noise she had heard had been from outside of the small staircase, from somebody searching for her. Perhaps the Blood Magicians were gone, and Della was coming to find her, to tell her it was safe to come out.

Still, Chhaya walked backwards, perching on the edge of the bed. She had promised Favian she would stay in the room until he came to retrieve her.

All of a sudden, the panel slid open behind her and Chhaya gasped. Favian had returned after all.

She turned to greet him, but her heart stopped in her chest. Entering the room were a man and a woman, both wearing the horrible dark cloaks she remembered from the night had mother had died.

"Your Highness," the man spoke with a wolfish grin plastered across his face. His long, light-brown hair shadowed his eyes, but his teeth were revealed. "At last, we have found you."

Swallowing, Chhaya looked around herself for anything she could use as a weapon. Her Magic was not yet strong enough to face two Blood Magicians, but from what Favian had discovered, they would not want her dead anyway. Not yet, at least.

"Oh, don't waste your time, princess," the woman reassured her with a mock pout. Her dark locks flowed over her shoulders as though they were alive. "You won't be able to escape now. Your very helpful bodyguard was able to lead the way to you—we know there is no alternative route out of this room."

Her heart plummeted into her stomach. Favian. They had Favian.

Chhaya opened her mouth to scream, that was her only option, but the Blood Magician moved faster, appearing behind Chhaya and placing a hand over Chhaya's mouth.

"Don't even try it," the other Blood Magician spat. "From down here, nobody will hear you." Still, she attempted to scream, producing only a pathetic, muffled, moaning sound instead. "And unless you want your soldier to suffer the consequences of your actions, I would stay quiet." She stopped immediately, forcing herself to relax in the grasp of her attackers.

"What a good little princess," the woman behind her whispered before pressing a cloth to her face. And with the sight of the Blood Magicians towering over her, all turned black.

Chapter Twenty Three

When Chhaya opened her eyes, it was to darkness. A cold material pressed into her from behind, and she leaned forward to alleviate the pressure. The hard stone floor under her was cold, and she was startled to find her hands tied behind her back. She shifted, trying in vain to remove her hands from the tight, scratching bindings.

There was a scratching sound, and a match was struck, lighting a small candle on the floor before her. "Good morning, Your Highness," sang a taunting voice in front of her.

Immediately, Chhaya froze. She knew that voice. Slowly, she looked up to face the person responsible for all of this, for the attacks, for the threats, for the death.

"Della?" she whispered.

"Yes, princess," Della replied with a wide grin, her eyes bright with joy. "I must say it's nice to see you not as the princess for once."

Not as the princess? What could she mean by that?

"I never asked you to treat me any differently—"

"No, of course you didn't, *Chhaya*," she spat. "You wanted to be treated like anybody else, didn't you?" She laughed then, a short bark of laughter that sounded more deluded than anything else. "But you are *not* anybody else, Chhaya. You are the Princess of the Khiona Kingdom. It is true. You are."

Chhaya could hardly think. What had she done that Della was so angry about? They had even offered her a job when she was old enough. "But we grew up together, Della," Chhaya stammered. "You... you are my best friend."

Della scrunched up her face in disbelief. "Are you truly so delusional, Chhaya?" She crouched down in front of her. "Do you truly not remember how I was treated by all of you?"

How she was treated? Chhaya could only remember happy memories from their childhood. For the most part, at least.

"My mother brought me along to work because there was nobody else to look after me. Instead of being *my* mother, she was forced to act as yours. Because your own didn't have the time for you."

Chhaya inhaled sharply. "How dare you?" she hissed.

"You don't want to hear the truth, Chhaya. You are living under a cloud of protection; you don't see what is really around you. And to make matters worse, you asked me to work for you!"

"My father did that to help you. He wanted—"

"Oh, and what fine help it was. Laundering your clothes. Bringing your tea. Pressing your clothes. Cleaning. Cooking. Running baths. I am a *maid*, Chhaya. It's hardly the finest line of work. Your father offered me the job because he felt he owed us. My family. For tearing my mother away. And you never seemed to care."

Chhaya swallowed. Della had it all wrong. They had not stolen her mother away from her; they had only hired her. And Della came too; she had her mother there. Her father had offered them nothing but kindness. "I didn't know—"

"Of course you didn't know," Della interrupted. "You didn't notice. You never noticed. Princess Chhaya living in her perfect world, with others doing anything and everything for her. Of course you would never consider looking at another."

"I was *going* to say I didn't know you *felt* that way. But Della, nobody stole your mother away from you. Although whatever it is you are doing now, you are sure to lose her. Surely you cannot think you will not be discovered for tour crimes? I assure you, you will be arrested. How can you have your mother with you when you are in the dungeon as a prisoner?"

"A prisoner?" Della laughed. "Oh, Chhaya, I'm convinced you don't know what is happening here. Kalindi!" she called, and the same woman who had found her in the hidden room appeared.

"So, the princess awakens," Kalindi hummed. "Shall we show her the great deed she is going to do?"

"I was thinking just the same," replied Della, taking a small red jewel that looked quite like a ruby from Kalindi's hands. "Do you know what this is?" Della asked her.

Thanks to the Kingdoms of Talia, she knew. "The Stone of Essence," she answered, forcing her voice to remain steady.

Della and Kalindi raised their eyebrows and exchanged a look. "The princess is educated," Kalindi said, amused.

"This is only one part of it," Della told her. "There are two more. And you are going to weld them together again."

"You know I will never do that," Chhaya replied calmly.

"Oh, Chhaya, but you will," Della told her.

"You have me tied up. Why have you not taken my blood yet?" she asked. Nothing was stopping them—she had no access to any weapons, and Favian was not there to help her.

"It's not so simple," Della explained, waving her hand in the air as if her words were unimportant. "The blood must be given willingly. That was one lesson we learned from the death of your mother. So at least it wasn't entirely useless."

Chhaya swallowed bile, feeling her skin all but vibrating in anger. "Well, then, I suppose the Stone will never be one."

"And just why do you say that?" Kalindi asked her, an unsettlingly wide grin plastered across her face.

"I would never willingly give you my blood. And if you kill me, there will be no heir to the kingdom," she answered simply. "No heir, no Stone."

"You say that now," began Della, "but I wonder how you will feel when it is *his* life in danger."

From the darkness emerged the light-haired Blood Magician from the room, only this time, he was pushing forward a bleeding Favian, a deep gash in his arm that oozed crimson.

"Chhaya," he whispered.

Her heart squeezed in her chest at the sight of him. At least he was alive. "Let him go," she pleaded. "He had done nothing. Just let him go."

"Oh, you know we cannot do that," Della replied.

"Favian!" Chhaya called to him, the smallest hint of relief fluttering through her when he looked up at the sound of her voice. "Favian, are you alright?"

He mumbled something unintelligible before his head slumped down once again.

"Favian!" she called out to him again. This time a tremble crept into her words.

"Don't bother Chhaya," Della told her with a sigh. "He's unconscious. He couldn't respond if he wanted to."

Chhaya's teeth clenched. Her nostrils flared as she clenched her hands into fists. How could they do this to him?

She felt the anger rise in her stomach as she looked at him, lying hurt and helpless in the hand of the monster. *These* monsters. The monsters that brutally murdered her mother in front of her very eyes for the sake of power. Power that one being should never hold.

And then she glanced at Della, who she had treated like her closest confidant for her entire life, who she had treated like a best friend. And more than anger, she felt the hurt, the betrayal. She had loved her. Like a sister.

She closed her eyes and allowed the hurt to leave her, to travel outwards and to take control. When she opened them, Kalindi and the other Blood Magician were on the ground, unconscious, and Favian was standing upright as though nothing that ever happened.

Della, on the other hand, was nowhere to be seen.

"Favian," she whispered. "Thank the Goddess. You are alright." Hot tears escaped her eyes as Favian turned to her. But rather than untie her, his eyes narrowed, staring at her as though she was an imposter.

"Favian, we have to hurry," she insisted. "Della will get away!"

"Do not listen to her, Favian," a voice that sounded remarkably similar to her own cried from beside her. She turned to see *herself* looking back in horror. "*That's* Della!"

Chhaya widened her eyes. "What? No, I am Chhaya."

"That is Della, Favian!" the other Chhaya exclaimed. "I saw her take a potion to transform into me. She must have taken it from Gaia."

From Gaia? "No, Favian, I am Chhaya. I am."

Favian looked between the two of them and swallowed. They both looked the same, they sounded the same, and Della was familiar enough with Chhaya to mimic her mannerisms perfectly.

There was only one way she could prove it, one way for Favian to know the truth.

"I'm Aaliya," she whispered.

Favian turned sharply towards her, and even Della—as Chhaya—raised her eyebrows in shock.

"What did you say?" he demanded, his voice taking on a dangerous edge as he stepped towards her.

"It's me, Favian. I'm Aaliya."

Chapter Twenty Four

Within seconds, Favian had crossed the floor. He took Chhaya by the hand and ran, leading her to a stone staircase she hadn't been able to see in the dim glow of the single candle.

They emerged into a small passageway in the castle and, once again, Favian tilted a painting on the wall to reveal a door. Wasting no time, Chhaya threw herself inside. Della hadn't caught up to them yet, but it wouldn't be long before she and others would be on their tail.

"There are more of them," Favian said flatly, leading the way through the narrow passageway with only the candle he had managed to take from the small room they had been kept in for light. He had let go of her hand the moment she had clambered inside and made no move to hold it again.

Chhaya could feel a whirring in her stomach, nausea threatening to bubble up, but she refrained. Favian knew the truth now, but this was no time to discuss it. She would have to wait. She followed him without a word and bit her lip to refrain from speaking.

Finally, Favian stopped in front of her so suddenly that Chhaya was forced to grab onto the wall to prevent running into him.

"Stay here," he said, his voice more expressionless than the first time they had met. Her chest felt heavy, and her heartbeat quickened, but she did as he said.

Slowly, Favian twisted a handle and pushed a part of the wall, peeking his head out from the small gap that was created. A short moment later, he was holding the door open for her, his jaw clenched and his eyes thunderous, fixed firmly on the corridor rather than at her.

"This way," he stated after closing the hidden door.

Chhaya was surprised to find herself in the Rose Gardens not long after. "You took us all the way around the castle without me even realising," she commented, half to herself. But Favian remained silent. She was unsure if he had even heard her.

"We need to lead them away from the castle," he said as they came to the stone bridge over the river. Chhaya's heart sunk as they stood atop the bridge, the bright glow of the full moon lighting Favian's deep frown. This was where she had watched as he waited for her. This was where she had made the decision not to tell him the truth. And now, he knew it, too.

"The woods?" she suggested.

He nodded, and they set off.

"Are you injured?" she asked him in a hushed voice as they moved towards the trees.

"No," he replied instantly, without glancing back at her.

"You were bleeding," she added, struggling to keep up with his large stride.

"Only a scratch," he answered.

"Are you sure, Favian? Because it looked serious, and—"

"I am fine," Favian told her, turning around so quickly she marched straight into him.

For a beat, they stared at each other wordlessly. Until, again, he turned and walked towards the forest line.

"Favian," Chhaya called out to him, running up to him, her eyes filling with tears that threatened to spill at any moment. She grabbed Fabian's arm when he didn't turn around. "Favian, you have to understand..." But he snatched his arm away from her and stared into her with cold, empty eyes. "Favian..." The tears were flowing freely.

Never did she expect to cry over a man. Never. All these years of knowing how her mother's death had broken her father, and still she had fallen for this man in front of her. And ruined everything.

"We need to go," he said emotionlessly. It was clear he wanted nothing to do with her. But he was still her bodyguard. He still owed her father everything. And he would still get her home safely.

She followed him in silence, stumbling over tree roots and being scratched by the surrounding vines and branches of the forest, thankful that he was ahead of her and clearing the path.

He stopped too suddenly for her to react, and she walked straight into him and would have fallen to the ground had he not caught her.

Chhaya looked up at him in surprise. His arms were wrapped tightly around her waist so she would not fall, but he was staring deeply into her eyes. "Favian?" she whispered, but he pushed her backwards into the tree behind her, pressing her back flush against the rough bark of the trunk. Her eyes widened. "What are you—"

He clasped one hand over her mouth before she could say anything else, keeping the other hand on her waist.

"They must have come this way," a hushed voice grumbled as the sounds of crunching leaves grew louder.

A twig snapped nearby, far too close to them, and Chhaya's eyes widened in panic.

Favian kept his steady eyes locked onto hers. Even though he was angry with her, even though he would never forgive her, and even though their relationship was destroyed, his presence was still a calming one for Chhaya.

She tried to take deep and slow breaths, making sure to stay silent; even the slightest movement could cause a rustle of leaves that could reveal their location.

But still, her heart raced. She could feel it pounding so loudly in her chest that she was sure Favian could hear it. Anxiety pulsed through her, sending a constant tremble through her limbs.

With a shaky but quiet exhale, she looked up and met Favian's eye. Lifting her hand to her face, she took his from her mouth and intertwined their fingers. His eyes narrowed, but Chhaya didn't care. Already, her heartbeat was slowing, and she felt she could breathe again.

A snapping sound seemed to echo through the trees. They both stiffened. The snap was followed by a yelp.

"Quiet," hissed another voice. Della. "They were seen heading in this direction—they must be around here somewhere."

"But—" a voice attempted, but Della didn't allow them to speak.

"Don't return until you find them," she interrupted. "That ridiculous bodyguard of hers took a part of the Stone."

Chhaya's eyes widened immediately as she stared up at Favian, whose eyes were fixed on the tree behind her.

In silence, they waited. They waited as the faint glow of light that must have been lanterns faded into darkness, and the crunching of footsteps was too far to be heard.

Finally, when it was safe to speak again, Chhaya whispered, "you have the Stone?"

Upturning his lips, Favian tore his hand away from her. He stepped back and peered around the other side of the tree. Convinced the path was clear, he started moving again.

"Only a part of it," he muttered, finally.

Chhaya wrinkled her eyebrows. "You didn't tell me?"

"Why would I tell you?" he responded almost instantly.

Her heart squeezed. "We were supposed to be working together."

"Yes," he snapped, "we were. My deepest apologies for withholding information from you, Chhaya. Oh, I apologise. Am I to refer to you as Chhaya or as Aaliya?" Even in a hushed tone, his words dripped with venom.

Chhaya continued to follow him, her eyes dropped to the ground. "I deserved that," she muttered finally.

"You deserve much more than that. Your Highness."

"Favian, I understand you're upset, but—"

"Upset?" Favian turned. "Upset?" He took a step towards her, eyes glowing with rage. "You pretended to be somebody else. You acted as though you had feelings for me. As if *Aaliya* had feelings for me. You were aware of your actions, Chhaya. You allowed me to fall for you. In fact, you encouraged it. I shared with you—with Aaliya—things about myself I had never shared with anybody. *Anybody*.

"And after all of that, you deceived me, manipulated me. Did you take joy in allowing me to trust you, both as Chhaya and as Aaliya? Knowing after all of that, I would either have my heart broken or never discover the true identity of the one I loved? Did it amuse you to know I would spend the entirety of my life searching for somebody that did not exist?

"I cannot say why you did it or why you did not tell me the truth, but as of right now, I do not want to know. And 'upset' is certainly not the way to describe what I am feeling right now."

He breathed heavily in front of her, his chest moving up and down rapidly. The usual glistening grey of his irises was now dark. Without waiting for a response, he whirled around, releasing her from his intense gaze, and continued making his way through the trees.

He thought she had deceived him. He thought she had lied to him.

"Favian—"

"Stop it, Chhaya. Aaliya. Whoever you are." Favian glanced back at her again, only this time the fire in his eyes was replaced by defeat, by acceptance. His shoulders were slumped, and in this moment, with the moon glowing through the gaps in the trees, the shadows under his eyes were as clear as day. "Just stop it."

Suddenly, Chhaya felt a jolt of anger course through her. She took a large step towards him and placed a hand on his arm, turning him to look at her. "Think whatever in the Three Kingdoms you would like to about me, Favian," she told him in a low voice. "That I am a horrible person for what I did to you. That I am a crazy person. That I am a liar, a manipulator. Pathetic, useless, helpless, whatever it is you may think of me. But Favian, and you had better listen when I tell you this, don't you ever," she grabbed the front of his shirt with her hand, pulling him closer towards her, "*ever* think any of that was a lie. Because even if I hid behind another name, I fell for you just as you fell for me. The only difference was that I knew who I was falling for."

Favian, unmoving, glanced down at where her hand was still gripping tightly onto his clothes. She quickly released him, taking a step back and rubbing her arm.

"It was no lie," she assured. "Do you understand how difficult it was to be on a 'date' with another person when you were the only one to fill my thoughts? To have you so close to me and yet be unable to *be* with you?

"So, Favian, you may hate me as much as you would like. But you need to know none of that... none of what I said—what Aaliya said—was a lie."

They stared at each other in silence until another twig snapped in the distance. "We need to move," said Favian in a low voice, immediately snapping into action.

"Where?"

"I know somewhere we can stay, at least for the night. It is not safe in the forest, and we are at risk of being discovered."

Favian led them through the trees until they came to a small body of water, a small lake Chhaya had never seen before.

"What is this place?" she asked.

"Where I grew up."

The orphanage her father had placed him in until he was able to start his training to become a soldier. It was run-down now and certainly looked as though it hadn't been used for at least a decade.

Favian creaked the heavy door open, and they walked into the darkness. "When I had officially become a soldier, there was an attack here. Blood Magicians. I was part of the troop that was sent out here. When we arrived, it was like a nightmare come to life. There was blood all over the floor, bloody handprints on the walls, lifeless bodies all over the place; young children and babies."

"I am sorry you had to see that."

"So am I. Not many people know it is still here, so we should be safe. You should get some sleep; I will keep watch just in case."

"We can take turns."

Favian looked as though he was about to argue but sighed instead. "Fine. You may sleep first, and we will swap over later."

Chhaya could not sleep. The uncomfortable floor did not help matters, but she knew the hard stone was not the cause of her insomnia.

Feeling restless, Chhaya got up from her spot in the corner of the dark room. If she couldn't sleep, at least she would give Favian the opportunity.

The floorboards groaned loudly under her steps, and she flinched, hoping she had not disturbed Favian. They had decided the best idea would be to stay upstairs to give themselves more reaction time if anybody did happen to find them and came in through the front door.

Favian had agreed to remain outside of the bedroom door while she rested, but when she twisted her handle and creaked open the door, the corridor was empty. She frowned, looking to both sides, but saw nothing.

Slowly, in an attempt to stop the floorboard from creaking under her, she crept forwards, looking over the rotten wooden balcony that looked over a large proportion of the ground floor. But still, there was nothing.

Her heart quickened. Had something happened to him? But he had been just outside her door in this old and squeaky house—surely she would have heard if anything had happened?

Suddenly, a dull thud from downstairs made her jump. She placed her hand on her racing heart and sighed in relief. He had only gone downstairs, likely to ensure the area was clear.

"Favian, you scared me," she said, hurrying down the stairs. "I thought-"

"Sorry, princess," Della answered from the bottom of the stairs, a bright smile stretched across her lips. Chhaya froze, halfway down the stairs already. "The bodyguard is not here." In one hand, she held two pieces of the stone in one hand while the other dripped blood. She had cut herself. Which meant she had used her Blood Magic.

"Della, if you have hurt him, I will die before giving you my blood," Chhaya said in a surprisingly steady voice. It seemed Della was alone, at least for now, but she still didn't have much of an escape plan.

"Relax," Della chuckled. "Why would I hurt him?" She took a step closer, her eyes glistening and her lips twisted upwards. "Just to feel that rush when the blood listens to my every command? Just to feel the thrill of his blood suffocating his heart? Just to feel it pouring from his skin? To feel the deep gashes being made and the blood gushing from them?" Chhaya shivered at the horrifying look of pure happiness on her face. "Usually, I would. But for you, Chhaya, I have left him alone. After all, you are giving me a much greater gift. Your blood will be sweeter, richer than anybody else's. Yours will be given freely."

Chhaya swallowed.

"Are you going to give us the blood, Chhaya?" Della asked her, examining the blood running down her hand.

"No," Chhaya answered, taking a slow step back.

Della snapped her eyes up. "Well then, princess. After you." She waved her hand, gesturing for Chhaya to walk ahead of her to the door.

Her hands shook, and her legs trembled, but Chhaya had no choice. Slowly, with one hand supporting her on the bannister and her eyes fixed on the girl before her, she made her way down the stairs, past Della, and to the door.

This would be her only chance to run, but she wouldn't, not without Favian.

"Outside," Della demanded, her voice closer than Chhaya had expected.

Chhaya opened the door, and her mouth dropped, her heart sinking straight into her stomach.

Held up by two other Blood Magicians, Favian hung limply, on the brink of unconsciousness. A deep gash ran long across his chest, weeping profusely with scarlet blood.

"You—you said you wouldn't hurt him," Chhaya stammered, her lip quivering.

"I did," replied Della casually. "But I *didn't* say I wouldn't let them have some fun. He's alive. You have the chance to fix this."

"Chhaya," Favian murmured, his voice weak and barely audible.

"Oh, how sweet," Della laughed. "Even in such a state, he is calling out for his beloved princess."

"Chhaya," he rasped again, his words slurred and slow. She looked at him and felt the bile rise into her throat. But still, she forced her eyes to look at him. "Did you mean what you said?" he asked her, his lid only half open as he looked at her.

"What?" she asked.

"In the forest," he choked.

Her eyes widened. What she had said about her feelings for him. "I did."

Favian nodded, his movements sluggish but determined. "Then you do not have ancient blood running through you." He closed his eyes, and his head dropped. The Blood Magicians on either side of him struggled to keep him upright as he fell limp in their hands.

"Favian?" she asked in a panic.

She moved towards him, but Della wrapped tight fingers around her arm. "Blood first, princess." On Della's order, Kalindi reached into Favian's pocket and pulled out the final jewel. It shone in the light of the full moon above.

What did Favian mean about ancient blood? Of course she had ancient blood in her veins; she was the princess.

"What have you done to him?" she cried, tears spilling over.

"We just want your blood. And we'll leave him," the Blood Magician to Favian's right declared.

Just like in the basement, just like in the ballroom, Chhaya felt the anger rise inside of her, filling her with rage as she watched these monsters shove Favian as if he were a cloth doll.

She had no ancient blood.

She allowed it to happen. She allowed the anger to explode from her, not bothering to attempt to control it.

And then there was darkness.

A heavy pair of hands were on top of her, on her shoulders. But they weren't weighing her down. No, instead, they were lifting her up. She tried to open her eyes, but her eyelids were too heavy.

She ached all over. Even the attempt to lift her neck sent a sharp stab of pain through her, and she groaned.

"Chhaya," a deep voice whispered in her ear. Was she dreaming? "You did it, Chhaya."

Favian.

"Am I dead?"

There was a soft exhale of amusement against her face. "We're both okay. You did it."

Finally, Chhaya forced her eyes open. Favian was still covered in blood, but the gash on his chest and the bruises were gone.

Placing an arm around her waist, he helped her to sit up. With every small movement, she felt her muscles tremble and throb.

"Where's Della?" she rasped.

"Dead," Favian responded flatly. "You destroyed the Stone with your Magic, and at the same time, the Blood Magicians all collapsed. It seems in order to access the Stone's Magic, they were forced to link their lives to it in some way. When the Stone died, so did they."

"It's over?"

"It's over," Favian confirmed.

"But I don't understand. How did my Magic do that?"

"Remember when I told you your Magic was fuelled by your emotion?" he asked, his glimmering eyes staring into her own. She nodded.

He leaned in, his face closer to hers than it had ever been. Even after all they had been through, the faint scent of lavender lingered on him. He placed a hand on her cheek, gently rubbing away a stray tear she hadn't noticed with his thumb.

Slowly and ever so softly, he pressed his lips against hers.

Chapter Twenty Five

A light knock sounded at her door.

Chhaya felt a rush of blood to her fingers, and they tingled in excitement. Surely it had to be Favian.

"Come in," she called, sitting up in her seat and running a hand through the tangled curls in an attempt to make them somewhat presentable.

Upon arriving back at the castle, as Chhaya had been informed, she had slept for three days. For three days, her body had needed to recover, and for three days, Favian had sat by her bed, waiting for her to wake up, while other visitors had come to check in on her, including her father, Gaia and her friends.

She faintly remembered opening her eyes to see his Favian's, but she had not had enough energy to keep her eyes open or even to speak.

This morning, she had woken up feeling fresh and alert. But Favian had not come to see her.

The door swung open, and in walked her father, carrying two hot cups of chai in his hands. "I'm glad to see you awake, beta," he told her with a smile and a quiver in his voice.

Chhaya returned the smile, but she could not help but feel a twinge of disappointment that Favian still had not come to see her.

"Papa," she whispered. "I'm so sorry."

Her father's eyes dropped as he handed her the steaming mug and sat beside her. "I am the one who should be apologising, beta. I should never have used you the way I did. No matter my intentions, I had no right to do so."

Chhaya wrapped her arms tightly around her father. "Shall we agree we were both wrong and carry on as normal?" she whispered hopefully.

Her father leaned away to look at her face. "Thank you for humouring an old man."

She sank back and took a large sip of the silky liquid, sighing at the taste of the extra cardamom and sugar on her tongue.

"Favian told me everything," her father told her, suddenly serious again. "I should never have offered the job to that girl."

"Papa, it isn't your fault," Chhaya insisted. The sting of betrayal was very much present, and Chhaya felt her heart twist every time she thought of the girl she had once considered her closest friend, but she wouldn't allow her father to accept any guilt over something that was not his fault. "We all trusted her. Who could have known what was truly happening in her mind? That she would give herself over to such dark forces?" She shivered as flashes of Favian, Sebastian, Kat and her mother, all bleeding, flooded through her mind. "We thought she was a friend," Chhaya whispered, "not a power-seeking Blood Magician."

Her father patted her shoulder with a comforting hand. "Nevertheless, it's over now. And I wanted you to know that I am sending home the remaining bachelors tomorrow."

Chhaya felt a twinge of guilt; she had entirely forgotten about them. "Are they safe?"

"They are all fine, Chai. Only a few Blood Magicians entered the castle, and it seems they were all fixated on finding you." His eyes dropped, and the dark circles under his eyes seemed more pronounced than ever. "Thank the Three Kingdoms that Favian was with you. I would have gone after you myself if you were alone."

Chhaya quirked an eyebrow. "Papa, where is Favian?"

He chuckled at her. "You didn't want Favian here at all in the first place, and now you are asking after him?" Chhaya remained silent, waiting for a response. "He left already, Chhaya."

Her heart dropped into her stomach. "Left?" she breathed.

"Beta, his job was done. He stayed to ensure you were alright, but when you woke up this morning, he started preparing to leave."

Chhaya pounded on the door to Favian's room. Maybe she wasn't too late. Perhaps he hadn't left yet. She pounded harder, but there was no response.

No. Surely, she hadn't missed him. Surely he would not leave her without saying goodbye.

She pushed open the door, no longer bothering to wait for a response.

The entire room was empty.

Her heartbeat quickened. She threw open the cupboard, but his clothes were gone. The desk was empty. Everything was *gone*.

Chhaya dropped onto the edge of the bed. After all of that, he had left her. He never really *had* forgiven her after all. The tears began to pour from her eyes, and she buried her face into her hands. She had ruined everything.

She shifted on the bed, and there was a small crinkling sound. She sniffled and rubbed the blur from her eyes, shifting once again. Yes, there was a definitive noise coming from the bed. She lifted the bedding, but there was nothing beneath.

Under the pillow, however, was a folded sheet of paper.

Without waiting a moment longer, she ripped it open.

My dearest Aaliya,

Her heart squeezed in her chest.

I am sorry. I am sorry to have left you like this, but it was too difficult to say goodbye. Now that the threat has vanished, it was time for me to leave. Your father offered me a permanent position, but I cannot see you marry another man and live your life with him. For that, for my own weakness, I am sorry.

Perhaps one day I shall return. Chhaya, you are the only true friend I have ever had, and for you, I am grateful.

I know you will lead a happy life with Aamir as your King. You will be a fair and just Queen and ruler of the Khiona Kingdom. The entire Kingdom is lucky to have you.

It is time for me to leave.

If you will do me one last favour, I left something for Sebastian in my drawer. I would appreciate it if you could ensure he receives it.

Until next time,

Your dearest bodyguard.

Chhaya wiped the tears from her eyes. How dare he? How could he think she could marry another? Flinging open his drawer, she picked up Favian's dark lenses. He had left Sebastian his lenses.

Chhaya felt the tears well in her eyes once again. She wanted to lie down. She wanted to cry and sleep and never leave this room ever again. But she couldn't.

Not while she still had a chance.

She ran from the room, taking the sunglasses and the letter with her. He could not have left long ago; the ink had smudged under her fingers when she traced the letters on the page. She raced out of the castle and through the door, running over the bridge and down the cobblestone roads, ignoring the surprised faces of the people who hadn't expected to see her for a few weeks yet due to recovery.

She ran to Gaia's workshop and burst through the door.

"Is he here?" she asked Gaia, who shook her head.

"He came to say goodbye but left only a few moments ago."

Chhaya frowned. He had come to say goodbye to Gaia but hadn't had the guts to say goodbye to her. She nodded and hurried out of the apothecary.

She jogged down the paths glowing orange from the setting of the sun, suddenly aware that although she had hated the running Favian had made her do every morning, it was coming in handy.

"Where are you going?" She heard a familiar voice ask. Sebastian.

She turned the corner to see Favian, bag on his back, crouched down to talk to Sebastian, who must have seen him on his way out of the Kingdom.

"Yes, where *are* you going?" asked Chhaya angrily as she marched towards them.

Favian jumped to his feet and turned towards her.

"Answer the question, Favian," she demanded, stopping only two steps in front of him.

He swallowed and looked down at the ground.

"Answer." She took a dangerous step closer. "The question."

He stayed silent.

She held up the letter. "You truly thought this was enough?" she asked before scrunching it up into a ball and throwing it at him. "You thought *these* would be enough?" She held up the lenses and passed them to Sebastian, whose eyes widened in awe as he immediately put them on.

Chhaya took another step closer, so close she could see her own reflection in his glistening grey eyes. "How dare you?" she whispered before smacking him in the chest. "How dare you?" She hit him again, stopped only from hitting him a third time by Favian grabbing her wrist in his hand.

"I did not tell your father about us," he said.

Chhaya scoffed. "My father will need to know if we plan to marry."

Favian lowered his eyes. "It would never work," he said. "You need a King. I am a bodyguard."

"What I need is *you*."

"Chhaya," Favian began, but Chhaya did the only thing she could think of. She placed a gentle hand on his cheek and pulled his head down towards her, pressing her lips softly against his.

He stood motionless, his hands stiff beside him, and Chhaya let go of him, taking a slow step away from him. "Sorry, Favian. I thought—"

She was silenced when he wrapped one strong arm around her waist, pulling her against him and placing his other hand in her hair, crashing his own lips down onto hers.

Chhaya's eyes widened for a moment before she closed them and melted into him, allowing one hand to roam into his hair while the other grabbed the front of his shirt, trying her best to pull him even closer.

They were both gasping for breath when they finally broke apart.

"You only know me through my letters," Favian spoke in a soft voice.

"I know you for *you*, Favian," Chhaya insisted. She reached up and ran her thumb across his eyebrow. "I know how your eyebrows twist together when you are concerned. I know how your shoulders tense when you are frustrated. I know how you clench your jaw when you are angry. I see the vacant look in your eyes when you feel alone. When you feel lost." A small smile spread across her lips. "And I know your eyes have widened ever so slightly now, your irises bright and swirling like lightning because you are surprised I know so much about you."

He pressed his lips together, his eyes studying her in a way she had never experienced. "I could never be who you need me to be," he told her, finally.

Chhaya put a hand on his cheek. "You already are."

Chapter Twenty Six

C hhaya would have been lying if she claimed she had ever pictured her wedding day. While almost all of her friends had always dreamed of a lavish wedding, of a beautiful event, Chhaya had never wanted that. In fact, she had been quite certain it would never even happen, much to her father's dismay.

But looking at herself in her mirror, with the hand-embroidered and jewel-adorned red veil draped across her head and single curls framing her face, she could not stop smiling.

There was a knock on the door, and Chhaya turned as her new lady's maid opened it. "Yes, she is here," her lady's maid informed the guest.

The door opened wide, and in walked Aamir, the one man Chhaya had been unsure would even be attending her wedding. For almost an entire month, he had been at the castle with the intention of marrying her. And today, a mere two weeks later, he was attending her wedding.

He beamed at her the moment his eyes caught sight of her. "You look beautiful."

Chhaya returned his handsome smile with a warm grin of her own. She knew she looked beautiful—she *felt* beautiful. In the red sari her mother had married in, wearing her jewellery and with her hands decorated with *mehndi*, there was no possibility she would not.

"Thank you," she answered."I am glad you chose to stay for the wedding."

"How could I miss it?"

Chhaya pressed her lips together. "Aamir, I would like you to know I truly am sorry—"

"Please," he interrupted, "do not apologise. As long as you are happy, as long as he is happy, there is no need for any apologies."

Chhaya felt her heart warm. Aamir truly was one of the kindest men she had ever met, and she counted herself lucky to know him, but he had not been the one for her. Perhaps in a different life, she would have chosen him as her husband, but they both would have been unhappy in the end.

"I did not come to disturb you anyhow," Aamir continued. "I merely wanted to wish you well. It is a long journey back to my town, and regretfully I will be unable to stay after the ceremony. In case I do not get a chance, I wanted to thank you for the past month for allowing me to stay in your home."

Chhaya frowned but nodded. She understood.

Another knock sounded at the door, and both of them turned to see her father enter. "You look beautiful, Chai," he told her, tears glossing his eyes. "Are you ready?"

Chhaya turned back to Aamir, who grinned. "I will see you out there," he told her before leaving the room.

Chhaya walked over to her father, kissing him on the cheek before taking the arm he offered out to her.

"You look beautiful, beta," her father told her, a warm smile dancing on his lips. "Just like your mother."

She looked up at him, tears prickling the corners of her eyes. How could she have ever thought he wanted anything other than her happiness?

"Papa, Favian is no duke—"

"Not another word, beta. Favian is a good person. He cares for you as much as you care for him and you will make each other happy. That is all that matters."

With a grateful nod and a smile, Chhaya took a deep breath. It was time.

The pillars were adorned with colourful garlands, and the Goddess' temple was ornamented with piles upon piles of beautiful roses, courtesy of the Palace's gardeners. There were royal purples, deep blues, bright pinks and a range of colours Chhaya could not even name.

But her eyes were fixed ahead, at the man wearing a red sherwani at the end of the aisle.

With every step, the fluttering in her stomach quickened, and with every step, she could feel how right this was, how perfect. As she looked at the man in front of her, she knew with all of her heart that they belonged together.

"Hello," she whispered upon reaching him. She looked back at the front row; Gaia nodded at her while Sebastian and Kat sent excited waves in her direction. Her cheeks were sore from smiling, but she could not bring herself to notice.

In front of them, the Priestess rose and placed flower garlands around each of their necks. As she began chanting, Chhaya leaned towards Favian. "You look very handsome."

"Chaand," he whispered back, his stormy irises fixed on hers as the Priestess chanted before them.

"Chaand?"

"You look radiant. Just like the moon."

Afterword

I want to say a HUGE thank you for visiting the Khiona Kingdom with me! I really hope you enjoyed the Stone of Essence as much as I loved writing it.

It really does mean the world that you took a chance on a small indie author like me.

As authors (especially indie authors), reviews mean everything to us, so if you did enjoy The Stone of Essence, I would be incredibly grateful if you could leave a quick review.

P.S. Make sure to sign up for my newsletter to stay up to date with my upcoming releases! The Stone of Essence is the first standalone novel in this world with two more to come this year, so sign up to be notified about them!

Thank You

I would first like to say a HUGE thank you to you—my readers. I really appreciate all of your support, your reviews and your messages. I cannot thank you enough for taking a chance on a new writer like myself. I truly hope you have enjoyed meeting Chhaya and Favian, and that you will come back to meet some more pretty amazing characters and find out more about the Bone and Soul Magicians!

To my friends and family: There are an overwhelming amount of you to thank. I know you all already know how grateful I am for your love and your encouragement, but I'm saying it again. Thank you. I really don't know how far I would have come without you.

I would like to thank the Hindi Film Industry. Without it, this book likely wouldn't have taken form and become what it is today. I grew up watching those classics, and they have had such a huge impact on the creation of this story.

There are so many people I would like to thank for supporting me and this book's journey that I think it would actually be impossible to name you all.

I will have to end by saying an overall Thank You: to my friends, my family and my readers. I love and appreciate every single one of you.

About Author

Maya Unadkat is a multi-genre UK-based author of young adult fantasy and romance novels. She has now acquired her Bachelor of Arts degree in French. When she was just sixteen, she discovered her love and passion for writing and when, at age eighteen, she was hospitalised due to appendicitis, she decided to begin working on her first novel. She hasn't stopped writing since. Her passions include stories, chocolate and Jane Austen.

.

Printed in Great Britain
by Amazon

35707832R00164